Christopher

Christopher

a novel

by David Athey

SOPHIA INSTITUTE PRESS
Manchester, New Hampshire

Sophia Institute Press
Box 5284, Manchester, NH 03108
1-800-888-9344
www.SophiaInstitute.com

Library of Congress Cataloging-in-Publication Data

Athey, David.
    Christopher : a novel / by David Athey.
      p. cm.
    ISBN 978-1-933184-82-1 (pbk. : alk. paper) 1. Young men — Fiction. 2. Quests (Expeditions) — Fiction. 3. Faith — Fiction. 4. Superior, Lake — Fiction. 5. Minnesota — Fiction. I. Title.
    PS3601.T485C57 2011
    813'.6 — dc22

                                    2011027395

First Printing

Christopher

chapter one

CHRISTOPHER LAGORIO awoke from a midsummer's night of nightmares.

The eleven-year-old blamed the bad dreams on Minnesota, because when his family had lived in Sacramento, he was always a hero in the dark, battling the ghostly beasts and dragons like they were nothing. And now, rubbing his eyes, he felt powerless against the creatures that devoured the starry heavens in his sleep.

Chris rolled out of bed, wondering if it was the end of the world. The boy hesitated, and then slowly shuffled to the open window. He leaned forward to look outside. The morning sky was thick with light-filled clouds that made Chris think of bread. The boy's stomach rumbled, and he gazed down at the water where the great Lake Superior was sun-reddened like wine.

Chris licked his lips as if he would feast upon all of creation. He had never felt so alive, so hungry, and so empty.

Scanning the rocky shoreline near the lighthouse, he saw a large family that was fishing. They were casting, reeling, and untangling a few lines. Chris wondered what it was like to have brothers and sisters, and he began to feel a familiar ache in his heart, and a temptation toward melancholy.

However, Lake Superior was all luminous, calling for a deeper response.

A smile began to cross the boy's face. And he whispered out the window, "Maybe I should go meet the Catholic girl."

chapter two

TERRA CORWIN lived in what was called the "cathedral-house" in a grove of pines near the deep water. The three-storey stone building was crowned by a large Irish cross. Christopher's parents had mentioned meeting "the strange Catholics." And some neighborhood kids had talked about the blond girl who never attended school.

Chris rode his bicycle down from the hill where he and his parents had lived for almost a year, having moved from California to Minnesota. He coasted through a stop sign, the wind singing a cool song into his ears, and then he pedaled north on Highway 61. The sun was rising brilliantly above the lake, and the waves whispered as if suggesting glad tidings. A few miles up the shore, he turned into the Corwins' almost-hidden driveway. Whistling like a boy trying to sound like a bird, Chris made his presence known so that his lack of an invitation would not cause a fright.

The girl was sitting on the front steps of her house, reading out loud from a great book. Her voice was prayerful and musical. Chris whistled and rode his bike closer, unable to keep from staring at the shimmering blond hair.

The girl pretended he didn't exist.

He hit the brakes and said amid the rising dust, "What are you reading?"

The Catholic girl looked up. "The *Summa*."

"Huh?"

She gave him a look of feigned impatience and hefted the volume into the direct light.

"Cool cover," the boy said. "I like the cross."

She laughed at the shallow response and allowed the full weight of the book to fall upon her lap. "I'm Terra."

"Hey. I'm Christopher. Some people call me Chris. Or Topher. Or Sacramento. My family is from Sacramento." He pointed at the book. "Is the *Summa* an adventure story?"

Terra laughed. "More of a love story. But it's not fluffy. It's all philosophical and theological."

The boy mouthed the words quietly, tasting the possibilities. "Philosophical . . . Theological." The words felt like meals and festivals. What did it all mean?

Terra lifted the great book to her heart and stood on the steps. "I think I'll go inside now."

Chris propped his bike against a pine tree. "Is it true you've never gone to school? The kids say an old wizard gives you private lessons."

She half-smiled. "An old wizard?"

"Is it true?"

Her eyes challenged him. "Do you believe it?"

"Sure," he said, grinning. "Why not?"

The girl was about to explain about her grandfather, the retired professor, when suddenly her mother opened the door. "Terra? With whom are you speaking?"

The girl paused for a moment, blushing, and then explained. "I think this boy wants to see the Catholic house."

Mrs. Corwin eyed Chris up and down. "I believe that you are the Lagorio boy."

He nodded at the lady, who was dressed in black. "I'm one of the Lagorio boys. My dad is the other. He's the older one."

Terra stifled a giggle.

Mrs. Corwin spoke in a serious voice. "I know your parents from the Club. They joined in the spring and seem like fine people, good additions to the Two Harbors area. Hmm. I've seen you riding your bicycle along the North Shore. You are always alone."

"I'm not alone now."

"Very well," the lady said. "Come in. We shall give you a tour. Wipe your feet."

The first floor of the cathedral-house was nothing special — at least not to the mind of the young visitor — the living room with its French furniture, and the kitchen with its Italian stone counter, seemed perfectly natural to Chris. "It's a house, all right," he said.

Mrs. Corwin led the boy along, with Terra following, from the kitchen to the master bedroom to the colorful sunroom. The lady in black stood and pointed. "That piece of stained glass is a real Tiffany."

"Spiffany," the boy whispered.

The lady flinched. "What did you say?"

Terra stepped forward. "Library. I think Christopher wants to see the books."

With narrowed eyes, Mrs. Corwin allowed the boy to pass. "Very well. Visit the library and read for a while. It may do you some good."

Up the stairs the boy and girl hurried, side by side, their hands almost touching.

The Corwins' library took up most of the second floor of the cathedral-house. Row after row of tall, wooden bookcases were filled with volumes in many languages. On the walls between the bookcases were paintings of landscapes and seascapes, animals of mythical proportions, shimmering fish, churches, saints, and lovers.

Terra led Chris to a scarlet love seat. "Want to sit here and read?"

The boy's attention was caught by a painting above. Two joyful nudes were reclining beneath a palm tree. "Man alive," he whispered, and couldn't stop staring.

Terra spoke in her most mature voice. "We can sit someplace else if the painting makes you feel uncomfortable."

Chris's cheeks burned red. "Why should I feel uncomfortable? I'm descended from a long line of naked people."

"Go find a good book," Terra said, "and I'll meet you back here."

"Okay." And he scurried away.

For a new reader like Chris, the library was filled with wall-to-wall miracles. He wandered around, browsing, and sometimes he and the girl would end up in front of the same bookcase. "You might like some of those," she said, pointing. "They were some of my first books."

Holy Grail Adventures was the first volume the boy pulled from the shelves.

Terra poked him in the ribs. "Where's your shining armor?"

"Ouch," he said, grinning, and pointed at her book. "What did you find?"

"More Aquinas."

"There's more than the *Summa*?"

Terra had a hungry look in her eyes that suggested she could read every book in the world. She said, "This one is a collection of prayers and hymns. So. Let's go sit on the love seat."

The reverie of reading together, in a room constructed to go on forever from world to world and beyond, made it easy for Terra and Chris to become good friends. And there was music in the air, drifting down from the third floor. Chris had never heard such music. It was sad, humble, ecstatic, and powerful. Who was up there singing? The boy wanted to know, and he wanted to visit that upper room, except it would be wrong to disturb the singer and the lovely reader at his side. Terra was eagerly praying with Aquinas, and Chris returned to *Holy Grail*

Adventures, while the thousands of books on the shelves beckoned in the soft light, offering their allure of wisdom and mystery.

After about an hour, the music stopped.

Terra smiled nervously. "You'd better go now."

The boy wondered if he'd done something to offend her. Had she felt ignored? The whole time they'd spent reading together had felt as if they had been perfectly connected.

Chris nodded. "Okay. I'll go." He ambled over to the stacks and placed the copy of *Holy Grail Adventures* between *Robinson Crusoe* and *The Travels of Marco Polo*. He paused there, his fingers lingering among the smooth bindings.

Terra whispered, "You're too late. He's coming down the stairs."

Her voice suggested that he try to hide. But where? He could not squeeze between the books.

Down from the chapel, where he'd been chanting his prayers, the retired medievalist appeared. He was tall and broad and wild-looking, stuffed into an old gray suit. He had a thick, curving mustache like two silver rivers flowing down his face. The old professor didn't seem to be aware that his granddaughter and a boy were in the library. He stared at the glowing red drapes framing the lakeside window, and then he marched, very slowly in strength, over to the suffused luminescence. He paused, as if for dramatic effect, and flung the drapes open.

"*Fiat lux!*"

Chris grinned, quite pleased with what seemed to be a game, and he responded with the first word that came to mind. "Silvenshine!"

The medievalist turned, surprised by the strange boy and his poetic outburst. "Goodness. What did you say?"

The correct answer was probably "Sorry" but that's not what Chris felt. He felt joyful and adventuresome. So he blurted out, "Golly-wanna-manna-sky!"

Professor Corwin wrestled with the syllables, trying, under his breath, to repeat and interpret the playful glossolalia. As if finding some sense in the boy's nonsense, the medievalist pronounced, "*Et vidit Deus quod esset bonum!*"

Chris glanced over at Terra and asked, "Is that good?"

She smiled, and nodded.

chapter three

AN ELEVEN-YEAR-OLD boy with a bicycle in summer is a creature of glorious trajectory. Chris's parents allowed him to fly away down the hill to the shoreline . . . to the lighthouse, to the ore docks, and back into the woods. Every shining day, the boy wheeled windward into the chill of the glacial lake, and into the warmth of the cathedral-house.

While Terra cuddled with Aquinas, Chris studied a thick book of local geology. He learned that the North Shore of Minnesota was a connection of ancient catastrophes. Fiery lava had arisen into mountains of cooled magma that were eventually eroded by gales of wind, and then crushed and polished by colossal, earth-shattering glaciers. Eventually, the ice was kissed away by the sun, leaving behind the ethereal, earthy stones. Chris learned that an ancient rift runs along the North Shore down to the Heartland, a rift that almost tore the continent apart. If the prehistoric shifting had continued, then Two Harbors and Duluth would have become cities on the ocean, seaports of saltwater instead of the deep fresh. Whales and sharks would have filled the waters, mightier swim-beasts than any in the current Mississippi, and the culture of Minnesota would have been much wilder. But the volcanoes and earthquakes subsided, and the rift was healed.

chapter four

AFTER READING together on the scarlet love seat, the boy and the girl began to get into the habit of going for walks. Terra loved to direct his attention to the small dramas that were playing out all over the place.

"See the tiger in the birch tree? Over there!"

The boy whirled around, his eyes searching for the swallowtail, but the tiger was gone in a flash.

"That's my favorite butterfly, Chris. Did you see it? Talk about amazing, the wings catching the sunlight! Oh, walk over here. Look at this."

The Corwins allowed part of their backyard to grow wild near the lake, and their reward was daisies.

"Aren't they wonderful?"

"Yup," the boy said, plucking a petal, "and they're good eatin', too."

"*Daisy* is not their actual name," Terra said, kneeling. "Chris, do you ever think about names and words and how they get changed?"

He chewed slowly. "Hmm . . ."

"Well, think about it. Like the word *goodbye*. It's been ruined."

The boy wanted to say, "Goodbye ruins my day when I say it to you." But he silently chewed the daisy.

Terra looked up. "God be with you."

Had Chris known the Mass, he might have answered, "And also with you." However, he just grinned and used one of his mother's old phrases. "Far out."

Terra frowned. "It's very sad what happens to language. I've seen it in the library. New books aren't as great as old books. In the old books, people will say, 'God be with you' instead of 'goodbye.' The original meaning makes a world of difference."

Chris thought about it. "I guess if you believe in God —"

"Of course I believe in God. Just look around."

The boy looked. The yard, trees, and lake were ablaze in the zenith sunshine. Chris could see that everything was too beautiful for words. And yet it was time to say something, because it was time to go home for lunch. He almost said goodbye, but bit his tongue after the release of "Good—"

Terra plucked another daisy. "In the old books, this flower is called a *day's eye* because it stares at God all day."

She handed the flower to the hungry boy.

"Thanks."

He gladly accepted the gift. And to please her, Chris did not consume the daisy. Instead, he held it to the sky.

chapter five

AT SUNSET, up on the hill, the boy made a small triangle of twigs, added a few dry leaves and, with the first strike of a match, he had a decent flame.

"This is better than fireworks," he told himself. "This is the real thing." And he felt, as millions of people have felt through the centuries, the spiritual connection between the soul and a good fire.

A few minutes later, not satisfied with the controlled burn, the boy fed the blaze a branch of jagged hemlock. The ancient tree, one of the oldest in the Northland, had fallen last winter after seven hundred years of sinking its relentless roots into the bedrock. The tightly wound tree, according to the warning of his father, would make a dangerous fire that would not stay in its pit.

"Far out," Chris whispered while the sparks thrilled the air like comet tails.

When the sparks alighted on the roof of the house, he thought they resembled stars, and then Christmas lights, and then bright drops of blood. "Wow . . . Cool . . . Uh oh!"

His parents rushed outside. His mother carried a fire extinguisher, and his father wielded a belt. While Mrs. Lagorio smothered the flames with mechanized snow, the boy had to remind his father, "In Sacramento, you were a pacifist. Your whipping belt is made of hemp. Look, your pants are falling down!"

Mr. Lagorio pulled up his linen trousers, and, after rethinking his philosophy, refastened the belt to his waist.

Having put out the sparks, Mrs. Lagorio set down the extinguisher and began rubbing the bottom of her throat. "Ohh, be still, be still, my sweet butterfly gland."

She was an endocrinologist, a diviner of the thyroid. A child of the Spirit of the '60s, Val Lagorio grew up experimenting with all sorts of herbs and mushrooms. She got very confused, but managed to get a medical degree in California.

Joe Lagorio was a business consultant, an ex-socialist who capitalized on selling merchandise for the Grateful Dead. He had stumbled into microchip stocks, made millions and lost millions, and, after a nervous breakdown, moved his family to Minnesota to seek the simple life. He spent most of his time with one eye on a PC and one eye on a Mac.

Joe and Val weren't bad parents. They ate dinner every night with their son, sustaining him on the finest organic, vegetarian cuisine. They made sure Chris got decent grades in school, and they gave him enough space, in the house and in the woods, so he wouldn't feel the need to rebel, run away from home, smoke dope, or make any of their mistakes.

Val groaned and rubbed her throat. "My poor little butterfly gland. It's fluttering and fluttering. Ohh, ohh, my whole system could fall out of balance."

The boy wanted his mother to stay balanced. "Sorry, Mom. I won't make any more fires."

"Ohh," she moaned. "My little butterfly wants to fly away . . . and throw my body into chaos."

The boy whispered, "I really am sorry."

"Ohh, my butterfly."

"Well, damn it," his father said, "we have to do the right thing here. Topher needs to learn his lesson. Where are the matches?"

The boy stammered, "In-in-my jeans pocket." He was afraid that he might get a whipping after all.

"Follow me," the father said and led his son away from the house to the bedrock ledge overlooking the town and the lake. Ghostly sailboats were out on the water, positioned for the fireworks celebration.

"Topher?"

The boy gulped. "Yeah?"

"If you're gonna grow up here in the wilderness, you'll need to get better with fire."

The boy shivered. "Get better with fire?"

His father's voice was both calm and forceful. "Try it again on this bedrock. Make a good circle of large stones, and then be careful with the fuel. No hemlock. Avoid pine trees and sparks. You have to be as careful as a priest. Okay?"

Chris didn't know what that priest remark meant, but he nodded. "Okay."

"I'm going to walk down the hill a ways and chill out. Hey, Topher — look at the harbor — the fireworks are starting!"

The boy did not look at the fireworks. Instead, he scrambled around in the darkness to find stones for a circle, and deciduous branches to burn.

Val Lagorio looked down from the house while her shadow of a son created a tepee of maple and placed some birch bark in the center. The boy struck a match, making his face alight with sun colors, and he reached down and carefully enflamed the papery birch. The curling sizzle licked into the maple branches, and soon the whole triangle was alive with a good, controlled fire. Lushly scented smoke spiraled into the air, reminding the boy of the incense that his mother burned whenever she was feeling sad.

He turned toward the house and thought he could see her in the picture window. The boy loved his mother, told her so twice a year — on his birthday and on hers. Now he wanted to invite her outside to enjoy the flickering light and warmth. He began to wave and then stopped because there was something in the fire that he needed to face alone. Chris turned away from his mother's gaze and focused on the flames that suddenly seemed to be leaping as if alive.

He stepped away from the fire. Instead of singing and dancing as others had done on the hill since the age of glaciers, the boy just sat on the cold bedrock. And then he leaned forward, not realizing he was on the verge of prayer.

chapter six

TERRA AND CHRIS were not allowed to eat in the cathedral-house library. Not one drop of milk, or a crumb of a cookie, would ever touch the sacred books. The library was for devouring words, nothing else. Whenever Terra and Chris needed other sustenance, after reverent hours of reading, they were welcomed downstairs into the kitchen, where the breakfast nook formed another world of comfort.

Mrs. Corwin enjoyed making snacks that smacked of a feast, and that day it was apple bread slathered with butter and elderberry preserves, and steaming mugs of ginger tea sweetened with brown sugar.

Terra smiled at the boy; he had a dreamy look on his face, feeling the supernal presence of simple graces. She spoke softly, "This is very nice."

Chris met her eyes. "I feel like we're in a book, like a perfect story in the upstairs library."

Terra laughed nervously. "A perfect story, before the bad things happen."

The boy shook his head. "No bad things can happen here."

Everyone knew that Mrs. Corwin's husband had left her for Europe, but it was impossible to see her as a victim, because she suffered his absence with such dignity. "Christopher, may I offer you some more bread and preserves?"

"You're an amazing lady," Chris said. "Thanks."

And his plate was filled again.

The boy whispered in Terra's ear, "Your mom's a queen. And so, you know what that makes you."

"Pudgy," Terra said, "if she doesn't stop baking every time you're here."

After each visit, Chris would linger around the backyard and the lake, strolling along the beach of shiny pebbles, allowing the convergence of cool air and warm air to kiss his skin more alive. The boy wished the girl could be outside with him, but she had afternoon prayers to say with her grandfather. It was a rule, and also something that she loved. Chris didn't understand the saying of prayers. His family never spoke of the Father, Son, or Holy Ghost. Strolling along Superior, beneath the treetops shining like day-candles, the boy allowed himself to feel the heavens . . . without really having to face them.

chapter seven

BY THE END of the summer, Chris and Terra had spent hundreds of innocent hours together. However, when the boy went to school in the fall, he was pummeled by the crassness of sixth-graders whose eyes and souls had already been scorched by porn. A pockmarked kid named Reilly made a comment about how Terra was "hot enough to email my attachment," and Chris slugged him in the gut. Twice. And gave him a bloody lip, too.

Principal Tolman's office, where Chris found himself a few minutes later, was decorated with posters proclaiming educational clichés such as "Reading Is Elementary" with a picture of Sherlock Holmes holding a magnifying glass.

"Sit down," the principal said.

The boy continued to stand.

"Sit."

The boy refused.

The old principal frowned, his ashen face already showing signs of cremation. "I've dealt with thousands of troublemakers, Lagorio. And you will not be the first in the history of Two Harbors Elementary to escape detention."

"I didn't do anything wrong," Chris said.

Tolman gave him a dry smile and leaned back in a leather chair that had faded during the Depression. He pointed a cadaverous finger. "You punched a fellow critter in the loins."

"Loins? I never punched him in the loins. It was the guts."

Tolman continued to point, finger trembling. "And you blackened the poor critter's eye."

"No, that's not true. I bloodied his lip."

The old principal almost smiled. "Well. Now we have our facts straight. You beat poor Reilly to a pulp."

Chris nodded.

"You admit your crime?"

The boy shook his head. "It wasn't a crime; it was a punishment."

Tolman put his twisted hand on the desk and tapped his crusty fingernails. He said, "I've got a regular Dostoevsky here. Boy, do you read grown-up books?"

Chris shoved his bloodstained hand into his jeans pocket. "My favorite books are about knights and ladies and great quests."

"And those books taught you to get into battles?"

"Yep. And they taught me how to win."

Old Tolman laughed, his face softening, showing the handsome history of his life. His eyes even twinkled, with a hint of holy mischief. And then he began to cough. He coughed so convulsively that Chris was about to go running for the school nurse. Finally, the coughing fit passed. Tolman caught his breath, and pointed accusingly at his computer.

"I never wanted the school to buy those things. I fought the Board — tooth and nail. And they beat me. It was unanimous. Now every classroom in my school has all of the evil in the world available at the push of the wrong buttons. We have so-called 'firewalls,' but fire always finds a way over the walls. Doesn't anyone study history anymore? Even stone castles burned. Even the rocks of Rome were scorched by Nero."

The boy stood silently, thinking about the cathedral-house, regretting how he'd made the comment about how bad things couldn't happen there. Bad things happen everywhere, all the time.

"You were right to beat the foul critter," the principal said, making a fist. "You were right to protect Miss Corwin's honor."

Chris sat in the chair facing the desk. He let out a loud sigh, and felt exhausted, having just won his second victory of the day.

"But you still get detention. A week, beginning tomorrow."

The boy leapt to his feet. "You said I was right!"

Tolman leaned forward, his face like a skull. "Just because you're right about something doesn't mean you don't have to suffer for it."

"What? That's not fair."

"I'll see you tomorrow at eleven-thirty."

"Are you serious?"

There was a pause, and it seemed as if all of the posters on the walls, including Sherlock Holmes and his magnifying glass, were awaiting Tolman's answer.

"I'm deadly serious. Now go to your class. And learn more history."

The boy lingered for a moment, waiting to hear that this was a joke. The principal was known to be something of a trickster. So where was the punch line that would set him free?

"Go to class, young man, and keep learning about things that don't make sense, even if they're true. Understand?"

Tears welled up in Chris's eyes. "No, I don't understand."

chapter eight

TERRA AND her mother and grandfather spent the autumn in Europe, searching for Terra's father.

He had been across the ocean for almost a year, having embarked on a pilgrimage to salve his conscience for being an inventor. He had sold lucrative patents to corporations and governments and was featured in *Time* magazine as one of the "Top 100 Most Influential People." The day after the article was published, he had a vision that showed how technology was being used by devils. And he felt as if he were dying, even after Confession.

Visiting ancient monasteries, giving away money to hospitals and orphanages, and wandering barefoot through the ruins of Christendom made Victor Corwin feel better. And then he felt worse, for having abandoned his family.

During the peak of Minnesota's changing leaves, when scarlet dominated all of the other colors, a postcard arrived at the Lagorio house from Paris. The handwriting was elegant and suggested carefully considered words. Chris read the postcard in his room, slowly whispering the news.

The Rose Window of Notre Dame is perhaps the best blossoming of the human art. And the High Mass elevated our souls even higher.

Chris, it's easier to find God than it is to find my dad.
I hope you are well, and reading.
                    Kind regards,
                    Terra

On the way to the airport, she had left a hardcover edition of an old catechism in the Lagorios' mailbox. The boy immediately read the first few pages, about how God loved, and then gave up when the book started talking about Christ and the Church. The only church that Chris had known in Sacramento was the fellowship of tall trees, and the only one he could believe in now was Lake Superior, with its congregation of great ships above and beneath the surface.

The day before Halloween, another postcard arrived, this one from Spain.

We have been walking the El Camino de Santiago. Mother and I have been struggling to keep up with Grandfather. I believe he could walk all the way to Jerusalem.

There is nothing like receiving Holy Communion in the old churches.

Several people have claimed to have seen my dad.

Chris, you should be deep into the catechism by now.
                    Kind regards,
                    Terra

The boy kept the catechism on the windowsill; in fact, he used it to keep the window perpetually open. The autumn air felt glorious, especially at night, when the boy buried himself under a host of blankets, and dreamed of the depths of Superior . . .

chapter nine

CHRIS OPENED the window wide.

The harbor down the hill was a study in gray. A still life of low clouds. The lighthouse seemed like a miniature, with just the slightest blink of light.

The twelve-year-old boy decided to stay home from school and read a large book he'd borrowed from the city library. *SU-PERIOR KILLS*. He was enthralled by the power of the deep, and he wrote down in his notebook the names of some ships that had been destroyed like nothing.

The Stranger
Belle Cross
Hesper
Isle Royale
Liberty
Niagara
Benjamin Noble
Oden
The Rebel

Chris returned to the window. The clouds had darkened. A storm was approaching, the sky gorged with snow-lightning just like some captains had reported in the moments before their ships had gone down. All hell was breaking loose above the water, and the boy leaned out, staring and shivering into the frigid gale, while Superior devoured the flashes of lightning . . . like nothing.

The first snow of the season was a blizzard, with schools closed and white roads rising. It snowed all day. Snuffing out the sky. Snuffing out the trees. Lake Superior disappeared. The land became all cloud, swirling. Chris leaned out the window and squinted into the icy tumult, hoping to see the cross on the cathedral-house. He could not see beyond his own backyard, however, and then a gust of wind nearly toppled him down to the drifts.

"Holy hell," he gasped and then grabbed the cold catechism from the sill and slammed shut the window.

chapter ten

NOVEMBER WAS a war of snow. Flurries whipped into storms of ice and lightning. Giant mounds, like ancient burial sites, hulked up and down the hill near the Lagorio home.

Chris ventured outside one Saturday afternoon to dig out some maple from the woodpile, hoping to make a sweet bonfire. Immediately he was attacked on the steps by pockmarked Reilly and two of his cowardly friends. The three kids in parkas had dug a fort into the side of a mound, and had brought along a bucket of water to dunk their snowballs, changing them into heavy ice balls. Chris got clocked on the side of his hatless head. "What the —"

"Kill Sacramento!" Reilly shouted. "Fire again!"

Dazed but not confused, Chris leapt away from the house and ran for cover while orbs of ice whirred past his face. He pumped his legs through the deep snow and quickly waded over to a stand of birch trees. The mid-size trunks offered both safety and safe passage for him to return fire. He made a large snowball, jammed it full of birch bark, and lit one side with a match. He tossed the whistling projectile through the air where it flamed like a falling star, shooting into the fort and scorching the front of a red parka. Reilly and his comrades cursed and shrieked. "Freaking Sacramento!" And they scurried around the mounds, back down the hill to their mothers.

Mrs. Lagorio appeared on the steps of the house, oblivious to the battle that her son had just won, and waved a shiny postcard into the sunlight. "Terra alert! Terra alert!"

Chris ran to the house and grabbed the brightness from her hand.

The Corwins were now in Portugal, in a place called Fatima, and the elegant words were larger than usual, and fewer.

> *The world is beautiful, and terrible.*
> *It is getting better, and worse.*
> *No sign of my dad. See you soon.*
> > *Love,*
> > *Terra*

chapter eleven

ON A DARK morning in the middle of December, Chris awoke for school, rubbed his eyes, and saw a fluttering light. He wondered: is there a bird in the room?

The light was like a hummingbird, flitting around his head.

His father shouted up the stairs, "Topher! You'll be late for school again. C'mon, get with the program!"

Squinting, the boy tried to sit up in bed. The feathery light was blinding.

"Hurry up, or you'll have to walk to school! I'm not a taxi service at your leisure. I have work to do!"

The light was everywhere in the room, and everywhere in the boy's head. He closed his eyes, and the light was there as well.

His father got distracted by a phone call, and eventually his mother flitted up the stairs. "Topher, are you okay?"

He rasped, "I feel like there's a fire in the room."

Chris's mother gently brushed the hair from his forehead and laid her palm flat against his sweaty skin. "Be healed."

He smiled at her blurry image. "Sorry. It didn't work."

"I'll make some black tea."

"Okay, Mom. Thanks."

All day long, Chris saw lights, hovering like golden hummingbirds; and a horrible thirst began to ravage his throat. His bones ached from head to toe, the pain rising and falling through the night.

His father said, "It's a Minnesota thing. He's depressed. Seasonal Affective Disorder. SAD. He'll snap out of it when the sun comes out. And when Terra returns."

The sun came out the next morning, and Chris's face was glowing, wet with fever.

His mother the endocrinologist pulled down the shade, sat beside her shivering son, and wiped his brow with a towel. "It's not depression. It's something beyond that."

The hovering lights and whatever was swimming in his skin became so severe that the boy was unable to sit up. He barely could open his eyes.

He was burning. It went on for several days.

Dr. Val Lagorio did not believe in doctors or pharmaceuticals. So she attempted to nurse her son back to health with Chinese herbs, Indian extracts, and maternal instinct.

"It isn't working," Joe said. "I'm driving him to Duluth. Val, you need to let him go to the hospital."

She forced a smile and spoke with make-believe confidence. "Topher will get better soon. I have the tinctures all figured out."

Joe shook his head. "Just because you believe in something doesn't mean your son has to die for it."

Val ignored the accusation and stood her alternative ground. "The mortality rate of hospitals is astronomical. He's much safer here. I have the tinctures all figured out. He's already responding."

The boy noticed a slight quavering in his mother's voice, and combined with his father's obvious fear, he willed himself to escape the tension in the room and fall into the bright dark sleep that had been calling him. Down. Down . . .

Chris met death three days before Christmas. He tried to fight it with punches and kicks, but it was like taking on a fiery monster. After that dream, he slept peacefully, without any pain or discomfort; and when he awoke, there was a blurry presence in the room that was not his mom or dad. However, the feeling from the presence was similar to that of his own flesh and blood. Did he have a sister? He couldn't remember. He blinked his eyes until everything became clear.

Terra was sitting beside the bed. She had a book in her hands and spoke very calmly. "You gave us a scare, you dork."

The boy smiled weakly. "Did you just get here?"

Terra brushed away a tear. "I've been right here for about twenty hours."

Chris raised an eyebrow. "Your mom let you stay in my bedroom?"

"Mother sat beside you, too. Along with your mom and dad."

Chris raised himself up without wincing in pain. "What about your father? Did you find him?"

"No."

"I'm sorry."

Terra smiled sadly. "Grandfather is here, downstairs having tea. You know, he prayed over you like crazy."

"In Latin?"

"In several languages. It was very serious. He was just about to call our priest."

The boy reached out and touched Terra's hand. She would have let it linger, except for the footsteps rushing up the stairs. The girl clutched her book with both hands while the adults appeared in the room.

"Silvenshine," Chris said.

The old professor was the first to answer, tears of joy streaming down his face. "Silvenshine!"

chapter twelve

WINTER. WINTER. Full of life. Scintillating world, otherworldly.

On Christmas morning, Chris's parents were downstairs by the fireplace, listening to New Age music.

The boy put on a brave face and padded barefoot down the carpeted steps, knowing that his presents would include computer upgrades that he wouldn't install, and herbal supplements that would be hard to swallow.

His mother, wearing a purple sari, cried out, "Sweetie! Good morning!"

His father, glancing up from a laptop, joked, "You haven't been very good this year, but we bought you some cool stuff anyway."

Computer stuff. Video games.

"Thanks, Dad."

And herbal supplements. Capsules the size of horse pills.

"Thanks, Mom."

She dripped some astragalus into his chai. "What a lucky boy." Val smiled and took a big gulp of her own medicine. "Yum, yum."

Chris hadn't gotten around to making a Wish List. It would have been all books that year, because he'd dreamed of building a library like the Corwins'.

However, even without a fulfilled Wish List, the boy was happy to be alive and realized that his parents loved him in their own ways. The fire was warm, the music was fuzzy, and the boy leaned under the solstice tree and pulled out the gifts that he'd made for his parents back in autumn. Wrapped in birch bark, the presents were replicas of famous Lake Superior shipwrecks. For his father, the *Oden*. And for his mother, the *Hesper*.

"Aren't you crafty!" Val said.

"Son, this is good work," Joe said, allowing the ship to sail upon his laptop.

"Love ya, Mom and Dad," the boy said.

"Love ya," they responded.

When New Year's morning arrived in a blaze of snow-blanketed glory, Joe and Val tiptoed into their son's room and placed another gift at the foot of his bed. The boy had become a very sound sleeper since meeting death in his dreams, and so it was more than an hour later when he rubbed his eyes and saw the shine on the floor. Two shines.

A pair of skis!

Chris scooped the skis into his arms and carried them down the stairs like spears and almost poked his father in the groin.

"Be careful! Geez! Castration is no way to start my year."

"This is an awesome present! Can I ski down to Terra's house?"

"No, not yet. You need to practice in the backyard, and master a few bumps, before you descend the hill. I don't want you flailing uncontrollably across the highway."

The boy grinned. "Flailing sounds like fun."

Joe frowned. "You remember the man who got run over last winter? That's not a good way to go. Struck down like a deer."

His mother appeared. "I can give you a ride in the Volvo, Sweetie. Volvos are very safe."

"But I don't want to be safe."

chapter thirteen

TERRA SAID, "A book! Thank you!"

Chris said, "A book! Thank you!"

The boy and girl sat on the love seat and read their stories for an hour in the good light of the Corwin library.

Although Terra already owned a copy of *Anne of Green Gables*, and had read it twice, she continually burst out laughing. Chris looked up from *The Fellowship of the Ring* and asked, "What's so darn funny?"

"This crazy girl — Anne. She's hysterical. I mean, she really suffers from hysteria. But she's so earnest and alive."

The boy nodded, pleased that his gift was a source of happiness. He said, "Being earnest and alive is good."

Terra looked at him in a way that seemed like a kiss — at least a kiss on the cheek — and then returned to Green Gables.

The boy reentered Middle Earth. The realm was seemingly created for his very soul, the mystery and adventure deepening with each page. There was magic in the words, and beyond, there was something bordering on the heavenly — with all of the glories, and dangers.

"Can you hear him?" Terra asked.

The boy looked up. "Him?"

"Yeah. He's coming down."

Chris nodded. "Yeah. Like a big old dinosaur."

The professor tromped down the stairs and into the library, singing, ". . . *beata Trinitas, et principalis unitas* . . ."

"Happy holidays, Professor."

"Happy holy days, Christopher."

The boy stared at the elderly man's face. "What happened to your mustache?"

"I gave it to the Pope."

Terra scolded, "Grampa! Don't say crazy things."

The professor chuckled and began to leave the room.

"Goodbye," Chris said.

"God be with you," the professor corrected.

Terra felt the need to apologize. "Gramps has been acting strange lately. We might have to bring him to a doctor."

"Oh? Maybe my mom could help him. She gives my dad things for his brain. Stuff like ginkgo."

"Ginkgo? That sounds like a Tolkien character."

"Yeah. Ginkgo Baggins, the healer hobbit."

The kids laughed, and kept on making up names that could have belonged to various creatures of Middle Earth if Tolkien had been sillier. Terra's favorite funny name was "Anne of Green Goblins."

The kids laughed and laughed. One of them would stop. And the other would start up again.

Chris's parents wanted him home by dark, so occasionally he'd glance out the window at the dying light on Superior. "Well," he said with a sigh. "I better get going pretty soon."

Terra looked out the window. "Right. You don't want to get lost and end up in Mordor."

"Or Manitoba," he said.

She pointed solemnly to the North and spoke as if recalling a great curse. "Beware of Anne of Green Canada."

"Yikes. If I see her, I'll put on my magic ring and make myself invisible."

"Good idea. Red-haired girls are not to be trifled with."

"Or blondes, either."

"That is true," she said, turning from the window. "Beware. Beware."

"Yikes," he said with a big grin. "I will beware."

Terra accompanied Chris downstairs to his boots, coat, and scarf. While the boy bundled up, the two kids began laughing again. For no reason. They were simply having fun. They laughed and laughed, and then hushed when they heard the professor and Mrs. Corwin up in the chapel. The adults were singing in their strange, mystical language, ". . . *beata Trinitas* . . ."

Terra was pulled to the song and hurried up the stairs, forgetting to say, "God be with you."

Chris tromped out into the twilight, carrying *The Fellowship of the Ring* in his backpack. He wondered if the Corwins would ever invite him to the upper room again. He had refused their first invitation, way back in the summer, and probably should not have said, "I have no interest in joining a cult."

Now he spoke in breathy, disappearing clouds, "Maybe I'll have to invite myself. I would like to see what sort of magic they have up there."

In the morning, immediately after breakfast, the boy strapped on his skis, the fish-scaled *Omni-tracks*. And using two sticks for balance, because his parents had forgotten to buy poles, he carefully made his way around the snow-buried mounds and down the hill. Skirting the icy cliff, Chris moved slowly, sliding as if walking with elongated legs.

He descended from above the harbor, scolded by a jealous crow and raced by a rabbit that skedaddled out of sight. The boy was going at just the right speed, stick-walking the *Omni-tracks* down the drifty slope, not too fast through the pines, and then a little faster through the birch, and then too fast through the brush at the bottom of the hill. The beginning skier hit the ditch-slope and went flying out into the middle of the road. He landed with a loud scrape, a splayed wipeout, and barely missed getting run over by an angry man in a pickup. And then a frightened woman in a Volvo appeared, window open. "Oh, sweetie. You're shivering. You'll need a boiling herb bath."

"Boiling?"

"Yes. We'll boil you good, sweetie."

chapter fourteen

ON NEW YEAR'S DAY, the Corwins' cathedral-house shimmered in the cold sunshine, the crystalline stones finding every color in the sky.

Professor Corwin opened the front door. He was wearing his gray suit, and there were signs of silver whiskers reappearing on his face. He stared solemnly at the wind-kissed boy. "Please remove yourself from those boots, Christopher, and join me in the kitchen."

"Yes, sir."

The boy basically leapt out of his boots, with visions of baked goods dancing in his head — he couldn't wait to snuggle up to Terra and engage in playful banter while feasting on the sugar. The kitchen was aglow and the table was awaiting his presence, splendiferous with warm cookies. Chocolate-chip and oatmeal-raisin. Chris had just enough manners not to openly drool, but he did lick his lips.

"Sit," the professor said.

The boy gladly obeyed. "This is great. Where's Terra?"

"Upstairs."

"She's still asleep? It must be ten by now."

"The time is ten-seventeen, and Terra is very awake. She and her mother are in the library."

"Oh. Is she waiting for me?"

The professor pulled two large mugs out of the cupboard. "We should stay in the kitchen. Would you like some hot cocoa?"

It was hard to answer the question about cocoa when he was dying to know what was going on in the library. The boy shrugged. "I'll drink whatever you're drinking."

"Two whiskies," the professor said. "Coming right up."

"Really?"

"No."

"Oh. Anyway, alcohol is bad for the thyroid. My mom says —"

"Christopher, are you allowed to drink caffeinated tea?"

"Yeah, but usually with echinacea or something else that makes it taste like —"

"Prince of Wales?"

"Umm, well, huh. Will the ladies be coming down to join us?"

Professor Corwin poured steaming water into the mugs. "They are having a very serious discussion. It could last until lunch, or later."

"Hmm," Chris muttered.

"Have a cookie," the professor said. "They just came out of the oven. I made them myself."

"You made them?"

"Yes. I made them for you. Now eat. And drink your tea."

The boy and the professor sat at the table and feasted on the cookies. Nobody was counting, but the boy ate three chocolate-chip and four oatmeal-raisin. He and the gentleman munched and sipped in relative silence, with just a few whispers of "Yum" and "Don't mind if I do." The time passed by without awkwardness or edge, and the boy was amazed by how the old professor seemed to be sort of a kid too.

Chris drained the last of his tea and wiped his mouth with his sleeve. "Did you like being a teacher?"

Professor Corwin's face was bright with melancholy. "That is a complicated question."

"Why is it complicated?"

"Because when I first started professing, ages ago, education was alive and well. It made my soul sing to hear Dante's poetry ring out from the hearts and tongues of the young. I would recite from *Paradiso* and the students would understand how their own spiritual lives were great adventures nourished by Christendom. Christopher, I was blessed to witness decades of illumination in the classroom. And then the '60s arrived, with all of its false light. And in the following generation of darkness and indecency, not many students signed up for Medieval Literature. The university caved in and started teaching cultural relativism. The Aztecs were said to be as holy as Saint Francis. It was nonsense. The relativists took over, however, and my courses were replaced."

Chris had many questions about this, but his mind was fixed on the idea of *Paradiso*.

"It almost killed me to leave Saint Louis and its glorious domed cathedral, where I attended daily Mass. Christopher, you must go to Saint Louis someday and be inspired in that cathedral."

"We should go there together," Chris said. "You and Terra and me. And you can recite from *Paradiso* along the way."

The professor smiled and whispered something beneath his breath.

The boy grinned. "What did you say?"

The professor grinned back. "Silvenshine!"

To celebrate the joy of language, and the joy of baked goods, they dug into the cookies again. This time with tall glasses of cold milk. Chris was a dunker, and Professor Corwin was a purist. And life was sweet, except that the sound of crying began to find its way down from the library. The boy eyed the staircase and let his mind wander up, among all of the great stories of love and suffering, to comfort his girl.

The professor asked, "Has Terra told you about her father? About my son?"

Chris nodded. "I know a little about him."

The old man's eyes filled with tears. He took a sip of milk and swallowed it down as if wishing it were whiskey. "Terra's father is like Leonardo Da Vinci, a great artist, but even more of an inventor."

Chris pointed up. "Terra is his greatest invention."

"Indeed. Although Mrs. Corwin did most of the work."

"Oh. Right. Gosh, for sure."

The professor sipped his milk. "My son made a killing on the three-dimensional printer."

"Three-dimensional?"

"Yes. Somehow he figured out how to rig an ink-jet printer to perfectly expel sand and adhesive and make any image that had been scanned into a computer."

"Like the image of a bird?"

"Yes. Any image. And within an hour, you would have a perfect replica in three dimensions. My son was always obsessed with the idea of three. When he was a little boy, he always asked about the Trinity. His face would scrunch up in innocent puzzlement as he tried to figure out how Three Persons could be one God."

The sound of crying intensified upstairs.

"Victor had a vision, a terrible vision after he had struck it rich, of terrorist groups messing with his inventions. And he felt the need for penance."

Chris responded as if he didn't know the word. "Penance?"

"You really do not know?"

The boy shook his head.

Professor Corwin spoke as gently as possible. "To do penance is to serve God in a way that hurts the self."

"Hmm. You do something on purpose that you know is going to hurt? Like the kids that get piercings?"

The professor finished off his milk. "A few years ago, Terra's father went on his first pilgrimage of penance. He began in Jerusalem with the *Via Dolorosa*."

"*Via* what?"

"The Way of Grief. The path to the Crucifixion."

The blank look on the boy's face made the educator pause and wipe away a tear. He tried to explain. "In the Age of Faith, it was very common for people to walk long distances — barefoot — in a slow rhythm of contemplative suffering, to visit the holiest places on earth, to ask holiness to rub off on them while shedding the old flesh for the Body of Christ."

"Is Terra's father still alive?"

"Oh yes. He continues to do penance all over the world."

"Terra won't talk about him anymore."

"She is hurt by his absence. And embarrassed."

"Embarrassed? Why? Her dad is a great inventor. She ought to be proud. I think I'll go upstairs and talk with her."

"Perhaps you should not."

"Why?"

The professor whispered, "Because there is another issue. The girl is becoming a woman. Be forewarned. If you trespass on this rite of passage, there will be hell to pay."

chapter fifteen

JANUARY HOVERED over the Northland in a light mist. The great lake did not freeze. Seagulls sailed above the harbor in a brightness that suggested springtime instead of winter.

Despite the relative balminess, Chris was buried in a world of cold. Terra wasn't speaking to him. Ever since the boy had crept up the stairs and listened in on her private conversation, the friendship was frozen. Twice he returned to the cathedral-house, and both times the professor was sent to the door to shoo him away.

"Sorry, Silvenshine. Terra is still very angry. You crossed a line."

"Only because I cared. She was crying."

"Yes, but even so, you should have waited until you were called."

The boy became sickly again, always shivering. He could not get warm, no matter how thick the sweater he wore. At school, the boy lost his reputation for being a tough guy. The kids revised the stories about his battles, suggesting that he'd been soundly beaten. "Sacramento is lucky that he's sick," Reilly proclaimed in the cafeteria. "Or else I'd have to kill him again."

Back when Chris was considered a warrior, his interest in literature was tolerated by the other boys. However, now that he was sickly, he was despised as being "a book wuss." He was

even seen talking to his teacher. And he was chosen to read his
essay in front of the class.

PIONEER WINTER
By Christopher Lagorio

*Pioneers must have liked each other, but all winter in a log
cabin can't be easy on your wife. Did you know that Mr.
and Mrs. NORTH founded the town of Northfield? Ha!
Northfield is south of here.*

*This is really the North. Once you get through Duluth,
you might as well keep going.*

*In a book called BUNDLED UP, one of the chapters is
about a guy with rutabagas. He buried them deep in the
ground. Surprise surprise they melted rotten. Everyone
forgets that the earth is one big volcano.*

*People froze to death all the time in the old days. They
never knew if the snow was really a killer storm. You
could be out walking with the trees and following the animal tracks on the ground. Everything is really beautiful.
And then the wind just turns on you. Lots of people got
caught and buried.*

*However they kept moving up North as if winter
would not kill anymore.*

*It was a pretty good life. If you were not too sick and
stuff, there were sleds and horses with jingle bells, singing
parties, and people still got married and had babies to
keep warm.*

I'm not sure if this was a history book or a love story.
The end.

chapter sixteen

APRIL IS the month of returning birdsong. Flock after melodic flock, the birds descended upon the melting forest, adding their voices to the rising song of the creek. Winter wrens, kinglets, golden warblers, and hermit thrushes all blessed the hill.

Free of the shivers, Chris went outside and sat on a stone beside the creek, and sang to the birds. Without words, the boy's song was a cross between a hum and a purr — enough to send all of the wings fluttering away. Except for the crows. They claimed the tallest pines and cawed down wrath upon the boy's head. He laughed, and they increased the volume of their wild cursing. This went on for almost an hour, until a salvo of caws ended with one squawking, swallowed note.

The forest fell into stillness. The only sound was the creek, but even that seemed to be rushing away.

The boy hushed himself, and awaited the approach of an invisible creature. The presence was large — enough to change the dynamics of the whole morning. Was it a bear? Chris had seen one in the fall. The sleepy bear had come bumbling into the yard, searching for a garbage container, before getting cursed and chased away by the crows.

This was no bear approaching.

Chris wondered if a wolf was on the prowl. He listened for the sound of loping, or the soft *pad-pad* of the predator.

The music of many waters rushed down the creek and covered a multitude of sounds. The boy focused and stared into the trees — the budding birches and maples — and saw no large animal. Just a red squirrel on a high branch, tail twitching as if it had seen a ghost. Or a wolf. Something was among the balsam fir, and the boy presaged the eyes. He could feel the energy of something large and carnivorous.

Chris wanted to run away. He also felt drawn to the creature. Death and wisdom seemed to be hidden together in the shadowed sanctuary of the Christmas trees. The boy wanted to know. He wanted to know what a wolf knew — its journeys through the ancient boreal, and its midnight songs to the winter stars, and the long loneliness of the blood hunt.

The lights appeared . . . like eyes pouncing on mysteries.

The eyes of a cat.

Chris blinked. He'd seen tomcats hunting in the woods. However, this was no tomcat. He'd once seen the face and fangs of a bobcat, springing for a grouse in flight. That was a feline to rule the North. And yet, this was no bobcat.

It was a lion.

Long whiskers hungering in a slant of sunlight, ears bent aggressively forward. It was a mountain lion, a rare firecat of the Minnesota forest, breathing steam and trying to discern if the boy was an enemy, a nuisance, or prey. The scene had played out since the place was a paradise of ice, with lions showing teeth the size of sabers, and barely alive human beings showing the survival skills learned out of Eden. And skills beyond surviving, the stillness of the soul in contemplation.

Here . . . now . . . is death. And here . . . now . . . is grace. Chris and the firecat stared at each other, locked in a divine presence that the lion seemed to know and the boy was yet to accept.

"Caw! Caw! Caw!"

The crows beat wings for the sky.

The boy fought the urge to flee as well. He squinted into the gentle, killer eyes and waited to see what the king of beasts would do.

There had been recent reports of a mountain lion roaming around Two Harbors, but nobody wanted to believe the teller of such tales. A dead horse was given as evidence, but the Sheriff had spit and said, "Stupid, drunken teenagers. Playing with knives. They'll pay for it."

Now the firecat moved forward, death and grace together; and the boy felt impelled to stand up from the stone beside the creek and run to the beast and fling his arms around the golden neck and whisper love — and whimper apologies — to that king.

But the urge to seek the safety of the house was just as strong, although it would be the worst thing Chris could do, the only way to provoke and suffer a real attack. Like the horse that had galloped.

Heart pounding at the chance to risk the law of the wilderness and embrace the beast as if it were kittenish, playful and a kindred spirit, Chris took one step toward the cat . . . and it was nothing but a tail swirling around into the fir trees — and gone.

"It didn't happen," the boy's father said at the dinner table. "You imagined it."

Val nodded, chewing seaweed. "We've all imagined things."

Joe laughed. "I once saw a leprechaun leap out of the San Francisco Bay and land on the Golden Gate Bridge."

"Thank the goddess those days are over," Val said. "Now we tend to see things as they really are. Which means we don't see many things."

"I really saw a lion," the boy said, staring down at his plate.

"Well, sure you did, sweetheart. You really saw a lion — in your imagination. Just like something you see when reading a story. Like some crazy story in the Bible. You were creating it in your subconscious."

"The lion came out of the Christmas trees," Chris said, looking up from his untouched food. "He was real."

chapter seventeen

THE NEXT DAY, Chris declared the end of winter. Tempting his health, the boy wandered outside in a T-shirt, jeans, and sneakers. His mother stuck her head out the door, her throat tightly wrapped in a scarf. "You'll catch your death!"

The half-rebellious son stomped to the door and held out his bare arms and hands. "I'm warm as a lion cub."

Val frowned, her cold fingers touching the heat of his hands. "How would you know about lion cubs?"

"Grrr," he said and bounded away from the house.

Chris was allowed to have his run of the western forty acres, with just one rule: he must "stay on this side of the creek."

He never felt trapped. He was one of those souls who could sit beside the melt water and listen all day long. And watch. Unlike television, with its chintzy manmade images, the creek was awash in a semblance of real infinities . . . fiery stones, pebbles, sand, bubbles and foam, the latter shape-shifting every split second into one flowing artwork after another. Minnows slick as moonlight. Trout flashing sunlight. Every round, square, and triangular inch of the creek was a free-flowing masterpiece of the moment. The boy was never bored. Wherever he looked, there were several million more reasons to be impressed. The creek was the exact opposite of TV or a computer screen, and Chris witnessed more wonders in a minute than most people see in a lifetime.

The crows joined their mad voices to the song of the creek, while deer added pauses and moments of silence. The possibility of a lion leaping out of the pines gave the boy another reason to pay attention, and to give himself up.

Nature was nudging him heavenward. And nature was ever falling.

Chris witnessed a murder of crows killing one of their own in the April dusk. From his side of the creek, he watched the feathered thugs go devilish on the other side. The injured bird caw-cursed for its life and was given no mercy, pecked to pieces. And then a red fox appeared and scared off the murderous flock. He plucked the flapless crow, his white fangs going all red, and the neighbor's dogs arrived — the black lab and the golden retriever — chasing a small, limping doe. They took her down near the water. The doe's eyes rolled into death before the boy could shout the dogs back to their master. "Bad! Bad! Go home!" The dogs, panting, ran again and pursued the fox.

It was a big day for flesh and blood. And Chris, from his side of the creek, saw enough of the shadow of death to fill a whole book.

A few weeks later, on a balmy Saturday, his mother called him out of the woods. She greeted him on the back stairs. "Guess who's here to visit."

The boy, overly warm from running, knew immediately. Shivering, he hurried into the kitchen, where Terra was standing beside her mother. The girl was all in green, the mother in black.

"We brought you some things to read," Terra said.

Chris wanted to give her a hug. He made his move, but the girl shoved a box into his arms. "Grandpa went crazy at the Saint Scholastica book sale. He thought you'd like these, especially *Orthodoxy* by Chesterton. Perhaps you could start your own collection."

Val answered politely, and a little pertly. "Thank you very much. Of course we already have our own library in the house."

Chris laughed. "You mean the shelf of books about thyroids?"

"You have a gorgeous home," Mrs. Corwin said, gesturing. "And I love your kitchen. What a wonderful back-splash. Is it Venetian? So intricate."

"Oh, thank you. That pattern is from Pakistan."

"Pakistan. Well, I have always loved color in a kitchen."

"Yes, for sure," Val said excitedly. "There are studies that show that colorful kitchens are very helpful for digestion."

"Really? How interesting. I'd like to hear more about that."

While the mothers talked about colorful kitchens and better digestion over a cup of chai, the kids went outside. They tramped over the rotting leaves from last fall, kicking up the sweet odor of mold and thawing earth. Side by side, the boy and the girl traversed an implied path through the forest.

Chris pointed and said, "Those birches are like maple trees, filled with syrup."

Terra replied, "Yes, I know. But if you truly want birch syrup on your pancakes, you must boil the sap twice and not expect too much. Remember, I grew up here, Sacramento Boy."

He pointed again. "Look! A yellow-bellied sapsucker!"

The kids laughed at the silly, pecking bird, and also admired the effort. The sapsucker enjoyed a few moments of sugar, and buzzed away in a whir of chirping. Chris and Terra continued along, tramping over lichen-hugged bedrock toward an elevation of red pines; but before entering that sanctuary, they paused to consider the green fiddleheads of ferns, uncurling in the spring light, singing their silence. The beautiful lack of sound seemed to swirl up through the swaying arms of the hundred-foot pines. The boy stared heavenward. "An eagle family nested up there in the past. But they flew away."

The girl arched her lovely neck. "At least they're in the area. We see them hunting for fish all the time."

The moment she finished speaking, an eagle blazed over the pines, wings whistling.

"This is amazing," Terra said. "I love it up here on the hill."

The boy said, "It's one of the best places in the world."

"One of the best? Not the very best?"

Chris wasn't sure how honest to be. The forest was a wilderness paradise, but he thought the Corwins' property was better. He adored the cathedral-house, the library, and the secret room upstairs. He wanted to tell her that, but it seemed inappropriate. As though he wanted to move in with them. As though he wanted to be adopted.

The girl could sense that something was muddling the boy's brain, so she took his hand and turned him north with a gentle tug. "Look at those trees . . . starting to get green."

The quaking aspen buds were just beginning their trembling lives in the wind. Chris smiled, and then looked down at the forest floor. He let go of the girl's hand and reached for a blue mayflower.

"No," Terra said.

"You don't want a flower in your hair?"

"Let it grow."

"Your hair?"

"The flower, you dork."

Chris liked it when Terra called him a dork, and he happily loped ahead of her in the direction of the creek. "See the Christmas trees? That's where the lion lives."

"The lion?"

He shouted, "Here kitty, kitty!"

She caught up with him. "You saw a lion? Really?"

"Heck yeah, I saw it. And it ran away from me."

"You were lucky."

He puffed out his chest. "So was the cat."

"You're such a dork."

"No, I'm not."

The kids walked around in the soft grass, pine needles and mud, their eyes on the ground. Terra said, "We should be able to find some evidence. Paw prints, or a tuft of hair."

Chris replied, "The lion's hair was the same color as yours. And his eyes were as pretty as yours."

"The lion had blue eyes?"

"No, I didn't mean that. I meant they glowed."

"Here in the Christmas trees?"

"Yep. Right here . . . or maybe over there. I wasn't paying attention to the exact location."

"You weren't paying attention?"

Chris began to sweat. "You believe me, don't you?"

Terra reached out and snapped a twig away from a low branch. "This is interesting."

"What is it?"

"Blood. Was the lion bleeding?"

The boy scratched his head. "I don't know. I didn't notice any blood. Maybe . . ."

The girl tossed the twig. "It doesn't matter."

"What do you mean?"

"You probably saw something."

"Yeah, I did see something. It was a lion."

"Hmm."

"You don't believe me?"

Terra searched his eyes. "Do you believe yourself?"

"Of course I believe myself."

"About everything?"

"Yeah . . . geez."

"Hmm. Let's not look for any more signs. Let's go to the creek."

He held back. "Don't you believe me?"

Terra tugged his hand. "Let's go to the water."

Slipping out of her grip, he said, "I can't."

"What?"

"I can't be friends with you. Not if you don't believe me."

The girl walked past him, brushing his shoulder. "I'm going to sit by the water. And I hope you'll join me."

The boy did not follow her. Instead, he shouted, "I saw a freaking lion!"

Terra stopped dead in her tracks, and held her stillness, while the breeze whispered through the pines. Golden light filtered down to the forest floor. The first insects of the year were arising. Terra watched the illuminated specks drift mindlessly in the wind like dust. Very slowly, she turned to face the boy. His cheeks were flushed, and his eyes watery. "Christopher," she said, "would you believe me if I told you that I've seen angels hovering above the altar in our chapel?"

Chris had never gone to church, not since his baptism. His heart pounded while Terra's eyes pleaded for an affirmation. What could he do? He didn't believe in angels. And yet, and yet, there was Terra's face. Were the angels above the altar so beautiful?

He panicked and changed the subject. "Sometimes I like to pretend that I'm a thousand years old."

"What?"

The boy raised his hands and made finger-horns above his head. "I wish I'd been a Viking."

The girl turned and walked away.

Chris rushed forward and grabbed her hand. "I've been studying the Viking culture and how to make a long-boat. But it's too big. So I'm going to make a birch-bark canoe. A short long-boat."

Terra tried not to smile and ended up laughing.

Chris led her to the creek. "One day you'll be looking out the window at Lake Superior, and I'll be there. Sailing."

"Oh yeah? Well, if you really make a boat, I'll sail with you."

"You can steer."

They sat on some dry bedrock, and listened to the song of the water for a while. Eventually, Terra asked, "Where will we go sailing?"

"Up to Isle Royale."

"And down to the Apostle Islands?"

"Sure. After that, we'll take the rivers all the way to Saint Louis."

Terra punched his shoulder. "I don't want to go to Missouri. It sounds like Misery. I want to steer the boat to Middle Earth."

"That sounds like fun."

"Yes. You can begin your new life as a hobbit."

The boy pouted. "A hobbit, not a king?"

"First things first, you dork."

chapter eighteen

IN EARLY MAY, on a Saturday afternoon, Terra and Chris were reading in the library when the girl pointed the *Confessions* at him. "Want to go visit a secret place?"

Thinking she meant the upper room, the boy eagerly nodded. "Let's go."

"Okay, leave your book."

Chris set *Holy Grail Adventures* on a side table and followed Terra to the stairs. He was surprised and disappointed when she hurried down instead of up.

"Follow me," she said, and led him out of the cathedral-house and into the bright sun.

On the northernmost border of the Corwins' property, a shoreline cave offered shade and, beyond that, an entrance to any number of great adventures.

"A cave! Far out!" Chris said, pausing and looking inside.

Terra smiled. "I thought you would like this. The French voyageurs referred to these places as 'purgatories.' "

Chris clambered forward, almost falling into the water. Rhyolite rocks, resembling salmon-like creatures, seemed to be spawning in the shallows. "I can't believe you never brought me to this purgatory before."

Terra pushed him forward. "You're here now."

"Amazing. A person could live here."

"My mom calls it The Tomb, but I don't think you could die in this cave. It's safe from even the worst storms."

"I love it," Chris said. "Let's move in here."

"Sit down, you dork. Here, on the back ledge. Watch your head."

Chris snuggled next to the warm girl. And he faced the opening of light pouring in. "This cave messes with your mind," he said. "It's cold and damp and dark, and yet it's so beautiful."

Terra nodded, her face awash with reflected light.

Chris wanted to kiss her. He wanted to worship her. And he wanted to run for his life.

Instead, he stammered a question: "Did-did you really see wings above the altar? In the upper room?"

She pointed at the lake. "Look at that."

Coming into view was a massive ore ship the color of rust, pushing through the water toward the harbor to load up tons of iron.

Chris observed, "That rusty ship needs an overhaul."

The girl quipped, "You mean an over-hull."

"Good one, Terra."

"Not really."

He grinned. "I liked it."

"That's sweet. You dork."

The ore ship brightened and darkened, as if expanding, as if breathing. Chris whispered, "It's so weird how Minnesota built the world."

"Built the world? Didn't God do that?"

The boy stared hard at the ship. "I learned about this in school. Ore was shipped to factories in places like Pittsburgh. They turned it into steel, and that got turned into railroad tracks and trains. Cars and trucks. Skyscrapers. Lots of good stuff to help people. And along with the good stuff came guns, tanks, and bombs."

Terra said, "That's the way of the world. Everything down here has its dark side. That's why my father . . ."

"Your father?"

"Never mind. Look at that."

The freighter, glacier-slow but steady, continued on its course and dissolved into smallness . . . becoming a reddish hint at the edge of the horizon. And then nothing at all.

Just Superior. As if on fire.

"We should get out of here," Terra said. "We never told my mom that we were leaving the house."

"Uh oh. Will she be mad?"

Terra grabbed his hand and pulled him from the ledge. "She trusts us."

"Cool."

"Yeah. And she'll still be mad."

Out of the purgatory, the boy and girl tried to hurry away, but found themselves lingering along the beach. Chris was endearing in his reverence for pebbles. And by the time he and Terra had trudged back to within sight of the Corwin house, their hands were full of agates, quartz, golden chert, and other northern crown jewels.

"They're so cold," the girl said, shivering.

"They sort of burn," the boy said. "It feels good."

They stood at the shoreline and performed the usual beach-combing ritual of catch-and-release. They tossed all of their treasures back into the water.

chapter nineteen

SUNDAY MORNING, Chris awoke before sunrise, went to the window of his room, and watched as the world was given its life again. Lake Superior lost its darkness, brightening with the sky. Colors of warmth appeared — yellow, orange, and red. A halo rose out of the water on the far horizon and soon became a crown of fire.

Blinking, the boy whispered, "Maybe I should go to Mass."

He was curious to witness what occurred in the upper room of the cathedral-house. Every Sunday, an old priest appeared and offered an exclusive ritual for the Corwins, in Latin, as if the Middle Ages were still alive.

Chris took a good shower, combed his hair, and put on his best clothes. He was starving, but did not break the fast, knowing that Terra would also be embracing emptiness in hopes of more. The boy hopped on his bicycle and flew down the hill. Braking at the bottom, he was about to turn north into the chanting wind, when he recalled the sign that was placed at the stairway leading up to the Corwin chapel: BEYOND HERE BE DRAGONS.

He knew the seafaring reference regarding unchartered waters and dangerous mysteries. However, what did that have to do with the Mass? Was it that dangerous? And to make things more confusing, Terra had scribbled in the word *no* so that the sign read: BEYOND HERE BE no DRAGONS.

Chris had wondered: does that mean me? I'm not allowed up there?

Heart aching, the boy went outside, his mind already set on having an adventure. He climbed onto his bicycle and glided down the hill and turned toward the lighthouse. "House of light," he whispered, and smiled, and began to feel better.

Chris dismounted his bike and walked to the shore, where he reclined on a large rock that was throne-like. Facing the sun, the boy closed his eyes and welcomed the warmth as well as the cool breeze blowing in from the east. The young knight drifted in and out of a daydream full of leaping leviathans that were all pursuing a golden cloud above a dark sea . . . and then Chris opened his eyes again to Lake Superior. The water was like rising waves of fish with sparkling fins that seemed all fire. An hour passed by like nothing, and another hour, the reverie of the Sunday morning deepening in the boy's vision; and it was all good — wonders upon wonders — and he wanted more.

He pedaled into town, and looked around. People were gathering together in all sorts of churches, and seeing them made Chris hunger for whatever they had. The boy circled the places of worship as if he could catch the Holy Ghost around the next corner; and then he suddenly stopped at another kind of haunt, the Two Harbors American Legion.

Chris sneaked in through the back door without being noticed, sat in the back corner, and observed the ritual.

The old-timers fought over a newspaper for a while, mostly interested in the obituaries.

Then the oldest guy began to tell a story.

"One time, Yort was fishing along the shore in his little wooden boat. And nothing was biting. The fish seemed to be outsmarting him."

The other geezers sighed, laughed, and cursed in a sort of chorus.

"Well, Yort had tried the usual tricks and lures to catch some fish. And nothing was working. The lake wouldn't give up a thing. Not even a bite."

Sighs, laughter, and affirmative curses.

"So Yort needed a new plan."

The storyteller took a swig of beer, pausing for effect. His friends also sipped, and raised a chorus of impatience: "Yah, yah, yah."

"Well, as it happened, Yort set aside his tackle box, and he set aside his fishing pole, and he reached into his duffle bag."

"Yah, yah, yah."

"And old Yort pulled out a stick of dynamite."

The chorus of impatience became a sort of responsorial psalm. "You bet! You betcha!"

"Well, Yort lit up the stick of dynamite. He made the Sign of the Cross as the fuse disappeared, and then he tossed the explosive into the lake. Down it drifted for a few seconds, down where the big sturgeon live. And BLAM!"

Amens seemed to fill the bar. Chris leaned forward in his chair.

"The boat lurched up on a bubbling wave and almost capsized. Yort was drenched. But when the lake became calm again, Yort looked around and saw a stunned fish. A huge, whiskered sturgeon."

"You bet! You betcha!"

"Well, the Game Warden appeared on the shore. And he commanded Yort to row in and pick him up."

Silence. Except for a few sips.

"That Game Warden was known to throw the book at people and put them in jail. And now old Yort was dead to rights. There was no way he could wiggle out of this."

Silence. Except for a few gulps.

"The Game Warden climbed into the boat and commanded the lawbreaker to row back out to where the fish was floating.

He was going to retrieve the sturgeon as evidence and make sure Yort went to jail for a long time."

Curses were flung about the bar, and the boy wondered why everyone, including himself, wanted Yort to go free. Didn't he deserve to be punished for breaking the law?

"When the boat got to where the fish was floating, the Game Warden reached out with a net. Yort should have felt defeated, but he was grinning. Suddenly, the sturgeon came to its senses and swam away. The Game Warden waved the net frantically and almost fell overboard. He hollered at Yort, 'It don't matter if that one gets away. I'm still gonna put you in jail for fishing with dynamite.' "

The storyteller paused and lit a cigarette. The smoke rose heavenward and hit the low, stained ceiling.

"Well," the storyteller continued, "while the lawman talked about jail, old Yort grabbed another stick of dynamite, lit it, and tossed it into the Game Warden's hands."

All eyes in the Legion were open wide, even though the same story was told every Sunday.

"The Game Warden cussed and threatened. And old Yort said to the law man, 'You gonna talk all day? Or you gonna fish?' "

chapter **twenty**

THAT AFTERNOON, Chris decided that he would ask the Corwins for a guided tour of their secret chapel. He rode his bike to the cathedral-house, looked up, and noticed how the stained-glass windows shone like multicolored pools of water. He believed that was a good sign, and he went to the door and rang the bell.

The bell tolled deep, echoing into the heart of the house, up through the library and the upper room. Nobody came to the door. The boy rang the bell again, wondering if he was early, or late. He was about to give up and go home, when the door suddenly opened and a woman appeared in a red dress and white apron. She looked like someone from Germany or Switzerland. She said, "Christopher, do you know how to polka?"

"Polka?"

"Yes, it's a dance."

"Hmm, I doubt if I —"

Terra appeared in the doorway in a yellow dress and white apron. "I forgot to tell you, Chris. Today is the Spring Fling at the community center. My mom just got off the phone with your mom, and it's okay for you to join us."

"A dance? I don't know. I was thinking —"

Professor Corwin squeezed into the doorway, dressed in funny short pants and red suspenders. "OOM pa pa! OOM pa pa! Let's polka!"

"Oh, I don't know. I was hoping to —"

The professor bobbed like a great bird. "OOM pa pa! OOM pa pa! Let's polka!"

Terra grabbed Chris by the hand, and led him down the steps — he nearly fell on his behind — and dragged him over to the blue Fiat. "You'll like the Spring Fling. It's a lot of fun."

He spoke nervously. "Will other kids be there?"

"I don't know. Who cares?"

"Will it be a bunch of goofy old people? And us?"

"Maybe."

"Hmm."

Terra squeezed his hand. "You'll love the dance. I promise. Polka is the happiest music on earth."

The Two Harbors community center, when the Corwins and Chris walked through the door, was hopping with happiness. Half of the dancers were dressed up in traditional polka attire, the festive colors brightening the room, and the other half were in jeans and flannel. The accordion, tuba, clarinet, drums, and trumpet were rolling out a barrel of fun. The dance floor was overflowing. Couples in their midnight years were turning counterclockwise toward childhood again. Terra and her grandfather joined the spiral galaxy of spinners, hoppers, and dippers, while Chris and Mrs. Corwin sat at an empty table.

Suddenly a glass of beer and a sparkling water were served to them. Mrs. Corwin raised her glass, coaxing the boy to raise his. "Cheers," she said, and took a frothy sip.

The boy drained half of the water, the fizzy bubbles tickling his throat.

Mrs. Corwin said, "Christopher, do you like beer?"

Was it a trick question? Meant to get him into trouble? "I don't know," he said, staring at her golden brew. "Probably."

"What do you mean, probably?"

He gestured toward the bar. "Well, it seems like most people like beer. I'm probably the same as them."

Mrs. Corwin wiped her mouth daintily with her apron. "Oh no, Christopher. You're different."

"Well, I'm in no hurry to start drinking or smoking, or anything. My father used to see leprechauns."

The woman sipped. "Good boy. Stay away from leprechauns."

The band transitioned to the *Chicken Dance*, and the dancers responded like little kids. Chris was intrigued by the spectacle of Minnesotans flapping their arms. He noticed the growing smile on Mrs. Corwin's face, and he said, "I'll bet you miss your husband."

The smile remained on the woman's face, while her eyes grew sad. "Marriage is not a romance, Christopher. It is a sacrament. Like the priesthood."

The boy nodded, wishing he'd kept his mouth shut.

"Do you think the priesthood is fun? It's a sacrifice, Christopher. No matter what vocation you choose — or get called to by God — you have to give up almost everything else. Oh, don't look at me like that. I have much joy in my life. Every vocation has its joys. Yes. And its sufferings."

Mrs. Corwin took a big drink and gestured toward a young couple on the dance floor. "Marriage is more like a liturgy than a romance."

The boy was puzzled.

The leader of the band shouted, "Is everybody happy?"

There was a joyful noise of shouts, whistles, claps, and stomps. The accordion began a laughing melody: *Stella at the Wheel.*

The boy wished he knew how to dance. And he wondered if Terra was going to teach him. She was having such a great time dancing with the old professor. Had she forgotten about him? Did she really expect him to dance with her mother?

Chris began to sweat, imploding under the pressure of being at a dance that he couldn't join. He thought he would excuse himself for the bathroom, and then make a run for it. His house was only a few miles from the community center. "Excuse me," he said and stood to make his getaway.

Mrs. Corwin would have allowed him to leave and would have phoned the Lagorios to inform them of their son's decision to walk home. However, Terra and the professor appeared, their faces flushed and glowing. The old man was puffing for breath and wasn't able to say anything. Terra playfully chided her mother and Chris, "Why aren't you dancing?"

The boy blushed and looked down at the floor, searching for an excuse. "Umm. I have two left feet. And neither one of them knows how to dance."

"C'mon, you dork. You'll learn fast. No matter how many feet you have, they can do the polka."

"Oom . . . pa . . ." the professor panted, " . . . oom pa."

Chris was not only a dork, but a klutz, at first, stepping on Terra's feet a few times, until his body picked up the pulse of the band. The trick was to follow the heartbeat of the booming tuba and ignore the gypsy-quick accordion. It also helped to let Terra do the leading, at least for the first two songs. After that, Chris was as suave as a boy could be at a polka dance, dipping the girl like an old pro and not pausing too long before moving on with the next steps, always aware of the other dancers and their places in the ever-changing circle.

Chris didn't know what he was doing, exactly, except for making his best friend happy and making himself happy in the process. Even Mrs. Corwin seemed to have forgotten all of her troubles and was twirling like the queen of Bohemia.

The final dance of the afternoon was the *Kissing Polka*. While it was playing out, Chris didn't think about the words. He was too busy floating through the air with the prettiest girl in the world. And when the song ended with a final blast of the trumpet, the dancers all exchanged a kiss. Including the kids. A quick touch of the lips. It just sort of happened in the flow of the moment.

"Thank you for the dance," Chris said, and bowed.

"Thank you," Terra said, and curtsied.

Mrs. Corwin noticed the kiss, and proclaimed to herself, "This boy is going to hurt us."

Overhearing the prophecy, Chris replied, "No. I'm going to help you."

chapter twenty-one

IN EARLY JUNE, the boy and girl reclined in the pebbles beside Superior, a little north of the Corwin house and within sight of the purgatory cave. Terra reached into her shoulder bag and pulled out a surprise gift. "Here. An early birthday present."

He reached out and accepted a hardcover copy of *The Cloud of Unknowing*. "Thanks. But my birthday isn't until September."

"I know. I just thought . . ."

The boy held the book to his chest. "I love the title. I can't wait to read the whole thing."

"*The Cloud* is less technical than the catechism. More mystical."

"Far out."

Chris opened the book to a random page. "*And so, humbly trust the blind stirring of love in your heart. Not your physical heart, your will.*"

The girl shaded her eyes and looked toward the horizon, seeing a gull above the lake. She did not hear the boy's question.

"Is *The Cloud of Unknowing* a love story?"

Terra ignored the question and asked a different one. "Are you excited about attending your new school in the fall?"

Chris was startled by the question. He shook his head as if in denial. "I haven't really thought about it. I didn't think I'd live to see seventh grade."

"You're going to be a teenager," Terra said.

"Yeah. We're getting old. Look, here comes a bird."

The gull approached from the northern shoreline, calling out to them.

Terra sighed. "I wish we had bread for her."

"I wish we had bread for us, too," Chris said, his stomach rumbling.

The gull hovered for a few moments, politely asking for food with its eyes. And then it flapped its wings forcefully.

"I'm sorry," Terra told the bird. "I don't have anything for you today. You'll have to forgive me."

The gull gave her a pleading look.

"I know flying is hard work. But you'll have to catch your own lunch."

Screech!

"Can't you dive for minnows?"

Screech!

Terra loved all creatures great and small, but this gull was trying her patience. "Shoo! Go away!"

Screech!

"Go fishing! You have a big lake full of food."

Screech! Screech! Screech!

Terra tried to wave the gull away. The bird fluttered above her and continued its ravenous demands. Terra raised her other hand and clapped loudly. It didn't work. The bird screeched louder. It might have been playing a game, or it might have been crazed. Terra continued to clap. She shouted and even cursed. Chris had no idea that she was capable of using such English.

In something of a panic, the boy ripped out part of a page of *The Cloud of Unknowing*. He held the paper crumb between his fingers and offered it up to the open beak.

The bird hesitated, and cocked its head to the side. Hunger made the paper resemble bread, the whiteness wrapped around a few words:

spirit of a person
only one of these
created thing.
love when through

Chris reached higher. "Here. Eat."

There was a final screech. The gull ripped the morsel from the boy's hand and wheeled out over the waters. A hundred yards out, the whirring wings began to circle back, as if the bird were returning to screech a complaint or a thank you, and then she suddenly flew off, disappearing into the sunlight.

Chris turned to Terra and gave her a grin that almost made him seem above it all.

She punched him in the chest.

He lost his breath and felt as if a bone were cracked. "Auggh," was all he could say.

"How dare you," Terra said. "That was a collector's edition of *The Cloud*. My grandfather bought it in London, years and years ago, long before you were born!"

"Auggh. Sorry. I'll make it up to you."

"And what about my grandfather?"

The boy rubbed his chest. "I'll make it up to him, too."

Her eyes demanded penance. "How?"

He winced. "I don't know. I'm sorry. You'll have to forgive me."

The girl had never looked so fierce. "I forgive you. But I've just about had it with you."

chapter twenty-two

ONE WEEK LATER, Chris phoned Terra and stammered, "My family is moving to Duluth. Umm . . . today. I should have told you sooner."

The girl said nothing. She already knew.

"Don't worry, Terra. It's not that far from Duluth to your house."

"It's twenty-eight miles."

"Is that all? I can ride my bike."

"Whatever," she said icily. "Don't kill yourself on my account."

chapter twenty-three

THE LAGORIOS moved to the east end of Duluth, where some of the best architecture in the world — Greek, Roman, Renaissance, Victorian, and various Revivals — formed a neighborhood that didn't seem Minnesotan. The Lagorio house was a Tudor Revival that stood halfway up the hill with a partial view of Lake Superior. Chris stood at his new bedroom window, squinting and craning his neck . . .

On the other side of the Tudor Revival, across the street, were the Ruins — archways from a demolished school — the remnant sandstone a dark shade of terra cotta.

The boy couldn't understand why his parents wanted to live in the middle of a big, crumbling town. Joe could work anywhere with his computers, even in the deepest woods. So was it his mother's fault? Did she really need thousands and thousands of thyroids? Her business had picked up from the moment they'd arrived, as if everyone in Duluth were feeling cold and sluggish.

Terra danced in his mind as if she would never become a mere memory; and he tried to imagine her in his future. The doleful boy sent her emails, trying to express what could not be understood for many years. And she never answered.

Early June could have been glorious for Chris in a town full of wilderness parks and trails that ascended deep into the northern sky. But for a boy out of love, June was a month of slunking.

Chris even started watching television.

He slouched on the couch and stared blankly at the situation comedies, and never laughed. In school, he'd heard a few teachers make fun of the shows on TV, with advanced vocab words such as *insipid* and *vacuous,* but had no idea that his teachers could be so correct. Chris had become accustomed to the sublime in the landscape around Two Harbors and by spending time with Terra in the library. He knew the world was "charged with the grandeur of God." And he liked how the grandeur challenged him. It was a good fight, enlivening. But the things on television were another story, doing their damnedest to destroy the real.

The boy started eating potato chips.

He bought them at the gas station and sneaked them into the house, into the basement. And then, after getting hooked on the *Jerry Springer Show,* Chris began drinking cola. Insinuating the sugar into his bloodstream, he was able to laugh. But not with joy. He chugged more sugar and yelled at the TV screen. "Oh, just pick one cousin and stay with him! Can't you be weird enough?"

From channel to channel, the boy searched for images worthy of humanity, and he soon became sick. The potato chips and cola made him feel better for a few buzzing minutes, and then it became worse. And worse.

He began to watch soap operas.

He cheered for the lusty villains and leered at the heaving cleavage of the victims. Soon he was addicted to the Spanish Channel, muttering at the romantic travesties, "*No es bueno . . . no es bueno . . .*"

And then cable news.

"Topher," his mother said, appearing in a fuchsia sari, "what are you watching?"

"Nothing."

She stepped closer. "Is there any good news?"

The reporter reading the teleprompter said, "There is no evidence that the red yeast rice did anything to reduce cholesterol levels."

Val exploded, "She's reporting a study that was funded by the pharmaceutical companies! That's not journalism! That's propaganda for the drug cartels."

The next day, the cable was removed — actually cut away from the house.

And Val made her son eat large amounts of seaweed, sprouts, and things that might have been vegetables.

The boy was grateful. His strength returned, and he began to spend more time outside. He learned to love the parks and trails of Duluth. He found hidden gorges and mystical waters and precious white pines that had eluded the lumberjacks by growing among the dangerous ledges. Chris contemplated among wildflowers at the top of the Duluth hill and fathomed the lake from a new perspective. Superior the great, emblazoned with colorful sailboats upon its lovely blues. The sight of the boats made him remember the boast that he'd made to Terra about sailing to her house.

"I'll sail on my bike," he whispered.

Not bothering to tell his parents about the journey, the next morning Chris jumped on his bike and began peddling down the hill, and then gliding, faster and faster, speeding beyond his ability to stop; and when he intersected a crossway of careening cars, it was too late. A rusty Escort clipped him, flinging the boy toward a lilac bush, where he crashed into the fragrant branches.

While the Escort made its escape, Chris wondered if Terra would be more likely to forgive him now that he'd flown through the air for her; and he hoped his leg was broken to garner more sympathy. "Augghh," he moaned when a "What the heck" neighbor arrived. "Augghh," he moaned a few minutes later when his "Goddess have mercy" mother arrived.

The boy milked it. "My leg! My leg! Augghh. I broke it for Terra."

"Pick up your bike and walk home, Sweetie," his mom-doctor said, after examining him. "You have some scratches and a bruise."

He arose slowly. "That's it?"

"Yes. And you're grounded until further notice."

chapter twenty-four

KENYANS.

Running the Minnesota marathon like winged creatures, they led the race as if they weren't even running, as if the road along Lake Superior were nothing but a pure sweet breeze.

Chris watched from down by the lake, admiring the grace and endurance of the winning Kenyans. For the next hour or so, the other runners, those with a closer relationship to gravity, came stumbling down the road, limping, sweating, and gasping.

Val Lagorio was volunteering at one of the tents, offering herb tea instead of the usual sugary sports drinks.

Chris waved and gave her a smile — he was no longer grounded — and he hurried home to prepare for his own run. The boy, inspired by the levitating Kenyans, was going to run to Terra's house.

He laundered his athletic socks, gym shorts and a white T-shirt, even adding some chlorine-free bleach to bring out brightness. He ate a perfect balance of protein (egg whites from free-range chickens) and complex carbohydrates (flax-oat muffins). He went to sleep before sunset, tossed and turned for a while, but not too fitfully, in order to preserve his strength. Eventually he drifted into a dream . . . above the harbor . . . library . . . stairway . . . Holy Grail . . . Dragon . . . fire . . .

Just before dawn, his eyes flashed open, his head full of light.

"Silvenshine," he whispered, lacing up his shoes.

Chris began his personal marathon by walking across the street to the Ruins. He stood beneath the dark archway until it caught the start of sunrise; and away he went. The boy ambled down the hill, winding his way over to Our Lady of the Rosary Cathedral. He paused, thinking that he might go inside and get some kind of blessing, and instead picked up the pace.

Tischer Creek added music to his descent, and he continued downward, perhaps a little too fast, to Superior Street, where he crossed over and veered north on the sidewalk, barely avoiding a man walking a yellow lab. Chris raced along the fence line of the Congdon Estate, famous for its obscene wealth and murder. He thought about how Terra's house was both grand and somehow humble, the perfect structure.

The first few miles of the marathon were easy, a cool jaunt in the suffused glow of the sunrise. The boy's legs were happy. His lungs were happy. His whole body was thrilled, and he felt certain that he could run like this forever. He accelerated and chased a crow that was lurking on the sidewalk, chased it into the sky.

Chris rounded the bend at the Lester River and was greeted by the everyday star rising out of the water. The direct light was nourishing, empowering, and the boy pushed himself to an almost sprint, past Brighton Beach and its glistening boulders, and he suddenly had a decision to make: Expressway or Scenic Drive.

"Scenic Drive," he said, grinning.

Up Old 61, through the forest above the sun-risen lake, Chris accelerated into a sprint, his heart pounding happily while the waves rolled in to shore, slowly, one surge for every three strides of the boy.

Five miles into the journey, the forest began to thin, replaced by houses with large yards. Chris imagined that the residents loved their views, especially with elevation above Superior, and he daydreamed some memories for a while about his world on the hill above Two Harbors. It had been a kind of heaven and had helped to sooth the pain of having been uprooted from Sacramento. He smiled at the memory of the mountain lion, and rewrote the details in his imagination as if he were a lion trainer who had made the wild beast do tricks and dance among the Christmas trees.

The boy ended the daydream when he saw some little wooden cottages for rent. They were painted in oranges and pinks that suggested Florida instead of Minnesota. The sight of the tourist traps was deflating, and made his lungs convulsive. The race toward reconciliation with Terra was already losing its charm, and the boy, gasping, had to decelerate to a slow jog like a tottering old man.

On a ledge above Lake Superior, Chris felt half-dead and nearly lost his balance. Negative thoughts swirled through his mind, and he became certain that the journey was a farce. From a plodding jog to a shuffling walk, he tried to catch his breath. Lightheaded, he wasn't sure if the scent of pine and wildflowers was real or conjured within by something that wanted to compel him forward.

Forward into the scent of pine and wildflowers.

Forward into the sun, ever rising. Above the waves, ever rolling.

The boy was buoyed up. His head became clear on how to finish. He just had to be smart and keep his own pace. No more sprinting. No more dead runs.

Chris had traveled seven miles and was more than a quarter of the way toward his destination. He was being nimble, remembering the Kenyans and their easy gliding through the air. If only he could keep this rhythm for the distance, he'd arrive with enough energy remaining to form the words that would make everything worthwhile. "I'm sorry." And he allowed himself to imagine a more excellent phrase: "I love you."

He laughed, knowing that phrase was years away.

The boy stumbled. "What was that?" A dead woodchuck. The reek of road kill filled the boy's lungs with a rotten breath. He turned and kicked the furry corpse into the ditch. And then he thought: maybe I should bury the poor thing. But with what? My bare hands?

He glanced up the road to see if there were any houses among the trees, or a tourist trap, any place that would have a shovel. Sentimental, he wanted to give the creature a human burial. He leaned over to look at the woodchuck. Already the ants and flies were feasting.

Chris winced, and ran away at a dangerous speed. He was sweating profusely, and the blazing sun was asking for more. The boy felt as if he ought to turn around and try to walk home; or better yet, hitchhike.

He shook his head, trying to be logical with the fantasy of the journey. What would happen if he finally made it to the Corwin house? If he had any strength left to ring the bell, and if he wasn't doubled over barfing on the flowers, what would he say to the wide-eyed girl when she appeared? "Hi, Terra. Can you carry me to the bathroom? Do you mind if I take a shower?"

And it became more absurd. Whose clothes would he wear after showering?

He imagined himself in a pair of her grandfather's trousers. And gray jacket. And he burst out laughing.

Over the French River bridge, the morning continued to brighten and heat up. Traffic increased as well, with "cabin people" from the Twin Cities driving north in SUVs and week-end pickups, hauling rainbows of ATVs, canoes, kayaks, and bicycles.

The cabin people had always been an irritation to Chris. They tended to circle northland lakes with flashy developments, trying to turn the Garden of Eden into the Mall of America. And they often trespassed, especially the ones with ATVs. Almost every weekend in past summers, a three-wheeling gang would wind their way up to the Lagorios' house and drunkenly ask to use the bathroom.

That reminds me, the boy thought. I really need to go.

The great outdoors makes for an easy outhouse, but Chris wasn't one to whiz just anywhere. He had respect for both the land and the landowners. He would hold his wastewater, no matter how much it hurt, until he found a place for a proper release. Despite having grown up in the woods, his parents had taught him some manners, especially when it came to things like public exposure. Chris was sure that he could hold it until he found a house. He ran faster, but that only angered his bladder. Instinctively, he reached down to literally hold himself from leaking — just as a car full of cabin people drove by, including teenage girls in the back seat, laughing hysterically.

The boy waved with both hands, as if to prove they'd been in the air the whole time. And he suddenly felt a little leak. Panic surged through his brain. Chris stopped dead and stared down at his gym shorts. Was that a wetness beyond his drench of sweat? Was that a hint of yellow? Please, no! The boy dashed away from the road and into a stand of aspen. He wasn't as hidden as he could have been, had he entered pines, so a few more cabin people got a good laugh at a "local hick in the sticks." But the relief of relieving himself was so profound that he didn't care who witnessed it.

"They all go, too," he whispered. "Everyone has to go."

Back on the road, the boy loped along for an easy mile. The sun was nearing its peak, climbing and climbing. Chris also ascended, higher and higher into the north, even when the terrain began to go downhill. The boy ran toward his goal, dreaming of reconciliation. He imagined some of the things that Terra might say. He thought she might scold him for a while, or punish him with a silent pout, and then welcome him with open arms. And open books. They'd spend the afternoon in the library, on the love seat, literary souls easing back into their friendship. And then, Terra would want to kiss him again.

"Slow down, slow down," he told himself, realizing that his flesh had gone all goosey and he was shivering.

Heat stroke, he thought. I've overheated into chills. I've pushed myself too far.

Chris was wrong. It wasn't heat stroke that was making him shiver. It was Lake Superior, with a northeast wind blowing down the cloudy road from Canada. Chris limped forward, going numb. Fluid filled his nostrils and slid down his lips, the unwelcome taste of salt filling his parched mouth.

Gross, he thought. He pressed a finger to one of his nostrils and blew out the snot, followed by a blast from the other side.

More cars drove by. More laughing faces.

Trembling, on the verge of tears, the boy forced his slow legs to carry him forward. Ten miles into the crazed marathon of his own making, he approached a golden-brown bump on the shoulder of the road. The colorful obstacle seemed beautiful until his blurred eyes made out the features of a female deer. Fresh road kill. She wasn't yet bloated, except for the natural plumpness of being full of milk. Chris stopped and looked around for the surviving fawn.

The boy scanned the trees and underbrush on both sides of the road. The terrible thought entered his mind that the frightened fawn had perhaps hurtled through the woods — over the cliff and into the lake. Chris shuffled through the ditch into the pines and birches, panting with worry. He made his way to the overlook, and stood shivering on the cliff. The blue water went on and on, with a hint of a blue-green horizon.

The boy could not look down. All he could do was pray for the little fawn. If only God existed — like the angels over the altar — if only everything really existed.

Chris turned away from Superior and ran through the trees, falling twice in his haste.

The rain began pouring the moment his feet hit the pavement. The wind gusted against him like slaps and punches, pounding his body to the very bones. Now Chris ran blindly, barely feeling the road, past the gaudy signs for TOM'S LOGGING CAMP and past Stony Point Drive with its wave-misty boulders that would have been a perfect place for a rest in good weather.

The boy ran like mad, sprinting through the freezing rain as if daring it to kill him, and daring his own body to kill him.

Falling face-down on the cold, wet shoulder, the boy heaved for breath. The heavy rain washed over him, the wind pounded his flesh, and the two little fawns watched from the tree line, their ears held high and alert. The fawns had never heard a boy cry. They'd heard the screech of hawks, the howl of wolves, and the wail of loons. This seemed wilder.

The fawns watched for five or ten minutes, keeping very still, with an occasional twitching of tails. Warm and dry beneath layers of pine branches, the abandoned fawns took in the scene of mourning until Chris finally crawled to his knees. Then the silent, nearly invisible creatures walked dangerously close to the cliff — ears attuned to the waves smashing the rocks — and gently nibbled the soft wet grass.

The boy stood and leaned into the wind and rain. With his eyes half-closed, he made himself believe that he was just a mile or so from Two Harbors.

He limped up the North Shore, into the teeth of the weather. Lake Superior, even in late June, was only forty degrees; and the wind-chill raging against him felt autumnal or perhaps the final bite of winter. The boy coughed and sneezed. The cold filled his overworked lungs.

"Just another mile . . . or so . . ."

Shivering through the dark corridor of pine, staggering like a drunk on the verge of death, Chris strained his eyes through the curtains of rain. "No, it can't be," he gasped. "This place . . . is only halfway!"

The landmark was one that had divided his mother and father, a shack on the side of the road called Russ Kendall's Smoked Fish. Joe Lagorio loved it. Val, however, was not a fan of smoked fish. "The smoking process makes the meat carcinogenic. Just like any form of smoking, it will kill you. Do you want to die?"

Chris preferred life. However, the smoked king salmon, with a side of fresh bread, was to die for.

The boy stood in the murderous storm, on the verge of collapsing, hoping the fish shack was an illusion. His knees were shaking, and he gasped, spitting the words, "I must be farther than halfway. I must be. I should have passed this place long ago. Damn it."

And yet, he thought, if the shack was really there, he could spend the emergency money in his sock. He could eat some fish and bread and cheese, and drink some water. Strengthened by the feast, he might be able to conquer the blasted weather and get to Terra's by dusk.

Chris accepted the fish shack as a real place, and staggered to the door.

chapter twenty-five

THE SOGGY ten dollars was enough for honey-glazed salmon, a hunk of bread, a chunk of cheese, and a bottle of Deep North Water. The latter was enjoyed first, with no glass or cup. Chris sat at a table and chugged. Then he carefully chewed the salmon, and eased it down with the succulent bread. The boy was amazed by how quickly he felt strong again. He broke off a small piece of the cheese and placed it in the side of his mouth, allowing the mild cheddar slowly to dissolve and give him a sense of fullness.

"Everything okay?" asked the owner.

"Yeah. Very good."

For the next ten minutes or so, Chris feasted, growing stronger and warmer.

A family of cabin people entered the shack. The mother, in dark sunglasses, was reassuring her teenage son, "Yes, this is the place, all right."

The son, in jeans and a maroon sweater, spoke as if spitting. "This isn't the same place. Where are the aquariums? Where are the lobsters and eels?"

The father stepped up to the counter and ordered several pounds of Lake Superior trout. He asked the owner, "Do those fish have bones?"

"Yes, sir. Fish have bones. Best to protect yourself with bread to be safe."

"Fine, then. A loaf of the bread, and a pound of the cheddar."

"Sharp?"

"Not sharp as a bone," the father said, laughing.

"Ughh, what losers," the cabin kid said, sauntering over to Chris. "And you look all wet. What have you been doing?'

"Me? Oh, I don't know. I'm sort of on a quest."

"A quest? Like Jonny Quest?"

"What?"

"It's a cartoon."

Chris sipped some Deep North Water. "Sorry, I don't know much about cartoons."

The cabin kid sat across the table. "So . . . what sort of a quest are you on?"

"You know," Chris said, shrugging, "the old-fashioned sort — battling dragons and trying to help the girl. Like a knight."

"You've been battling dragons?"

"Well, um, no. But the weather has been sort of brutal."

The cabin kid smirked. "I don't think weather counts as a dragon."

His mother called out, "Connor, hon, you want a Mountain Dew?"

"Yeah, make it twenty ounces."

Trying to impress the kid, and trying to convince himself that the journey was fraught with great danger and therefore glorious, Chris said, "I encountered some wild animals along the way."

"Werewolves?"

"No, not exactly. There was a dead woodchuck . . . and a dead deer."

"Did you kill them with your bare hands?"

"No. I just kind of stumbled over them."

Connor reached across the table and took a piece of bread. "Dude," he said, "you are like the worst knight ever."

"Hon," his mother called out, "they have only twelve-ouncers of Dew."

"Then get me two of them. Sheesh."

"Well, I suppose," Chris said, "you have a long day ahead of you. Where is your cabin, exactly?"

Connor grabbed another piece of bread, then stood up, munching. "Wouldn't you like to know, Sir Sweatalot."

While the cabin family gathered up their goods and noisily exited the shack, Chris allowed his fists to become gentle hands again. They were shaking a bit, however, because of how much he'd wanted to beat the living dew out of that Connor kid.

"Sun's coming out," the owner said. "Should be a perfect day for a quest. How far are you going, brave knight?"

Before Chris could answer, there was a honk out on the road. He looked through the wet window to see a blue Fiat barely avoid crashing into the cabin people. Mrs. Corwin swerved around their gray SUV, honked again, and continued south toward Duluth. And there was Terra in the passenger seat! Did she see him?

Chris thrust up his hand to get her attention. "Hey! Stop! Stop! Come back!"

The Fiat curved around the bend and disappeared.

"God, God," he muttered, trembling angrily. "That's it. I'll never go on a quest again. Not when it seems like everything is against me. Nothing ever seems to go my way."

"Hey, kid," the owner of the shack said. "My help's coming in at two o'clock. You need a ride somewhere?"

chapter twenty-six

WALLOWING IN his room, slouched on the floor, Chris stared into a corner and allowed the most depressing thoughts to have their way with him.

Almost.

The window was propped open by the catechism that Terra had given to him, and the scent of lilacs filled his room with a presence that stirred a longing and lifted the dispirited boy to his feet, down the stairs, and out the door.

Dragonflies, recently freed from exoskeletons, zipped through the sunshine, followed by a crested flycatcher in hot pursuit. The bird gave a little *greep* while it flashed through a maple. Chris ambled around the house and across the street to the Ruins. He sat on the steps and imagined ancient civilizations . . . What happened to all those people? Greeks. Romans. Anglo-Saxons. Kings. Queens. Knights. Maidens. "All dead and gone," he said, while a swallow swooped through the archway and sailed away.

The boy stood and stretched his arms, feeling old before his time. He couldn't believe he was going into seventh grade in the fall. Seventh grade! It seemed like graduate school. Would it spark his imagination, or would he be bored to death? Chris left the Ruins and began walking across yards and scrambling over fences on his quarter-mile journey to the wildest place in town. Along the way of woods to Sunshine Creek, he noticed, without thinking, how every vein in each leaf was a lifeline — a photo-synthetic map to the green side of God. And a flash of unfallen lightning sparked the wings of a blackbird. And a water-song arose from the welcoming creek. While the boy ascended the trail, he paused in a clearing to witness the clear sky become a great cloud, blue-white and feathered, stretching above Duluth like the hint of an angel's real power.

When June fell sweltering into July, Chris continued to explore the green shadows of the city, the inner workings of wilderness just beyond the busy streets. He found the first raspberries and strawberries of the season, drank from water that seemed streamlined from the sky, and one evening when it was time to return home to be scolded for having missed dinner, Chris witnessed clouds that turned blood-red, gorged with sunset like some grand catastrophe of grace.

The boy decided he could live in this place.

One night in the backyard of the Tudor Revival, Chris considered a blade of grass . . . and saw a dewdrop, clear to the starry skies, become a double galaxy.

"Topher?" his mother called out the door. "Are you out there?"

"I'm here," he answered. "Don't worry. I didn't run away."

"Just checking, Sweetie." Val closed the door and turned on the outside light, extinguishing most of the heavens.

"Damn," Chris muttered.

And a luna moth appeared, alighting near the porch.

"Poor thing," the boy thought. He'd studied moths in school and out of school, and knew the luna moth would never see the moon's full cycle, searching the sky in a lifetime week. Chris believed it was cruel for life to become death in a few quick flutters. "Damn, damn," he muttered. And yet, the seraphic eyes on the wings seemed like a glimmer of immortal vision. Chris stayed with the moth through several hours of the night . . . and then dreamed he had his own wings and seraphic eyes.

The next morning, the boy strolled up the tree-wild street, thinking he'd visit the public library on Mount Royal. He wondered if they would have a copy of *Holy Grail Adventures*. He felt the story was calling to him again.

Chris had just begun to climb the Mount when he was struck by a sort of vision. Standing on the sidewalk was a curvaceous girl in a blue dress.

She spoke gently to the boy, "Are you lost?"

"I, umm, don't know."

"Are you new to Duluth?"

"Yeah. Ahh, not really."

"Will you be attending Woodland Middle School?"

"Hmm. I'd have to ask my mom."

She pointed at the building. "Well, that's Woodland."

"Umm . . ."

The girl's face grew concerned, as if she were thinking: is this boy mentally challenged? Should I take him by the hand and escort him to the appropriate authorities?

"My name is Christopher," he said, stepping up to the sidewalk.

"Christopher," she echoed. "It means Christ-bearer. What a great name."

"Oh. I live over by the Ruins."

The girl extended her hand, and held his tightly. "I'm Mary Joan Mudgett. My uncle teaches at this school."

Two large men walked out, carrying toolboxes. They had been working on the set designs for the school's Fall Festival. The seventh- and eighth-graders would be presenting a musical, *Out of the Woods: A Comedy*. Mary Joan's father, the larger of the two men, wasn't smiling, seeing his daughter grasping the hand of a strange boy. "Mary Joan!" he called out.

Her uncle also shouted, but playfully, "Can that boy sing? Dance? Act?"

Chris shoved his hands into his jeans pockets, and began shuffling away. "I'm on my way to the top of Mount Royal."

Mary Joan said, "Nice to have met you, Christ-bearer."

Chris turned around, almost tripping, and waved awkwardly.

"Who is that kid?" her father asked.

"He looks like the creative type," her uncle said. "Let's put him in the show."

"Yes," Mary Joan said, smiling. "Let's put him in the show."

Chris spent all of July and August in the public library at the summit of Duluth. He walked up there every day, and always paused in front of Woodland Middle School, hoping to see the curvaceous girl in the blue dress. He hadn't forgotten about Terra Corwin — she was his first touch of the possibility of bliss — and yet this new girl, Mary Joan, had an allurement of additional bliss. Mary Joan was more of a woman than a girl. Chris even dreamed of her. He woke up soaked and embarrassed.

Taking refuge in the library, no longer striving to live in the realms of magic and courtly love, he settled for local history. He dove into the volumes about Duluth, "the Zenith city of the unsalted seas."

Before its fall, Duluth had more millionaires per capita than any place in America. The wealth was created by ships coming in, and ships going out, the port connected by waterways to the depths of both the Atlantic and Pacific oceans, making it the center of the shipping earth. The mansions rose on the hill, and barons of all kinds, especially of lumber and iron, built a city of great beauty, and industrial ugliness, melded together on the shore of Superior. Every so often, the economy would sink, and then rise again. Duluth got rusty and yet continued to shine.

"Here I am," Chris whispered, looking out the window of the library. "I'm all yours, Duluth. Can you give me the greatest adventure?"

chapter twenty-seven

IN SCHOOL, the boy found himself seated behind the girl in the blue dress. She wore every other color, too. Her dresses were all homemade, but not dowdy — more like costumes, with puffy sleeves and bright sashes and glitter. Mary Joan Mudgett was mostly polite to Chris, but sometimes acted as if he had the plague. The thought crossed his mind that maybe she knew about his dreams. Were such things possible? Could a girl really know something like that? Chris blushed when he thought of such exposure. And he was steeled in his disbelief in God. How horrible to be so well known. It was difficult enough to have teachers marking up his papers. He couldn't bear to have a Supreme Being giving him a grade.

The midnight dreams of flesh filled him with incendiary shame. What the hell was his body doing? Why couldn't he control it? He burned and burned . . . for what purpose?

He supposed the girls were having a rough time, too.

Mary Joan Mudgett, however, seemed to be beyond it all. She was secure in her homemade dresses, knew all the answers in every class, and when the skinny girls were risking kisses and impulses more dangerous, she was a walking, talking, perfectly confident NO.

"NO," she was always saying to the scraggle-boys who tried to ask her to a movie or a walk by the lake. "NO." The girl was immovable, larger than life in the seventh grade. The only time she let a boy touch her was during the performance of *Out of the Woods*. And even then, playing The Huntress, she grimaced during her dance with the Mute Minstrel — played by Chris.

And the audience roared.

The eighth grade was more of the same: a comedy of pubescent errors for all of the kids — except for Mary Joan. She was so mature. And beyond mature, the girl had accomplished the seemingly impossible: she knew who she was. That self-knowledge, and the spiritual power that accompanied it, made Mary Joan irresistible. And the memory of Terra Corwin began to fade.

One day in the middle of February, Chris was shivering in the boys' room, when he noticed a Bible tract near the urinal. He would not have given the tract any attention — they were routinely scattered around the school by sons and daughters of zealots — but this tract was different. It was homemade, colored with crayon. Chris picked it up and read the title: *SAVE YOUR FLESH*.

The fourteen-year-old laughed. "Save it for what? A rainy day?"

That night, Chris looked out the frosty window, his soul contemplating the starry sky. "Far out . . . far out . . . it's all on fire."

The boy was smart enough to know that the stars were not overflown fireflies or sparks from the hearth of angels. He knew, from long ago in Sacramento, that the stars were nuclear suns, each one powerful enough to scorch the world to nothing — not even ashes.

"Good God . . ."

Chris considered the poetic shapes of the constellations, how the glittering bodies could be almost anything, or even shift into the shapes of buildings, such as castles or churches. However, those thoughts were whimsy, a kid's imagination making nice with danger. The stars, the uncountable billions of deadly suns, were not in fact nice. And if God were a trillion times more scorching than all of the burning suns put together, then who could survive a visitation from on high?

Chris blinked at the Great Bear, the Lion, and the other cosmic marauders. "And God would be a trillion times infinity bigger."

The boy's head became feverish, the big questions flashing like lightning. He struggled to think: how did people believe in a shrunken God so tiny that it could enter their hearts? If God existed . . . an all-consuming fire . . . then nobody could survive the touch of such a destroying Creator.

"Man alive . . ."

Turning away from the heavenly window, Chris vowed to avoid any real contact with the Killer Love that would be the death of him.

Instead, the next day, he asked Mary Joan out on a date. He approached her in the lunchroom, where she sat with the other farm girls. One of the lines of segregation at Woodland was drawn according to the city limits. The few farm kids huddled together against the usual insinuations about bad hygiene and various smells.

Chris shuffled up to sweet-smelling Mary Joan, paused as if remembering his line, and stammered, "Wanna go with me to Cariboob?"

He meant to say Caribou, as in the Caribou Coffee Shop on the top of Mount Royal.

Mary Joan didn't answer, chewing the last of her goat-cheese sandwich.

Her two friends giggled.

Beads of sweat glistened above the boy's eyes. His cheeks burned. "Ma-ma-mary . . ." he tried again, "I'd like to t-take you to . . . Cariboob."

Mary Joan ignored the giggles and wiped the corner of her mouth with a napkin. "NO."

Chris felt the urge to flee, but two of his buddies came up behind him to add support. George had a monstrous nose and chin, tiny eyes near the sides of his head, and a mess of brown hair sticking up like antlers. Everyone called him Moosehead. The other kid had a premature streak of gray in his hair. His name was Lonnie, and everyone called him Skunk.

Moosehead snorted, "Go for it."

Skunk lisped, "Yeah, Sacramento, go for it."

Chris focused on the crucifix peeking out of the upper cut of Mary Joan's dress. He cleared his throat, and stammered, "I wa-nanna buy you a coffee, or a teat. I mean treat!"

"NO."

Mary Joan and her friends smiled with a sense of power, and the boys retreated from the table.

What was that power?

The guys felt as if they were battling something beyond their ken, and gave up easily. They were never able to verbalize the many dimensions of the struggle between the sexes and for sex. They spoke of girls as being "hot" or "smoking hot" or "nice" or "smart" or "easy" or a "crazy bitch," and yet Chris never used any of those words for Mary Joan. She was a person who would need more than a word or two of description. She was a girl-woman, farmer, actress, seamstress, intellectual, spiritual power who would need a whole book to flesh out her unique multiplicities that drove him into a stammering stupor of desire.

Toward the end of eighth grade, Chris approached the girls' table again. Moosehead and Skunk followed closely behind. They had never been on a date, and they secretly hoped that Sacramento might be able to talk his way into a triple date. The other farm girls were cute and mysterious, too.

"Okay," Mary Joan said, before the question was even asked. "I'll go to Caribou with you."

Moosehead snorted, "Me, too?"

Skunk lisped, "Us, too?"

Mary Joan's girlfriends were shocked. "All of us? A group date?"

"NO. Just me and the Christ-bearer."

chapter twenty-eight

WITHIN THE festival of atoms, the heavens were at play, bursting forth into all shapes and colors and sounds.

Columbine blooms were moving in the wind like winged bells.

A bumblebee was ringing in a bluebell, a musical pollination.

A squirrel conducted the air from pine to maple in a whirl of Mozartic laughter.

In a higher branch, a red-crowned sparrow sang as if he were the king of music.

All the wild ones of God, even in the city, were singing as if life were ever-rising and never dying.

Walking up the sidewalk to Mount Royal, Mary Joan sang out, "The wildflowers are everywhere! Free gifts every May! Isn't God wonderful?"

The boy nodded, not sure if that was deceptive. He wanted to affirm Mary Joan's belief, without pretending that he fully shared it. However, he had the Bible tract in his pocket — *SAVE YOUR FLESH* — for good luck.

Mary Joan in her blue dress, and the way she walked as if the round earth had been formed to accentuate her curves, made Chris want to run away, down the hill to Lake Superior, and throw his body into the icy, lust-snuffing water. And he also wanted to wrap his arms around Mary Joan's lushness and kiss the living daylights out of her.

With those two impulses battling for control, no wonder he kept stumbling at Mary Joan's side, hands in his pockets, mumbling things like, "Uh-huh, umm, yep, those are nice buds on those trees."

When they arrived at the coffee shop, other teens were already crowded into the booths, slurping hot and cold drinks. Boys on one side of the shop. Girls on the other. When the slurpers saw Chris and Mary Joan, they whispered among themselves and also across the room. The boys and girls said the most horrible things, and yet they meant no real harm. They were all intrigued by the sight of a couple that might be flirting in the realm of romance, the almost-secret world of love, sweetness, and danger.

"Maybe we should go someplace else," Chris said.

"Why? The line isn't very long. It'll be our turn soon enough."

He paused, frozen by the whispers. He didn't want to lie, and he didn't want to tell the truth about his embarrassment. So he said, "We could stay here. Or we could go back in time."

Mary Joan smiled. "Go back in time?"

He nodded. "Yeah, to that new place."

She laughed. "It's new? And yet back in time? What are you talking about?"

The boys and girls in the booths wanted to know what he was talking about, too. They leaned forward and listened closely.

"Let's go to *Old Hound Dog*."

One of the kids in the booth began to pant and bark. Others joined his doggie chorus.

Mary Joan rolled her eyes. "Oh, please. Let's get out of here."

Old Hound Dog was an ice-cream shop that was decorated with larger-than-life posters of Marilyn Monroe, James Dean, Jane Mansfield, Marlon Brando, and other tragic stars. The place was popular among college students and retirees. The jukebox blinked and glittered with selections ranging from *Dream a Little Dream of Me* to the *Great Pretender* to *Blueberry Hill*.

The boy paused near the jukebox. "Will your mom be okay with this? Do you need to let her know where we are?"

Mary Joan nodded. "I'll call her about our change of plans. She'll be thrilled to meet us here."

Mrs. Mudgett had dreamed of being a famous actress, but had settled for parts in the community theater, along with directing the Christmas and Easter pageants at her parish. When Mary Joan phoned and reported the change in venue for the "non-date," the exuberant woman exclaimed, "I love that place!"

"Settle down, Mom. It's MY non-date, not yours."

"Well, well," she said dramatically, "maybe I won't show up at all. Perhaps your non-date can drive you home in his non-car."

"See you soon, Mom."

"Maybe."

"Bye, Mom."

Chris and Mary Joan sat on checkered stools at the counter and waited for someone to take their orders.

An Elvis-looking man eventually appeared, his apron splattered with a dozen flavors. He smiled as if offering the whole world. "Whatcha want, kiddos?"

"Neapolitan, three scoops in a sugar cone." That's what Mary Joan wanted. And Chris, with his stomach aching with nervousness, said, "The same, umm, please."

The apron-wearing Elvis nodded and strutted over to the glass freezer to scoop up the goodies.

Because Mary Joan knew who she was, and wasn't afraid to be happy, she spun around on the checkered stool as if it were a merry-go-round. She raised her arms. "Whooeee!"

Multiple thoughts whirled in Chris's brain, all mixed up in a mess of adrenaline, shame, and desire.

Mary Joan is acting different.

She's not who I thought she was.

She's wilder.

Hmm.

Maybe I like wilder.

Everyone's staring at us.

I wish Mary Joan would stop spinning.

Elvis is gonna kick us out.

Her dress is rising while she spins.

Look at those thighs. Look at those thighs.

Oh no.

Oh no! I'm getting excited.

God, help me stay cool.

Fix the dress, Mary Joan. Fix the dress.

No . . . Let it go.

It's perfect.

When Mary Joan stopped spinning, Chris was worried that she would see his growing excitement.

Every boy goes through this. The battle of the bulge. Even the best of boys in the most gracious of homes cannot completely control the flow of blood through the body. How could Chris not respond naturally to a woman-girl like Mary Joan? Just watching her eat ice cream could sizzle a saint.

Dizzy from her spin, Mary Joan pointed her sugar cone at the boy's heart. "I knew you were different."

"Me?"

Mary Joan nodded and resumed working on her ice cream, finishing off the vanilla and moving on to the strawberry.

The boy was dying to know. "How am I different?"

The strawberry was like sweet lipstick on Mary Joan's face, and if Chris hadn't been so nervous with divergent thoughts, he might have leaned over for a kiss.

"You're a deep thinker," Mary Joan said. She paused, licking her lips, and then nodded proudly as if taking some credit for his soul. "You're not like the other boys in school. Last week in the lunchroom, I heard you talking to Skunk and Moosehead about the proposal to build a new zoo that would rival the one in San Diego."

"Wild animals should not be caged."

She smiled. "You also said that you didn't want Duluth to compete with California. You said Duluth shouldn't get too big for its britches."

Was there a double meaning in that? Had she noticed his britches?

"Hmm . . ." Mary Joan's eyes narrowed. She focused on his jeans. "What's that in your pocket?"

The boy was horrified. Damn it, he thought, what will she think of me now?

Horror has many levels, and the horror in Chris rose higher when he noticed that Elvis and several college students were watching and waiting to find out what he had in his pocket.

"What is it?" Mary Joan asked.

The boy's cheeks were burning. His whole body was burning. He followed Mary Joan's line of sight from her pure green eyes to his pants — yes, he wanted to die. Please, he thought, God kill me now.

But Mary Joan was just looking at the Bible tract. She could only see part of it, the crayon-red proclaiming: *SAVE YO.*

Chris thrust his hand to his pocket, grabbed the tract and raised it above his head. "*SAVE YOUR FLESH!*" he shouted to everyone. "*SAVE YOUR FLESH!*"

Mary Joan's eyes grew wide, not expecting such religious enthusiasm from him.

Elvis tsked, "Man, don't be preaching in here. Some customers don't dig it."

Mrs. Mudgett was standing in the doorway, trying to decide what to do. She hadn't expected her daughter's non-date to be so evangelical. She called out, "It's time to go home to the farm, dear. C'mon, now. We don't want to worry the goats."

chapter twenty-nine

ON THE LAST day of school, after the bell had sounded the call to freedom, Mary Joan appeared at Chris's locker and said, "I'd like to take you out to the barn."

What could such a sentence mean? Chris had two instantaneous interpretations, one having to do with sweeping out hay, and one having to do with rolling in hay.

Mary Joan hadn't meant to be confusing and immediately began to clarify. "The Barn Theater in Wrenshall is having a festival next weekend. My mother and I are going, and I thought you might like to see some films that have more depth than the usual."

The boy leaned against his locker, his mind still rolling in the hay. "Heck yeah, I'll go to the barn with you."

"Saturday night is a double-feature. Both films were shot in Minnesota. The first one is about pioneer farmers, and the second one is about star-gazing. Does that sound good?"

"I'm all over it," he said.

She smiled. "Fantastical."

He focused on her crucifix. "Visions in a barn. That's not the usual."

"Yeah. You'll be amazed."

On Saturday night, Mrs. Mudgett drove the non-daters in a white Mustang. Chris thought that was a strange car for farmers to have, and yet it also made sense. The ride was loud and swervy, with Mrs. Mudgett entertaining them the whole way to Wrenshall. She sang tunes from *The Wizard of Oz* and *South Pacific* and turned her red-scarved head toward the back seat for applause. The singing was agreeable to the boy, because he didn't have to talk. He glanced out the window at the green-golden trees, and then at Mary Joan's bemused face, and back to the trees. The sun was low, losing its blaze . . . the valley was darkening . . . and the Mustang reverberated with *The Sound of Music.*

The boy was intrigued by the Mudgett family. There had been farmers around Two Harbors, but they tended to be quiet and more stereotypical. How on earth did a person like Mrs. Mudgett fit into the world of agriculture?

"We've climbed every mountain!" she sang. "And now we're here!"

Just outside of the town limits of Wrenshall was a sky full of an old red barn, transformed into a big-screen theater. Mrs. Mudgett parked in the grass near a portable outhouse, and they all rushed out of the car. The last of the day's glow filtered out of the western horizon and into the barn. The entrance was studded with Christmas lights, and nearly twenty people were waiting in line for tickets.

Chris reached for Mary Joan's hand. It was warm and fitting, and he let go when they joined the single-file line of film buffs. The boy had brought enough money to pay for all three tickets, but Mrs. Mudgett would have none of that chivalry.

"This is my treat," she announced. "MOO-vies in a barn!"

"Mom," Mary Joan whispered, "shh."

"Three MOO-vie tickets! Fabulous, fabulous! Thank you. Keep the change."

The man behind the milk-can gave her a wink. "Enjoy the films."

"Films? Oh no, that's not how to market this event. This isn't a film festival. This is a MOO-vie festival."

Mrs. Mudgett, who believed that God had personally called her to Hollywood before she got roped into getting married, was creating quite a scene. Laughter surrounded her. Not snide laughter. Everyone was simply having a good time, excited about the simple and powerful mix of high art with lowly hay bales. The barn was bustling with old hippies, college students, film connoisseurs, and a few "regular folks" who'd seen the promotional story in the *Tribune*.

The locally produced films would be simulcast all over the barn, with a screen near the ticket counter where the cows once stood in their stanchions, another screen in the tractor storage area, and the biggest screen up in the hayloft.

Chris took Mary Joan's hand again and led her up the creaking, wooden stairs, with Mrs. Mudgett following behind, no longer mooing but exclaiming, "We should get some popcorn! Don't you want to stay down here and sit on bales? Mary Joan, slow down!"

The loft was scented with hay and pine, and the ticket-holders walked a red carpet toward the big screen. The boy felt as if he were walking a greater aisle — in this world or some other world — and ended up at the fourth row, where three plastic chairs were still available. Mary Joan's mother reiterated that she'd prefer to sit on hay bales, when the screen flickered and exploded with light. "Oh, this is good," she said, changing her mind. She sat heavily and leaned back. "This is wonderful! We'll have a perfect view."

The first film of the evening shimmered into the air in black and white, but so well textured that it seemed like a flood of deep colors. Chris's attention was drawn above the screen, where the rounded rafters of the barn glowed like golden ribs, as if the night had been swallowed into the belly of the world's most entertaining whale.

Lake Superior was the backdrop for the opening credits. The film was called *The Shivering Land*, and the narrator explained how the North was viewed differently by the Indian tribes, the French explorers, the missionaries, the industrialists, and the various ethnic groups that worked in the factories and mills. "And then," the narrator said, building tension while the camera flew over the water and forests, and hovered above a cultivated field, "there were the pioneer farmers who tried their hands at fruits and vegetables."

"That's us!" Mrs. Mudgett said. "We grow fruits and veggies."

Mary Joan tried to shush her. "Shhh."

Her mother whispered loudly, "I think the film-makers are sitting in the back row. I saw two guys dressed in black. They enjoy it when you show emotion for their art."

"Shush," someone scolded from the back row.

Mrs. Mudgett smiled and let the images wash over her. Sky, forest, field, and home. The music was also good, a single violin with a dancing melody that suggested a second violin.

The boy felt that he was somewhere in the realm of love. It was a very strange place, vacillating between a solemnity and a farce. He turned his head to see the light in Mary Joan's eyes and the joyful smile on her face. Yikes! Her teeth had vanished! Mary Joan continued to smile through the emptiness. What was wrong with her? Chris saw a vision of a toothless old woman, as if time had rushed by — a hundred years in a minute. The old woman laughed in his face, and handed him a square of chocolate. "From my mom," she whispered. "It's dark, very full of cocoa."

Relieved that time had not so drastically traveled, Chris popped the chocolate into his mouth. And his teeth also disappeared.

The pioneer farmers suffered the big screen in old photographs, damaged eight-millimeter footage, and dramatic re-enactments. The strongest emotions, however, were conjured by an interview in a nursing home. A wrinkled and dappled centenarian, a man who'd seen it all, described the blizzards, bears, wolves, floods, mosquitoes, diseases, lumber barons, and ever-present death that he had endured.

"I love this," Mrs. Mudgett said, her face drenched with tears.

Mary Joan and Chris and everyone in the audience were also inspired to tears, the visions of the centenarian creating the sense that a barn full of a nursing home was part of a much larger view, making the hayloft that much nearer to the heavens.

"They've all passed on," the last pioneer said, his voice dry and raspy. The boy noticed that the old man's eyes were moist and clear. Chris almost said a prayer that he'd live to be so ancient and noble. The film-makers transitioned from the centenarian's eyes to Superior again, with evergreens rising through the water, and golden wheat fields, and rainbow gardens and flowers blooming everywhere, their petals heavy with snowflakes and yet still growing.

The final credits rolled while the title song, *The Shivering Land*, lilted hauntingly and lifted the last images of the far North . . . fading to black . . . and one final burst of light that stayed with the audience.

Nobody seemed to know what to do. Even Mrs. Mudgett was perfectly still. And then, illuminated by the grace of great art, the crowd stood and gave a standing ovation.

Chris rubbed his eyes, and clapped, and rubbed his eyes, and hoped his own life would be worthy of such paradisal images.

chapter **thirty**

VAL LAGORIO stood in the living room, trembling with maternal instincts and caffeine, when her son arrived back home from the festival. It was midnight, the latest he'd ever been out. "Topher, are you okay?"

"Hi, Mom. Of course I'm okay. The Mudgetts are awesome, and we had a great time. Everyone cried."

Val noticed a smudge of chocolate on her son's face. "I'd like to know more about these people."

"I'm going to their farm tomorrow. I'll give you a full report."

She smiled, her eyes tired and half-closed. "I don't need a full report. Just a good synopsis."

"Okay, Mom."

The next morning, the boy rode his bicycle up the hill to Mount Royal, and then continued into the high woods and meadows. Blue morning glories and purple steeplebushes graced the ditches, and other flowers and weeds color-danced in the wind, in-heavening the world with their short time on earth. Grasshoppers played their electric music, nearly drowning out the trill-buzzing crickets. Hordes of horseflies galloped through the air in search of a blood feast, and found some ecstasy in the scruff of Chris's neck. The boy pedaled faster to outpace the pursuers, and then slowed again and glided for a while, not wanting to work up a stinking sweat. The boy suffered the sting-arrows of the insatiable insects, hoping the loss of some blood would be worth making a good impression on the whole family.

The Mudgetts lived on twenty acres they called Sweet Woods. Surrounded by wetlands, the acreage had good elevation and drainage that allowed them to grow a healthy variety of grains, fruits, and vegetables. They free-ranged chickens, milked goats, plucked apples, made arts and crafts, and earned just enough money to continue being a family on the land.

From the second floor of the farmhouse, the Mudgetts could almost see Lake Superior. The tall trees blocked the view — or rather, provided the perfect view for people who love trees.

Mary Joan watched from the window while Chris rode his bike up the gravel road to the farm. Her whole body was happy to see him, and that made her a bit nervous. Was the red dress and pink head-scarf too much? She turned from the window, and took her time descending the stairs.

Mrs. Mudgett greeted the boy at the door. "MOO! Did you love the MOO-vies last night?"

Before he could make any noise in response, Mary Joan appeared. "Mother, please don't moo at my guest."

Chris laughed. "Hey, Mary Joan, it's okay."

"It's not okay."

"Come in," Mrs. Mudgett said. "We have the table all set. I hope you like everything goat."

"Everything goat?"

Mary Joan grabbed his arm firmly and led him toward the dining room. "Don't freak out about how we live. And it's all right to ask my sister questions."

"Your sister?"

Three people were seated at a large oak table: the father, the son, and a very pregnant sister. The latter's bulbous belly kept her a few feet away from the table.

"Whoa," Chris whispered.

The pregnant girl, seventeen, strained to stand up. "Hi, I'm Chastity."

Her twelve-year-old brother said, "Hi, I'm Promiscuous."

The father smacked the boy's head. "Grant. Watch yourself."

Mary Joan smiled stoically, knowing that once everyone was seated and chewing on all things goat, then this non-date of not-meeting the family would be bearable, and possibly even enjoyable.

Mrs. Mudgett announced, "This is Christopher Lagorio. He was my date last night at the MOO-vies. Isn't he a cutie?"

The father, son, and pregnant daughter all nodded. Yes, the boy was a real cutie. Scruffy as a billy goat.

"Sit," Mrs. Mudgett commanded. "Let's eat!"

Although the first fruits, berries, and vegetables of the farm were still in the ground, the table was full of the work of human hands and the gift of animals. Fresh goat milk, butter, cheese and yogurt glistened in the sunshine pouring through the window. Mr. Mudgett bowed his head and made the Sign of the Cross, followed by everyone except Chris. "In the name of the Father, Son, and Holy Spirit, bless this food to our bodies, and us to thy service. Amen."

Grant dug in and scooped a huge portion of yogurt that plopped to his plate. He said to the guest, "Have you kissed my sister yet?"

Mary Joan gave him the death glare.

Grant grabbed some cheese. "I meant my other sister."

Mr. Mudgett gave him a smack. To no avail. Grant muttered, "It's not my fault my sisters are hot."

Chastity opened the cover of the casserole to reveal the main dish. "Goat stew," she said, with melancholy.

"Pan was a good one," Mr. Mudgett said. "He lived a long, productive life. I hope his old legs aren't too tough."

Grant dug in. "Pan butted me all the time. I'm gonna really enjoy this." And then he spoke directly to the stew. "Payback's hell, eh, Pan?"

Mr. Mudgett smacked the boy again.

To no avail. The boy gave the stew the finger.

Trying to help, but making things worse, Mrs. Mudgett began to sing *Oklahoma*, in her own way: "MOOOO-klahoma!"

Chastity leaned farther away from the table, feeling nauseated. Grant gnawed on a piece of Pan's hind leg and said, "Kick me now, homie."

Some guests at such a feast might have been horrified. But Chris couldn't stop grinning.

"This is very good," he said.

And the table became silent.

There was a long pause, with everyone staring at the guest. Mrs. Mudgett's eyes began to water, and she dabbed them with a napkin. "You really like it?"

"Yes. The cheese is tasty, without being too salty. And the yogurt has a touch of sweetness."

"Maple syrup," Mr. Mudgett said proudly. "I tapped it myself last winter."

Chris nodded. "And the goat. The goat . . . Well . . . I must say, this is by far the best goat I've ever tasted."

Mrs. Mudgett burst into tears. "Give him some more!"

Grant snickered. "I think he's a goat-eating virgin."

"That's true," Chris said, blushing.

Mrs. Mudgett wept with joy. "Well, give him some more!"

The rest of the meal was full of the same. The action never subsided, with the animated conversation ranging from organic food to music to politics to education to pure nonsense. Chris was surprised by how quickly the time passed. Suddenly the dishes were cleared away, and everyone went outside to sit on the porch. Mrs. Mudgett made sure that Mary Joan and her non-date got the swing. "Oh, how cute," she said. "I should get the video camera."

"NO," Mary Joan said. "And no more singing, either. I want to hear the ducks and the geese."

Grant passed gas. A little *quack*.

Everyone gave him the death glare, and it actually worked. The twelve-year-old controlled himself for a while.

Chris contemplated the landscape, admiring the garden, fields, and orchards. He asked, "How do you survive on a farm this small?"

"We're very fertile," Grant said, glancing toward Chastity.

"Don't make me come over there," Mr. Mudgett said.

Quack.

Mr. Mudgett rose from his chair to give the boy a smack on the side of the head, but the boy leapt from the porch and was gone. "I'm going to see how the chickens are doing!"

"You're a chicken yourself," Chastity said. "*Bawk! Bawk!*"

Everyone laughed. And Chris thought this must be one of the strangest families on earth.

"Uh oh," Chastity said, holding her swollen belly. "A kick. Wow, what a kick!"

"That's what you get for bawking like a chicken," her mother chided.

Mr. Mudgett nodded. "No more animal noises." And then he addressed the question raised by Chris. "How do we survive out here? We put our eggs in many baskets. We sell chickens and eggs all year, turkeys during the holidays, apples and pumpkins in the fall, maple syrup in the winter, berries and vegetables in the summer. Do you know about the Farmers' Market?"

"Sure. My mom goes to all of those things."

Mrs. Mudgett was pleased. "Oh, does your mother buy blackberries?"

"Yeah, we eat those."

Mr. Mudgett nodded proudly. "Our blackberries sell for fifteen dollars a pound. That's black gold, Christopher. Especially with free labor. You can see how often Grant gets into trouble. Well, he works off his transgressions with farm work."

"He has forty years to go," Chastity said.

More laughter.

Mr. Mudgett gestured toward the land as if blessing it, and receiving a blessing. "Organics. Your family eats them, Christopher. And so do many of the families in town. We actually do quite well."

"We sell arts and crafts, too," Mary Joan added, quickening the swing. "Christmas and Easter and Thanksgiving decorations — we can't keep up with the demand. And my mom is like a professional painter. She does nature scenes and portraits. You should see the one she painted of my sister."

Chastity made a funny face. "Uh oh. The baby's doing back flips."

Chris stared at the girl's belly, looked away, and stared again. "Do you . . . I mean, are you . . . um . . ."

"Do I know the baby's father? Yes, of course. There is only one possibility. Are we getting married? No. Do I feel like my life is over? I've never felt more alive. Am I keeping my baby? Yes. Are my parents throwing me out of the house?"

"Don't be silly," Mrs. Mudgett said, her eyes watering happily. "We're not thrilled with the timing, but we're thrilled that God has given us this baby."

Chastity rubbed her belly and cooed. "What do you think I should name him?"

The guest didn't hesitate. He said the first thing that came to mind. "Christopher."

Everyone laughed.

Except for Mary Joan. She smacked the side of her non-date's head.

chapter thirty-one

THE DULUTH hillside was north of darkness at five in the morning, summoning a dozen tongues of birdsong . . . and Chris arose like a monk to witness the rising sun. He dressed in white linen, ate nothing for breakfast except a few sips of Deep North Water, and went outside to take the long way to Holy Spirit.

Filaments of fire were strung across the driveway, trembling spider webs catching nothing but a flutter of wind — blue wings — a spring azure butterfly ascending, just born and already searching the sky for a mating dance. While Chris shuffled at the pace of a death march, pausing as if to say goodbye to the world, he noticed yellow honeysuckle at the edge of the road, and bell-shaped flowers ringing out in blue silence.

"Beautiful . . . everything," he said, as if already missing the things of the earth.

Higher up the hill, cloud mountains appeared in the sky, suggesting kingdom upon kingdom . . . and Chris arched his neck and imagined castles, cathedrals, and dragons.

Greep. Greep.

A gleaming flycatcher, perched in a pine, caught the young knight's attention. Chris wondered what was hanging from the beak of the dragonfly-slayer. "Probably something for its nest. Oh, gross. That can't be the best thing to build with."

It was a snakeskin.

"Let it go, bird. Let it go."

Greep, greep, the bird replied with the snakeskin writhing in place. *Greep, greep, mind your own business.*

Chris continued his slog to the top of the hill, and then looked down at Lake Superior with its ominous luminosity arising through the mist. Superior was beckoning as if claiming beauty deeper than anything at a church.

"Keep going," the knight told himself. "Don't get distracted now. You can do this."

The Mass in his mind was beyond Superior, the deepest grace and also the gravest danger . . . BEYOND HERE BE DRAGONS.

"Welcome, welcome," the greeters said, two old ladies with denture-perfect smiles.

"Am I late?"

He was, and the old ladies answered, "Come in. Come in."

The Mudgetts were in the front row, where they sat fifty-two times a year plus Holy Days of Obligation, allowing themselves to be signs of stability despite their many problems.

Chris crept into a back pew, and tried to follow along with the Holy Sacrifice. He stood when everyone else stood, and sat when they sat, and kneeled when they kneeled. He felt like a dork, being so ignorant of the religion of his birth, but he knew enough to stay out of the Communion line. In fact, he was too terrified to move. By some trick of the rose window, or the sunlight mixed with candles, Chris saw fire in the Host and smoke rising from the Cup. And when Mary Joan received the Holy Gifts, he could see her whole body engulfed in a deadly light. However, she survived, all radiant, and returned to the pew, slowly becoming flesh again.

"I have a bone to pick with you," Mrs. Mudgett told the priest after the liturgy. It was coffee and donut time in the church basement. "Father Karl, the media kills the culture, as you pointed out in your homily, but I think we should talk more about the good things."

The priest sat passively at the table, licking a glazed donut. Mr. Mudgett raised his deep growl of a voice. "Hollywood is the biggest failure in the history of the world. With billions of dollars in wealth, they've produced maybe ten good movies in the past hundred years. Ten good movies. That's it."

Grant nodded, and tried to name them. "*Cheech and Chong, Howard the Duck, Dumb and Dumber . . .*"

His father ignored him and continued. "Never in history has an industry produced so little, given the potential. What a waste. It's all controlled by Powers and Principalities."

Father Karl knew he was being theologically upstaged, but he didn't mind. He washed down some sweet glaze with bland coffee.

Mrs. Mudgett was ravenous for double-chocolate. She'd been thinking about it all through the homily. She grabbed the donut and proclaimed it, "Yummy nummy!"

Her husband continued to growl his lamentations. "Porn on the computers, poison on TV, filth in the movies, every evil thing for money. Writers, producers, directors . . . all of them peddling death in one form or another."

Chastity rubbed her belly and softly cooed.

Mary Joan snuggled up to her sister and rubbed, too. "Forty more days. And forty more nights."

Chris tried to score some church points. "Forty days and nights," he said. "That was in the homily. I was listening in the back row. I heard about the forty."

"From the *Book of Constipation*," Grant muttered.

His father raised an arm.

The priest laughed it down. "*Book of Constipation*," he said, shaking his head with humor and sorrow. "Been there, done that."

Mrs. Mudgett giggled, buzzing on sugar. She felt the urge to take center stage, but wasn't sure what to do. Suddenly it came to her. She slapped the table in front of Chris. "You need to get confirmed! You need to get with the program!"

"Mother," Mary Joan whispered, "don't force it. Let him speak for himself."

"Well, umm," the boy said, gathering his thoughts. "To be honest, I'm not sure how anyone survives Communion."

Father Karl put down his donut. He was impressed by that answer, and responded at the level of discourse that the young knight deserved. "May God grant you perfect timing to fully enter the fullness of the light."

And that will be the death of me, Chris thought.

chapter thirty-two

MONDAY MORNING, Chris got a call from Moosehead and Skunk. They wanted him to be part of their summer lawn-mowing business.

Skunk lisped, "Business is crazy, Sacramento. You should join our team."

"Hmm."

Chris was already taking care of his parents' lawn in exchange for a small allowance. He was pretty good at it, a low-level horticulturist; at least he knew the difference between grass, weeds, and flowers. So why not join a business venture and rake in more cash?

"Sure. Count me in."

Moosehead bellowed, "Cool, dude!"

Skunk lisped, "Fantastic!"

It was lawn-mowing hell. Moosehead and Skunk gave Chris the worst jobs in town, lawns with inclines that would challenge a mountain goat to jump to its death. The mower that Chris pushed was not self-propelling, so he had to strain up and down the dangerous hills to earn his meager pay. He pushed Sisyphus — the cursed name he gave to the mower — and sometimes became so frustrated that he simply killed the engine in the middle of a half-mowed yard, sat and rested in the shade, and listened to the landscape.

Chris knew that wherever there were trees, there would be music . . . from a cicada soloist to a crow ensemble, chipmunks and their jazz, chanting doves, and birds of every rhythmic wing and beak adding their notes to the swaying of the trees. The boy stood and almost danced, a slightest sway to the notes of ecstasy in the air. He wanted to join in; the beckoning had been there since he was a baby. But there was work to be done and money to make. So he fired up Sisyphus, killing the music and filling the hillside with clouds of exhaust.

Chris prayed for Sunday to arrive so he could really rest. Except even on the Sabbath he had work to do, because he'd agreed to meet the Mudgetts at Mass.

Sunday morning, Chris dressed in white linen and noticed that a great cloud had descended upon the city, down from Mount Royal to the shore of the lake, hovering over everything, as if laying claim. The boy looked directly at the veiled sun, surprised by the apparently docile circle, knowing that in fact the flames were leaping and dancing in all directions.

The boy limped up to Holy Spirit, and arrived late again. The denture-grinning greeters were as kind as ever and allowed him to sneak into the back row in the middle of the homily. Father Karl was not God's gift to preaching, his words a flat-lining monotone. With jokes: "Sven and Ole went to Rome to ask the Pope if he approved of Catholics being involved with gambling. The Pope proclaimed, 'You bet.' "

Nobody laughed.

Except for Mrs. Mudgett. She guffawed as if the joke were the greatest ever told. She knew the difficulty of entertaining an audience, so she was extra-gracious. "Gah-ha-ha!"

Grant appeared in the back pew, and slid next to Chris. "Got a smoke, homie?"

"Shh. Shouldn't you be in the front?"

"I've been in the bathroom since the processional hymn. I don't think anyone has missed me. Can I sit with you?"

"Okay, if you behave yourself."

"You sound like my dad."

"You sound like a kid."

They both nodded.

Grant was able to behave himself for exactly thirty-nine seconds, pretending to listen to the homily. And then he leaned over and said, "This place is full of animals."

"What?"

The imp gestured toward a middle pew. "Look at the back of that old lady's head. What do you see?"

"I see hair."

"What else?"

"Just hair."

"Look closer. Can you see the otter?"

"The otter?"

"Yeah. Every lady has a different animal in her hair. Look over to the right. Mrs. Dahl has a lion."

It was true. The play of light and shadow had created the king of beasts in the woman's perm.

Father Karl mumbled something about gambling everything on the Blood of Christ.

Grant yawned loudly.

Mrs. Dahl turned and stared at Chris as if he were the guilty one, and gave him a menacing growl.

Grant laughed, and whispered, "The lion wants to kill you."

chapter **thirty-three**

GRANT WAS a hellion in most situations. But out on the farm, left alone, he could be a saint. The boy had a dozen chores to accomplish — from milking goats to gathering eggs to watering the garden — and he was happy to lose himself in such work. Especially on summer days when the curse of Adam was lost in the splendor of all growing things.

On the last Sunday in June, after Mass, Grant was thrilled to teach Chris how to farm.

"You've never milked a goat?"

"Nope."

"Man alive," Grant said, trying to speak with a deep voice. "You're going into ninth grade, and you can't even milk a goat."

Chris shrugged. "What can I say? Show me."

Grant nodded like a wise old man. "I should tell you about alfalfa manure. I'll bet a million dollars you don't know anything about alfalfa manure."

"You'd win that bet."

The young farmer led Chris and the goat to the milking pen. He fastened the goat securely, positioned himself on the stool, and reached out for Miss America. "She gives more if you massage the udder. Like this."

Chris wasn't sure about massaging udders. "Is that really necessary?"

Continuing the lesson, Grant said, "After the massage, you just grab her like this. Very gently. You don't want to pull. It's more of a squeeze. Very, very gently."

Miss America raised a hoof to kick Grant in the head.

"Be careful," Chris warned, stepping back, "she's about to —"

"Praise the Lord," Grant said. "Milk!"

"Well, look at that. Good work."

The bucket slowly began to fill with the grace of warm froth.

Chris had never witnessed such a balance of control with freedom. The Mudgett farm seemed like a good combination of petting zoo and wilderness. The free-range chickens were happy as larks and still fit to be fried. The farm was not sentimental; it was filled with an authenticity that posed the important questions. What does it mean to be human? What does it mean to have dominion? How do we share what's left of Eden?

Mary Joan appeared, wearing a new dress. A golden sundress. She filled it like fire, and Chris had to focus very hard to keep from staring. He pointed at the milk bucket. "Your brother is quite the farmer."

"That he is."

"Your family is so fortunate," Chris said. "If the economy collapses and the grocery stores close down, your family will be saved."

Mary Joan smiled proudly at Miss America, while Grant continued to squeeze and fill the bucket.

Perhaps because of the sundress, and the fire it caused within, Chris felt compelled to mess with Mary Joan's mind. He said in a challenging voice, "A few Sundays ago, Father Karl sent all goats to Hell."

"What? No he didn't."

"Yes, he did. Father Karl said you have to be a sheep to enter Heaven. The goats are going to burn."

Mary Joan shook her head. "You don't understand. You have to know what's symbolic and what's real."

"I'm just telling you what was preached in your church. I'm not making the rules. I'm just reporting the news."

"No. You don't understand symbolism. That's why you got a C in English class."

"I got a C in English class because I didn't turn in my homework. I understood the assignments. I just didn't feel the need to explain."

Grant chuckled over the frothy goodness while Miss America continued to give.

Chris reached out and rubbed the goat behind the ears. "Maybe I should start my own church. I'd allow all of the goats into Heaven."

"Including Pan?" Grant asked. "He was a real devil."

"NO," Mary Joan said, getting into Chris's face. "You won't be starting any new churches. You need to submit to the original one."

He looked down at her crucifix. "Submit?"

She lifted his chin, gave him a quick little kiss, and said, "Was that symbolic? Or was it real?"

"Yuck," Grant said. He picked up his bucket, grabbed Miss America by the horns, and hurried away. "No more kissing," he lectured. "We don't need any more babies right now."

chapter **thirty-four**

MR. MUDGETT was chopping and stacking firewood behind the house. In exchange for doing various handyman jobs around the area, he was sometimes paid with cords of oak, ash, maple, walnut, and fir. He enjoyed chopping and stacking, and allowing the wood to season like fine wine. Mr. Mudgett was a north-woods connoisseur, preferring three-year-old maple. And one of the wonderful things about living near cool Duluth is that you can burn a sweet-smelling fire all year long.

After the very real kiss, the chopping stopped. And while the libidinous boy was thinking about more than kissing, and how to proceed, Mr. Mudgett appeared from around the house. He approached the kids with a solemn look on his face. His red flannel shirt was drenched in sweat, dark as blood. And he carried the axe as if Chris were a tree.

Yikes, the boy thought.

The man told his daughter, "Go help Grant clean the chicken coop."

"What? He doesn't want my help. Grant prefers to work alone. You know that."

Mr. Mudgett pointed the axe at the house. "Then go help your sister."

"She told me not to bother her until dinner. She's reading a book about how to raise a child genius."

"Then go help your mother in the kitchen."

Mary Joan didn't mean to argue, but all of the answers were naturally contrary. "Mother's not in the kitchen. She's watching a video."

Mr. Mudgett was at a loss. "For the love of God, Mary Joan, isn't there somebody you can help?"

She glanced at Chris.

Pointing his axe north, Mr. Mudgett said, "Go pick some strawberries, Mary Joan."

"They're not quite ripe."

"Well, go on. You don't need to pick any. Just check on 'em. And look for bear tracks around the blueberry bushes."

The girl sighed, and walked away, golden dress shimmering.

Chris wanted to go with her. He'd be happy to check on the blueberries, strawberries, blackberries, and raspberries and give a full report on their various progressions in light of their relations with the sun. The boy's eyes followed the golden dress and perfect form within.

"A-hem." Mr. Mudgett pointed his axe at the boy's chest. "How old are you?"

"Fourteen, sir. I'll be fifteen in September."

Mr. Mudgett held the axe as if it weighed nothing. "Christopher is a very important name. Did you know that?"

The boy shuffled nervously. "Yeah, Mary Joan mentioned it."

"It means Christ-bearer."

"I know."

"You can't escape your name, Christopher. And no denying it, it hurts like hell to bear the Christ."

"Oh."

The axe seemed ready to fall. "And if you try anything with my daughter . . ."

"Oh. No sir, I promise."

chapter thirty-five

DANCING WITH Sisyphus up and down the elevations and descents, Chris destroyed his leg muscles and lay in bed aching every night. His muscles re-grew larger and stronger. One morning, his jeans no longer fit around his bulging thighs. And the thought entered his head that he should become a jock. Moosehead and Skunk were football players, and they talked about the glories of the game. Legal violence. And sex. Some of the cheerleaders were said to be everything that legend had them to be.

Chris had become very devoted to Mary Joan. And he loved the thought of other girls, too. Images came to mind. The Internet called out to him. He was tempted to indulge, and indulge . . . and Sunday morning always came in tongues of flame over Superior. The young knight dressed in white linen, limped up to Holy Spirit, drawn and repulsed by the Catholic Fire. He sat in the back pew and went through the motions, knowing there were wilder words within the body language. And the moment Mary Joan consumed the Host, Chris felt a jolt of satisfaction, and an agony that seemed centuries old.

The after-Mass non-dates at the Mudgett farm were tense, and delightful. The kissing had ended, thanks to the axe and his promise, but his cup at the table overflowed with goat's milk, and his bowl brimmed with yogurt sweetened with maple syrup and strawberries.

And the Mudgetts played all sorts of parlor games. Their favorite was the "Face Game," in which a player stood in front of the group while someone shouted out an emotion, such as "bewilderment." The player would then attempt to make a face that expressed bewilderment. The acting could be silly or sublime, or anything in between. For two minutes, people would shout out emotions. "Rage!" Or "sympathy." And the player had to make the appropriate face, followed by oohs, ahhs, and laughter.

Chris loved how the Face Game revealed the inner life of the Mudgetts. The father was in the game but not of the game, barely expressing. And his wife would kid him. "You call that joy? That's not joy!"

Half-smiling, Mr. Mudgett stood his ground. "That's joy enough."

And nobody ever lost, because there wasn't a scoring system. The game was its own reward.

Until Grant hollered at Chastity, "Do 'lust'!"

The pregnant girl hesitated, obviously hurt, but trying to hide it.

Chris immediately offered some help. "Are we allowed to pass? What are the rules? Can we request a new emotion?"

"Do 'lust,' " Grant insisted, smirking.

Nobody else thought it was funny. Chastity had suffered enough for an indiscretion and was being heroic in bringing the baby to term, knowing that the baby's father would never help to raise the child, and knowing that her chances of getting married to someone else were greatly diminished.

"I want to see lust," her brother insisted.

"She can pass," Mr. Mudgett said.

Everyone was silent again. Everyone was showing "awkward" on their faces.

Chastity squirmed, the baby kicking, or dancing, or trying to fly. "Fine," she said. "Here's some lust for you."

She turned to Mary Joan's non-boyfriend and gave him the eye. And gave him the licked lips, slightly parted. And gave him a low moan . . .

"Okay, okay," her mother said, blushing as much as Chris. "The two minutes are up. Let your sister have a turn."

Mary Joan was the best at the Face Game, as if she had taken years and years of professional acting classes. Or as if she knew who she was, perfectly expressing the whole range of the soul. She could transform her flesh into tenderness, anger, ecstasy, and agony.

"You're amazing," Chris whispered.

Mrs. Mudgett was good, too, but added a little extra to each emotion, making it somewhat silly with exaggeration. The children loved it. "Mom, is that 'flighty'? Seems more like 'insanity'!"

Wild laughter would lead to a refreshment break. Goat's milk all around. With dark chocolate.

And then it was time for "Words, Words, Words," another simple game that made the soul happy. Mr. Mudgett pretended that he didn't really care about words. He sat in his oak chair and carved a piece of dark walnut, the whittlings falling at his feet. He carved resonant images of the north — eagles, wolves, bears — with the finishing touch of a little cross in every one.

"Okay," Mrs. Mudgett sang. "Who's going first?"

Grant raised his arm.

"Oh. No, dear. Let our guest give the first clue."

Chris thought up a good word: *date*. And he smiled as if he were charm itself. "A boy and a girl go on a . . ."

The answer was instant.

"Cruise!" the women all shouted.

Chris shook his head, and tried again. "When a boy likes a girl, they go on a . . ."

"Cruise!" the women shouted.

"No, that's not it. Listen carefully. A boy will ask a girl . . . to go out . . . on a . . ."

"Cruise!"

The timer went off. "Sorry," the boy said. "It was a date."

Chastity laughed. "Exactly. A cruise."

"Hey, I have an idea," Mrs. Mudgett said, buzzing on goat chocolate. "Christopher, why don't you take Mary Joan on a cruise?"

Flinching, Mr. Mudgett nicked himself with the knife. "Son of a —"

Chastity, still a romantic despite her mistakes, exclaimed, "The Friday cruise is the best! Duluth from the harbor is so beautiful. Oh, you two would love it."

Mary Joan's eyes, perfectly transparent, dared the boy to take her on a harbor cruise.

"Hmm," Chris murmured, wondering if perhaps he should have given better clues. He glanced over at Mr. Mudgett, who had gone back to his whittling, finger bleeding. Was that a look of disapproval on his face? Or just the plain old pain of being a father?

"Mary Joan is not allowed to date," the man said, his voice like a stone tablet.

"Oh, it's not a date," the girl said. "It's only sightseeing. It's educational. And besides, we'll be surrounded by a whole boat-load of chaperones. And you can watch us with binoculars if you want."

Mrs. Mudgett nodded enthusiastically. "I approve of this. It will be perfectly innocent."

Mr. Mudgett nicked himself with the knife again. "Son of a —"

chapter thirty-six

THE *VISTA KING* was shrouded in a fog that unfurled with the north wind, making the deck invisible for a mystical moment, and then visible again.

Mrs. Mudgett waved goodbye to the non-daters, who were leaning over the railing. "Be good! Have fun! Don't go overboard! Ha ha! Do you have your phone?"

"I have my phone," the dutiful daughter said. "And I'll call you if we begin to sink."

"Ha ha! I'll be back in an hour to pick you up!"

"Okay. See you later, Mom."

"Bon voyage! That means have a good one!"

"Okay, Mom. Bye."

Chris and Mary Joan had boarded the *Vista King* with about fifty other people. Most of the cruisers seemed to be from Duluth, or at least from Minnesota, wearing sweatshirts that pledged allegiance to the Vikings, Twins, Gophers, and Wild. A skinny guy with rusty hair wore a T-shirt that said: "Demons have more fun."

Mary Joan whispered into her non-date's ear, "He's shivering, poor thing."

Her breath made Chris shiver as well. He wrapped his arms around her shoulders that were covered with a dark-blue cape. The ship lurched forward, rubbing their bodies together.

"Whoa," the boy said.

The girl laughed. "See? Going on a cruise was the right answer."

The horn wailed, and the *Vista King* slowly chugged through the inlet and toward the deep water.

A disembodied voice began to narrate the voyage. "Look westward and behold the city on the hill . . ."

Chris looked and saw absolute beauty, along with some eyesores. Duluth was built along a green ridge of various cliffs that stretched for several miles above Superior. There were mansions and churches and the Enger Tower that hinted of heavenly architecture, along with ugly, hulking structures that seemed to beg for demolition.

Mary Joan pointed at the sky. "Look at that."

The sun was pestering through the clouds.

And sunscreen bottles came out on deck. Pasty Minnesota faces were immediately greased for protection.

The descending sunlight formed a huge circle in the water, and the temperature began to rise.

"Perfect," Mary Joan said. "It's a perfect day."

While the *Vista King* chugged along, the narrator gave some facts and figures about Lake Superior, including that it reaches "the almost unfathomable depth of a thousand feet."

There was a pair of loons in the harbor, drifting, diving, rising, and wailing.

Mary Joan kissed her non-date on the cheek. "I love this."

Note to self, the boy thought: cruise, cruise, cruise!

"Superior is a great graveyard," the narrator intoned. "Buried in these waters are three-hundred fifty ships."

The guy in the demon shirt snickered. "Fifteen more wrecks, and we'll have one for every day of the year. A whole calendar of destruction."

The narrator continued. "Wind gusts can reach seventy miles per hour in the relative safety of the harbor — with waves reaching thirty feet. The lift bridge must arise to allow the giant waves to pass through."

The *Vista King* ventured further out into the harbor. A screeching seagull swooped down and checked the deck for fast food. There were a few pieces of popcorn to please the scavenger for a few moments. Then it screeched again. The guy in the demonic shirt kicked at the gull, missed, and fell on his butt. Several people snickered, and someone whispered, "That's what he gets." However, Mary Joan wriggled out of Chris's arms and went to assist the fallen man. She helped to tug him to his feet.

"Thanks, chickie-poo," he said, gripping her hand.

She tried to let go. "I am not a chickie-poo."

"Well, you're a baby doll," he said, holding tight, "and I've always liked a baby doll."

Chris leapt forward, adrenaline pumping. "Let go of her," he said. "Let go of my date!"

"Your date?" the guy sneered.

"Your date?" the girl questioned.

"YES," he said, with everyone on board watching.

Chris extracted Mary Joan from the demon's grip and led her to the front of the boat. The confused teenagers stood a few feet apart, and kept their thoughts to themselves for a while. And then, eventually, they were drawn together again by a wind that demanded snuggling. The wilds of Canada and wildernesses beyond were frolicking in the cold air like all of the magic of the North mixed together.

The boy took a deep breath. "*Mysterium tremendum.*"

The girl was impressed by the heroic-sounding phrase. "Is that Latin?"

"Yeah."

"Christopher, how do you know Latin?"

He glanced up the North Shore, where it was still misty. "It's a long story. And I can't interpret."

The narrator intoned, "This concludes the deep-water part of the cruise. Now we'll turn the *King* around and give you an IN DEPTH — no pun intended, ha ha — tour of the dockyards and storage facilities."

Several people groaned and complained about how fast the "good part of the cruise" had ended.

Chris agreed with them. "A boy and girl don't want to see a grain elevator."

"Yes they do," Mary Joan said. "Don't you want to learn about grain elevators?"

He knew the correct answer was yes, but he wasn't the best student, especially during the summer; and he wasn't the best date. "Look at that crap," he said when the boat floated into the maze of industry. Huge buildings with peeling paint and rust suggesting a bygone boom; and some of the structures had mottled cement walls that seemed to be crumbling. Piles of nondescript debris, mounds of scrap metal, rocks, gravel, coal, grain, and heaps of garbage everywhere.

Mary Joan lost some of her optimism. "Why is the shipyard so ugly? I mean, we do a lot of work on our farm. And our farm stays beautiful."

Chris gently put an arm around her. "I know why your farm is beautiful."

She seemed to know the answer, but asked, "Why?"

The boy flirted with grace. "You, of course."

The girl awaited his next charming move.

And with all of his strength, he withheld the kiss.

Until late July . . . when he went crazy in the heat.

chapter thirty-seven

"LET'S GO."

"Where?"

He pointed beyond the Mudgett farm. "Around the pond and into the woods."

Mary Joan nodded, smiling. "Okay. Should we bring a bucket to get the last of the berries? Or maybe I should get a basket and some lemonade so we can have a proper picnic."

"No. C'mon, let's go," he said, tramping away. "Hurry up."

"Wait a second," she said. "Slow down!"

Mary Joan sighed and then followed him while he rushed around the garden, through the sun-burnt grass, and down to the shoreline. The pond was circled by a treasure-path of marsh marigolds, and a couple of damselflies were mating — winging it — in the unblushing sky. The boy admired the latter image while the girl lingered among the former.

Around the pond they stepped lightly through the marigolds, and then down through a swale of bog with swelling vegetation and pools of water the color of earth. And up they tramped into a highland of hardwoods. The forest floor was still moist, however, from a recent rain, the fecundity of God spread everywhere in shadow-sparkled greens and golds.

Within a few minutes, Chris and Mary Joan were in the wilderness. A southern wind whispered through the trees and gave rise to cicada song and a dozen other chirpings, buzzings, and clamorings for life.

The boy was soaked with sweat from the temperature and the hotter fires of the flesh. He hurried through the birches, pines and maples, leaving the girl in the blue dress to follow his lead. They crossed an invisible property line and trespassed into the neighbor's woods. Shafts of sunlight shot through the branches while Chris burned a trail, searching for a good place . . . a good place . . . to do what?

Mary Joan cried out ecstatically, "Christopher! Blueberries! The last of the season!"

The boy felt a surge of frustration. Why was she pausing for blueberries when there were wilder delights to be had? Didn't she want to indulge in him the way he wanted to indulge in her?

He turned and shouted, "Hey, hurry up!"

Mary Joan knelt down and picked a handful of blueberries, and popped them into her mouth. "Yum. These are perfectly delicious. Just the right amount of sun."

The boy was smoldering. "C'mon, let's keep going! There's a clearing up ahead."

The girl stood and veered away as if on a hunt of her own.

Chris sighed. "What are you looking for now?"

"Raspberries!"

The boy followed her over to the bushes. He was hunger-panting.

"Yum yum," Mary Joan said. And soon her lips were red with berry juice. Chris licked his lips as well, preparing for a kiss and more. Sweating profusely, he approached the girl, and she veered in another direction. "Strawberries!"

And so it went. The boy prowled for flesh, while Mary Joan hunted for something else.

He panted. "I want to go . . . I want to . . . I want . . . I . . ."

The girl suddenly stood frozen and stared through the forest. Into the clearing . . .

Chris shifted his vision and didn't see anything. "What is it? Your neighbor? Does he have a gun? Is he a homicidal maniac?"

"He's not a maniac," Mary Joan whispered. "He's a mountain lion."

Chris took a jump-step back, not because of fear, but because he was struck by guilt. He continued to lurch backward, into the branches of a balsam fir. "Ouch, ouch! It's cutting me!"

Mary Joan strode over to the pine and was surprised by the fright on the boy's face. She spoke softly, "Christopher, you can come out now. The mountain lion is gone."

He stared at her crucifix. "He's gone. You're sure?"

The girl reached out and touched the boy's trembling hand. "It's okay. We're free to do what we want now."

Chris burst out of the tree, took Mary Joan in his arms, and began to kiss her.

She pushed him away. In fact, the strong farm girl shoved him to the ground. "What's wrong with you?" she said. "We're not even officially dating."

As if caught in the bars of a cage, Chris raised his shaggy head and roared. "I want more than a date!"

Mary Joan glared at the frustrated boy, and left him lying there on a bed of pine needles.

"Wait," he said, scrambling to his feet. "Slow down. We'll walk back to the farm together. Hey! Aren't you going to wait for me?"

"NO," she said angrily, quickening for home, "you wouldn't wait for me."

chapter thirty-eight

As if cued by a spirit of chaos or an angel of reconstruction, bellowing Moosehead called the next day. "Sacramento! You're one lucky dude!"

"Oh," Chris said in a flat voice. He was staring out at the iron-hued arch of the Ruins. "How am I lucky?"

"The groundskeeper at the nursing home cut off his toe! Yeah, man. He can't work for several weeks. You get to replace him."

"Why can't you or Skunk replace him?"

Skunk took control of the phone. "We sort of messed it up already."

"You cut off your toes, too?"

"Not exactly. We sort of crashed the tractor —"

"Sort of crashed it?"

"Yeah. We were sort of teaching ourselves how to drive it."

Chris imagined the scene. "The two of you were driving the tractor at the same time?"

"Yeah. I was riding on the back of the John Deere, telling Moosehead what to do, and we sort of crashed into a plum tree. No big deal, except one of the nurses saw it happen. We had to make up a story about Moosehead suffering from epilepsy. It's complicated. But anyway, our corporation —"

Chris laughed. "Corporation?"

Moosehead took the phone back. "We need you, Sacramento. This is the highest-paying job we've got. And the summer is almost over. Wouldn't it be nice to make some good cash before the leaves start to fall?"

All Chris wanted to do was to contemplate the Ruins.

"It's all resting on you, Sacramento. Don't let us down."

"Hmm. What about my other lawns?"

"We'll do them for you."

He could hear both of the boys breathing anxiously. "I don't know, guys. I'm sort of burnt out. My mom says my thyroid needs a rest."

Skunk lisp-shouted into the phone. "Listen! There is a woods by the nursing home, with a nice pond. You can take breaks there and smoke."

"I don't want to smoke."

Moosehead snorted, "Don't be a wuss-ass. The nursing home is the deal of a lifetime."

Chris paused for a moment, wondering how he should react to the insulting offer; and then he laughed. The absurdity of his friends was exactly what he needed to ease the pain of his latest heartbreak. "Okay, guys. How much does it pay?"

"Six dollars an hour," Skunk lied.

"Seven dollars an hour," Moosehead lied.

"I'll do it for eight."

It was a full-time job. From sunrise until sunset, while the elderly eased into eternity, Chris tried to stay ahead of the fertile earth. Although he drove the John Deere slowly over the grass, his cut-lines were crooked, because he was constantly distracted by the sky. Every few minutes, there was a new masterpiece above his head. Clouds of every shape and changing color. Chris saw a museum's worth of art every day.

The sky was also full of artful trees, the expansive grounds shimmering and shaded with hundreds of aspen, pines, oaks, and poplars. Chris had to trim around each one, and it had to be done very carefully, not damaging the trunks or scraping off a single scab of bark. The suited administrator had been clear about that. "You touch my mature trees, and you're history."

"I'll be careful," the scruffy boy had said. "I love old trees."

Chris especially loved the forest to the north of the nursing home, and the pond at the end of the path. First thing in the morning, and during his lunch break, he went to the hidden body of water and witnessed something akin to the visions of Adam.

chapter thirty-nine

CHRIS USUALLY fell quickly into dreams after a long day of keeping the earth beautiful. Pleasantly sunburned and wind-kissed, he kept the windows open and slept like the innocent, traveling through the subconscious from one restful adventure to another, not stirring in his bed until the first nudge of light called him back from the other worlds.

However, one sultry midnight, the turning constellations burned in his eyes, tossed him from worries to frets, and brought him to his knees. It was a posture he knew as a child in Sacramento, when his father had first taught him to pray. Now Chris reached for his headphones in hopes of finding some sleeping tunes, and accidentally found something else. On the floor under the bed was a small box of books. He yawned, "Oh yeah, I remember these," and then dug groggily through some of the starlit titles: *Holy Bible and Apocrypha, Book of Kells, Canterbury Tales, Orthodoxy, Le Morte d'Arthur, Visions of the Medieval Mystics* . . . gifts from Professor Corwin.

"Man alive," Chris whispered, grasping the *Visions of the Medieval Mystics*. He moved closer to the window and read a passage about Meister Eckhart and the shining Rhinelanders. Enthralled by the spiritual poetry, he repeated a phrase as if singing to the stars, "Within the festival of atoms, the heavens are at play."

Chris had almost forgotten about the present of timeless books, the cathedral-house and enlivening library, the northern shoreline, beautiful purgatory, and the mysterious upper room. His heart began pounding again with memories of Terra.

The boy closed the *Visions* and told himself, "You should give her a call."

There was a problem with that plan: Terra had no cell phone. He would have to call the land line. And what would happen if Mrs. Corwin answered the midnight ringing? Would she lecture him with a voice colder than Superior? If Terra did not pick up the phone, he hoped it would be the old professor. Chris would say: "Silvenshine! You should look out at the constellations. *Mysterium tremendum!* And may I please converse with your lovely granddaughter?"

The boy dialed the number, and his heart seemed to pound a dozen times during the first ring, accelerating by the second ring, and near to exploding with the third — "Is this . . . what it feels like . . . to have a heart attack?" — and after the fourth ring he decided to hang up and save his life; but he held on for one more.

"Hello?"

Chris knew that beautiful, song-like voice.

It was Mary Joan Mudgett. He had dialed the wrong number.

"Oh, um," the boy said.

"Christopher?"

"Um, yeah. It's me. Hey, Mary Joan."

She sighed. "Do you know how late it is?"

"Sorry. I couldn't sleep."

The girl sighed again, but pleasantly. "I couldn't sleep either. It's such a perfect night. The stars . . . Did you see the stars, Christopher?"

"Yeah."

"And the baby was crying for a while."

"The baby? Oh, Chastity! That's right. Did she have a girl?"

"A boy. She named him Francis."

"That's a great name."

"Yes. One of the best."

"Um, well, say hi for me to both of them. And to your whole family. And you, Mary Joan . . ."

"Me? What about me?"

The boy stared out the window at the wilderness of light above the lake. "I want to apologize. I hope we can be friends again. Are you going to East High School this year?"

"No, I'm doing homeschool. So I can help Chastity and the baby."

"That's nice of you."

"Chastity would do the same for me."

The image of Mary Joan pregnant made the boy blush, and he felt a rush of guilt. "Well, I should let you get your sleep."

The girl paused, and he wondered if she would say something punishing for the way he'd mistreated her. "I miss you, Christopher," she whispered, and then asked in a louder tone: "Will you be at Mass this Sunday?"

His mind raced. Return to Mass? With the pestilent dragons and the smoldering Holy Grail?

"I have to mow," he said.

"You have to moo?"

"Mow."

"Moo?"

"No, listen. I have to ride the Deere all day."

"A mooing deer? What are you talking about?"

"The nursing home."

Mary Joan sighed. "I've never understood you, Christopher."

"Me either," he said, turning from the window. And when he heard the click and dial tone, he whispered to himself, "I suppose it's way too late to call Terra."

While the fog rolled in from the lake and swallowed the stars, Chris knelt on the floor again. He boxed up the mystical books, and shoved them under the bed as if to keep them buried forever.

chapter **forty**

THE DAZZLE of Duluth was in its mist, the great clouds infiltrating everything.

"Damn," Chris muttered on Sunday morning. "The lawns will be wet."

He had been told to wait until the acres were sun-dried before giving blade to the grass. Dry acres were easier on the John Deere and also easier on Chris, because he would not have to double-mow or rake long lines of leftover debris. The mist delayed the boy's schedule and called him to the pond in the deep of the woods. There he stood under a weeping willow and waited for the sun to do its share of the work.

Later, during his lunch break, the boy returned to the full-bright pond. He squinted and considered the fiery arrowhead lilies — shooting heavenward — and witnessed a boatman bug whirling across the golden water as if encompassing four journeys at once, while a school of phenomenal minnows flashed silver near the shoreline. Chris ate his lunch slowly, carefully, as if the cold tuna sandwich might burn his mouth. And he whispered a short prayer, becoming aware of the enlightening in his soul: "Lord, let me not be a dullard among so much brilliance."

And toward the end of the day, when it was raining, he sloshed into the woods and stopped to consider an upfolded oak leaf, how it appeared to be a small, green grail. Chris witnessed a hummingbird drink from the cup. The sky poured and poured, and the wings disappeared. Chris stared at the pond fluttering up with tiny splashes as if a million humming-birds were diving in. And then the heavens burst into pieces, and there was a sun shower, the clouds all ruby-throated.

"Good God . . ."

chapter forty-one

ON THE FIRST day of ninth grade, during feeding time, Chris sat in the blue cafeteria with Moosehead and Skunk and a kid they called Blub. Blub had been promised twenty dollars from the surrounding crowd if he would eat a whole tray of slop.

"Fill me up," Blub said with an innocent, idiotic grin.

The sodden feast started with a milky pile of tater-tot casserole, topped with ketchup, pepper, mayonnaise, bubble gum, partially chewed lettuce, cola, tobacco, earwax, and asthma spray.

Blub dug in, and scooped the slop so quickly into his mouth that he actually seemed to be enjoying himself. In a matter of seconds, his tray was empty and he swallowed hard, smiled politely as if in a fine French restaurant, and proceeded to puke all over the table.

"Did I win?" he asked, gasping for air and wiping his mouth. "I cleaned the tray."

Moosehead snorted. "Doesn't look clean to me."

Skunk lisped, "Suck it up. Eat the slop again. Those are the rules."

"That's right," another boy proclaimed. "Otherwise you owe each of us a dollar. Everyone knows the rules. You puke, you pay."

The mob was speaking.

"Pay up!"

"Pay up!"

A runt who hadn't even made a bet, shouted, "Yeah, no cheating!" The runt reached for Blub's wallet. "You owe us each a dollar!"

Blub stared glassy-eyed at the hideous mess on the tray, and actually considered taking another bite.

The mob taunted. "Don't be a baby!"

"Ga ga!"

"Goo goo!"

"Suck it up!"

Blub was willing to swill hell in order to please the crowd. He leaned over the table and opened his mouth . . .

Chris pulled out a dollar and placed it next to the dripping tray. "Grace," he said. "Give him some grace."

The mob howled.

"What are you doing?"

"Stay out of this, Sacramento!"

Chris spoke calmly, strongly. "Blub deserves some grace with this bet. C'mon, guys. He ate everything on the tray."

The mob disagreed.

"No way! We play by the rules!"

"You puke, you lose!"

"He owes us! He has to pay up!"

With dry heaves and shaking shoulders, Blub accepted Chris's dollar and offered it up to the mob. "You guys win. I'll bring the rest of the money tomorrow."

The dollar disappeared into a horde of wriggling fingers.

chapter forty-two

ONE OF THE students at East who believed in a spiritual world was a junior named Trevor Nelson.

Trevor wore thick glasses, so thick it seemed he could see the world only darkly. His father the optometrist had offered him the best contact lenses, but the aspiring priest thought that was vanity. Trevor squinted constantly. And he began the school day by squinting at a poster hanging inside his locker, a Lake Superior scene at the break of dawn, the water welling up in unspeakable light, the sky full of hovering letters like birds born of ancient calligraphy:

I AM

THE RESURRECTION

AND THE LIFE

Slapping the older kid on the back, Chris wanted Trevor to know that he appreciated the sign of hope. Unfortunately, Chris didn't know his own strength. The slap on Trevor's back sent the thick glasses falling. And despite a manufacturer's claim of invincibility, the lenses shattered into pieces on the floor.

"Sorry. I didn't mean to —"

The older boy fell to his knees and tried to gather the fragments. "It's okay. It must be God's will."

"Are you sure?"

"Go to class. Don't get in trouble because of me."

A half-hour later, Chris was sitting in art class, daydreaming out the window . . . when the teacher clicked the Power Point. Charcoal swans became the face of Michelangelo. Speaking in an almost secretive rasp, Mrs. Anderson said, "The white light and the black light, the *rayon blanc* and the *rayon noir,* collect together in the same droplet of paint, and make something like blood on the skin. Excuse me. Mr. Daydreamer? Do you want to learn about art or not? Wake up and look at this."

"Um, yeah. It's beautiful," Chris said, not quite seeing it.

Spit!

"Beautiful as hell," a kid slurred in the back row. The kid was a tobacco-chewer named Duane Schmidt. All day long, Duane had been drooling boggish liquid into a Mountain Dew can. His nickname was "Dip" but nobody ever called him that to his face.

Spit! "Art sucks."

Mrs. Anderson clicked her Power Point. "Notice how Monet's water lilies show us the life within the life on the pond."

Spit! "I don't see any life in the pond. Where are the tadpoles? Where are the eels?"

After class, Chris tried to be friendly to the sullen tobacco-chewer. He said, "That was a strange lecture."

"Worthless. There were no eels in that painting."

"Well, I think the class will get better when we do our own paintings, eh, Dip?"

The innocent moment slithered into a more dangerous conversation. "What did you call me?"

"Dip. That's what everyone calls you."

Duane smiled with vengeance. "I'll be seeing you around, Lagorio. Or should I call you Sacramento?"

Chris didn't notice the negative energy. He joked, "You can call me anything you want, Dip. Just don't call me late to art class."

Spit! "You're quite the man, Sacramento."

"I try," he said, laughing.

After school, Chris didn't go to football practice. Despite the constant invitations from Moosehead and Skunk, and despite how tall and strong he'd grown, he'd decided not to try out. The after-school light softened and chilled as the days passed by. And at the end of September, Chris was told that the nursing home no longer needed his services, because the old grounds-keeper had returned with a reattached toe.

"I'm going to miss that place," Chris muttered. "Oh well. I'll probably go back in sixty years or so."

He found work raking yards for neighbors, and then ambled every afternoon to the top of Mount Royal. Despite his mother's warnings, Chris was becoming addicted to "the shadowy, money-sucking bean." He liked the boldest brew at Caribou Coffee, and sipped it slowly by the fireplace while listening to the various conversations. Neglecting his school books, he was more interested in how each person in the coffee shop was an epic, the conversations like turning pages. He found it intriguing that the college students were very similar to high-school students, the stories mostly featuring romances won and lost. Sometimes the stories made him melancholy, made him think about Terra and Mary Joan, and what might have been.

It seemed like the elderly coffee drinkers were melancholy, too. Chronicling their own lives and the adventures of their children and grandchildren, the elderly were flesh-and-blood libraries. Chris wrote down fragments of their conversations in his history notebook. And sometimes he wrote in verse, the rhymes giving a resonance like ancient poetry.

The widow lives in the mansion of a shipping baron.
Her old dreams have been drowned by the seafaring
Husband that left her for the land and waters of the dead.
And she tells the story to bring him back — alive again.

Two grandmothers took notice of the young writer, and the bespectacled one asked, "Do you go to Cathedral High School?"

The boy shook his head. "East."

The other grandmother gave him a maternal smile, impressed by his filled notebook. "Are you a senior?"

The boy blushed. "Freshman."

"Oh my. You seem so mature."

"I'm fifteen. Just a freshman."

Freshman. The word took hold of Chris and made him re-consider his place on earth. Who was he? A fresh man. How wonderful!

"Christopher Lagorio," a voice carried across the room. Trevor Nelson was seated in the other corner, and he appeared to be a new man, his glasses replaced with contact lenses. He was snuggled up to a beautiful ninth-grade girl, a vampiress with her coven; or perhaps they were just typical teens playing dress up. Trevor, with a Bible, was apparently trying to evange-lize them. "Come join us, Sacramento!" he shouted.

"I'm good," Chris said, smiling and keeping his distance.

The young knight observed that the vampires in Duluth were like the vampires in California, with their black lipstick, pierced tongues, and other facial atrocities. Ears waxed with iPods, the coven was ignoring Trevor, all plugged in to their own trendy darkness, and munching on whole-grain bagels. Chris won-dered what game they were playing in those black uniforms. Did they really want to suck blood? Were they really searching, in their own weird way, for the Holy Grail?

The next day, in history class, Chris and some of the vam-pires were forced to trudge through Russia, trying to keep a step ahead of Rasputin. The teacher, Mr. Koffski, stood cadaver-like in plaid against the blackboard.

"Blah . . . drone . . . blah . . . peasants . . . blah . . . czar."

Pause.

"Everyone got that?"

No answer.

"Drone . . . wife . . . blah . . . rubles . . . drone . . ."

Pause.

"Understand?"

No answer.

"Blah . . . blah . . . drone . . . drone . . . Rasputin."

Spit!

Dip Schmidt, who had been quietly suckling his tobacco in the back row, suddenly ejected some black juice into his pop can, rousing the classroom.

Chris stirred from a daydream of being in a snowy birch near the lake. He wasn't sure why some of the students were giggling. He raised his hand and asked, "Mr. Koffski, is it true that Russians worshipped birch trees?"

The teacher let out a loud sigh. "Some Russians worshipped birches. And some Russians worshipped the same God that you fear."

While Chris scratched his head and tried to figure out what that comment about fear was supposed to mean, Mr. Koffski clicked the Power Point and showed a picture of Karl Marx. The caption read: SAVIOR OF THE PEASANTS.

Spit!

Most of the class erupted into laughter. Dip raised his pop can to toast his supposed cleverness, and the slick aluminum fell into his lap and spilled its contents. Dip lurched to his feet, showing the most horrible crotch to everyone. At first, he was embarrassed. And then he relished the reaction he got with pelvic thrusts.

Several girls screamed, including a vampiress.

Mr. Koffski tried to regain control of the classroom. "That's enough. Settle down now." He clicked the Power Point. "Look at the screen. There's the Revolution, in all of its violent glory."

The pelvic thrusts continued, along with the laughing and screaming. Mr. Koffski said, "Duane, go to the principal's office!"

The kid sneered. "You know my dad's on the school board."

The room became silent. The teacher was obviously shaken by the open threat. But he said, "After teaching in this place, I have no fear of being sent to Siberia. Or Dante's hell."

The students laughed, and Chris said to Dip, "In your face, buddy."

The tobacco-stained miscreant slouched out of the room, muttering, "I'm going to kill you, Sacramento."

The bell began to ring, and Chris said to the noise, "Not if I kill you first."

While one adolescent went to the principal's office, the other went to biology class. There the young knight learned that he was a growing mass of cells that were constantly dying and re-generating, so that every twelve years he became another person. A new creation. Born again.

Man alive, Chris thought, scribbling notes for the next exam.

The day after Halloween, Dip threatened to kill him again. The stain-faced miscreant wore his usual costume to school: the asinine low-pants, as if he were some sort of gluteus gangster.

Chris saw the shameless boy in the hallway and let him know that too much was showing. "Crack kills," he joked.

Dip turned and raised his hand like a pistol. "I'll give you the crack of doom, Sacramento. I'll snuff you out."

The threat was half-assed. Chris laughed, unafraid, and went on with his life, studying for exams and renewing every cell in his body.

The young knight began to fall in love with his own body. He bought a set of free weights and hefted away every evening, stripped to his underwear, watching in the big mirror while his muscles pulsated and ached for more, more, more.

The fresh man, all through the dormancy of winter and the returning fertility of spring, hefted the weights as if lifting the whole world, his glistening image expanding beyond the frame of the mirror like an incarnation of the insatiable.

chapter **forty-three**

WEDDING BELLS resonated over the Duluth hillside. The first Saturday in June resounded with bliss, while Chris battled unruly yards. Church bells rang all day while the boy pushed his lawnmower up and down the slopes, his muscles exploding with power.

A gray and red pickup pulled into the driveway of a half-mowed yard. A big head with a buzz cut shouted out the window. "Hey, you!"

Chris killed the mower. "Are you the guy with the lawn up by the ski jump?"

"Nope. I'm the guy with the football team." The coach chomped gum as if trying to kill it. *Chomp, chomp.* "Are you the kid they've been talking about?"

The church bells rang with joy.

"Talking about? Me?"

Chomp, chomp. "Are you Lagorio?"

"Yeah. I'm Christopher."

The football coach chomped and nodded, and admired the muscles. "See you on the field, Lagorio."

"Well, hmm. I don't know."

Chomp, chomp. "I'll see you on the field."

"Hmm. Maybe."

"Fantastic," the coach said, half-smiling. "Now get a damn haircut."

"What?"

The wedding bells played on and on.

Chomp, chomp. "And stay the hell away from girls."

chapter forty-four

PIXIE JOHNSON was a cheerleader who sky-tumbled as if the very air had been created for her nubility.

All of the football players were enamored of her flexibility, the universe in her skin stretching the possibilities of pleasure.

Chris heard her spiraling voice while he mastered the field, bashing his body against the other Friday-night boys. Distracted by the red-headed cheerleader when she leapt heavenward, he wanted to run over and catch her.

Pixie wore a body-kissing black leotard, had a paw print on her cheek, and shouted, "Go, Lagorio!"

The boy was a natural, knowing when to accelerate, pivot, cut back, and lower his head into the guts of bothersome line-backers. His lawn-mowing thighs were propulsions of power that sent him smashing into the end zone.

"Lagorio! Lagorio!"

Pixie cheered louder than the other girls, as if making a claim on the new blood.

Chris, panting after his second touchdown and feeling faint, had barely made the varsity team. His father said he couldn't do it. "You're more of a dreamer, son. You'll get your head busted playing football." His father was doubly wrong. The boy made the team, and it was impossible to get his head busted while he warmed the bench for the first three games. He hardly paid attention to the action on the field. Instead, he focused on the red-haired Pixie, who seemed capable of everything.

Suddenly Coach Lundblat barked the boy out of his fantasy. "Lagorio! Get your ass over here! You're going in for Gutherson. If you fumble, you better say your prayers. Understand?"

Number 33 snapped on his chin strap. His wild heart was pounding, but not because of football. He wanted to impress the girl who kept tumbling into the sky.

Chris had never considered sports competition as a good way to spend time on earth. Bruises, concussions, broken bones and blood — he knew that much about football. But when he was given the ball on the battlefield, with Pixie Johnson singing out his name, something beyond the prospect of injury arose in his soul. It was like an instinct, a need to kill or save for a cause, and he lowered his helmet and pummeled the steam-breathing linebackers. He racked up a hundred yards and a couple of touchdowns.

Pixie smiled at him after the game. "You're amazing."

He nodded. "So are you."

The following Monday, he approached her in the cafeteria. "We should meet at Caribou after practice tonight."

Thinking over the offer, Pixie played with her colorful hair, and replied in a flirty voice, "You and me and coffee? Oh, no thanks."

The answer hit the boy's chest and knocked the wind out of him. He tried to breathe, bewildered, wondering how he had misinterpreted her interest.

"Let's skip the 'Bou," Pixie said. "Just come over to my house after supper." She paused, acting all innocent. "We'll watch old episodes of *Little House on the Prairie*."

He laughed. "*Little House on the Prairie*?"

"Yeah. With my mom."

That didn't seem like a situation that would lead to what Chris desired, but he said, "Okay. Sounds good."

The Johnson family lived in a tough neighborhood, and their two-story wooden house had no view of the lake. The ramshackle abode was hot in the summer, cold in the winter, and shook as if it would crumble every time the jets from the military base roared over the city. Pixie's father was a failed pilot who'd fallen into the paper industry. Her mother had been a beauty princess, but never a queen, having been second and third runner-up several times. She'd enrolled in beauty school and become a stylist.

Pretty Pixie and muscular Chris watched *Little House on the Prairie* on a beer-stained couch with drunken Mrs. Johnson. She whispered to her daughter. "He's cute. I like his hair. Brown and curly. Oo la la."

"Mother, watch the TV."

"He dresses nice, too. That white shirt is linen. You gotta love a boy who wears natural fibers."

"Mother . . ."

"What? I just think he's cute."

Mrs. Johnson munched peanut brittle, gulped beer, and during the commercials she kept offering brittle to the football player.

"No thanks," Chris said.

"Are you sure?"

"I had a big supper."

"Did your mom make steak?"

"Cauliflower casserole. Raw."

"Yuckie poo. Here, have a snack."

"I'm not hungry. Really. We also had a healthy portion of bean-sprout salad."

"Oh my gosh!" Mrs. Johnson spewed brittle in disbelief. "No! No! No!"

It was the episode in which little Carrie falls down a mine shaft. It was almost as good, on a romantic level, as a horror movie, because Pixie leaned into Chris's shoulder and held his arm for support.

Mrs. Johnson gulped her beer. "Thank you, Lord! Oh, thank you! Poor Carrie! She needs a bath, but she's okay."

Sob . . . gulp . . . belch.

The *Little House* hero of the episode was a drunk. Blessed with an epiphany after breaking his bottle of whiskey, the outcast had devised a sober plan to save the girl and renew the faith of her family and Walnut Grove, proving the goodness of Providence.

Click.

Mrs. Johnson turned off the TV, and staggered down the hallway to the bedroom, leaving the teenagers alone on the couch. "G'night night," she stammered. "Don't fall down no wells."

Pixie wiped a tear, and buried the next tear into the boy's shoulder. "I'm sorry," she muffled. "Maybe it was a mistake to invite you here."

Chris didn't know what to do. He had fantasized some things he'd like to do, but offering his shoulder made him feel somewhat chastened. And full of desire. Pixie had the body of a goddess, and he was a rising star on the football team. Alone together, drenched in the aphrodisiac of harvest moonlight, sex should have been happening. In the boy's mind, it was time to know what all the mythology was about. Moosehead and Skunk already knew the mystery, if their stories were true, and when Chris thought about those guys having their way with goddesses, the images literally made him nauseated. Yet for his own body to be joined to Pixie seemed perfectly good and natural.

He gently stroked the cheerleader's shiny red hair. She turned her face to his, and they kissed. Pixie smiled and held back the next sob. Her wet lips glowed with moonlight. He kissed her again. Pixie's lips opened to the momentum of passion. The moonlight seemed to intensify. Chris pressed his weight upon the girl, laying her down. She giggled and squirmed while he nibbled at her neck, going for the jugular. Was it pure instinct to hunger for the lifeblood? Like a polite vampire, he gave her the slightest hickey.

This is the life, the boy thought, tickle-kissing every inch of exposed skin.

The young knight returned his attention to the mouth that had cheered for him in battle. And in the middle of a breathless tongue-kiss, he sent his hands searching under Pixie's clothing for something better than a touchdown, something more akin to the holy.

Pixie repositioned her body, making everything more accessible. "I've never done this before," she whispered.

The girl was not going to stop him. He could distreasure her. He was free to take. And she was free to give. Two wills, willing the same thing.

"Baby," he breathed on her neck. "Baby."

She froze. "What did you say?"

"Nothing."

Pixie gave the boy a mighty push, and he fell to the floor.

"Ouch!"

"Sorry, Chris. Are you okay?"

"I'm fine. I'm fine," he said, trying to catch his breath.

Pixie looked down at him. "Can I ask you a question? It's serious."

"Um, okay," he said, thinking it would be something about what the kids called "protection."

"Chris, do you ever think about your soul?"

The boy shrugged.

The girl continued. "I think about my soul all the time. I always feel like it wants to fly away."

Please don't talk, Chris moaned inside. *Don't talk about the soul, not now.*

The girl continued. "I feel like I'm always holding its wings, keeping my soul close to my heart. Do you ever feel that way?"

The boy looked up at her thighs. His eyes seemed created for the secret luster of her flesh. He quickly climbed back on the couch, and on top of her.

Pixie wanted to continue talking about her soul, and Chris was willing to listen — later. For now, he kissed her more passionately, keeping her mouth from forming any more words. The boy and girl returned to their silent song of songs.

"Chris, stop. Stop!" She stared innocently into his ravenous eyes. "Chris. Do you believe in things? Things that really matter, like soul-mates?"

"Huh? What?"

"Soul-mates."

A flash filled the window with more than moonlight, and then was gone. Pixie knew that her father had just pulled into the driveway. "We'll talk more later" she said to the boy. "Now go sit in that chair."

"What?"

"On the other side of the room. Hurry!"

The downstairs door opened and closed. A fatherly voice called out, "What the hell is this?"

The boy stood and slunk over to the beer-stained chair.

"We can still be soul-friends," Pixie whispered. "That's more than 'just friends.' "

Chris didn't know what to say. "All right," he muttered. "Whatever you think is best."

"This place is a sty," Mr. Johnson slurred. He climbed the stairs to the second floor, swearing every few steps, and found his wife passed out in the bedroom. "Wake up, Lorraine."

"Christopher," Pixie whispered. "You should probably run."

The boy rose to his feet, but stayed in the TV room.

Mr. Johnson kicked the bed. Lorraine whimpered, "Careful, careful, the walls will cave in."

"What the hell do you mean, the walls will cave in?"

"She fell down the pit."

"Who fell? Pixie? What pit?"

"It was an old mine, Gus. Nobody knew it was there. It was just waiting to swallow her up."

"Is Pixie home? Or is she out wrecking her life?"

"She's home. We had good family time. Except she fell down a pit. It was awful."

"You're drunk."

"You're drunker."

"Damn. Is there any beer in the fridge?"

Lorraine spoke dreamily. "Gus . . . where were you when she fell down the pit? We could have used your help."

He sighed. "Where's Pixie?"

"In the TV room."

"She didn't sneak out?"

"Of course not. We had family time."

"Is she still watching TV?"

"Don't be silly. *Little House* is over. There's nothing else good to watch. Oh, it was horrible. She fell down a pit."

"Who fell?"

"Carrie. Then her sister Half A Pint went running for help."

Chris burst out laughing. "Half A Pint?"

Gus raised his voice. "Is Pixie alone?"

"No, silly. We had family time. You should've been here. Why do you make us spend every night alone?"

Gus staggered out of the bedroom and down the hall. The boy put his hands in his lap, while Pixie checked her blouse. She looked up and smiled nervously. "Hi, Daddy."

"The president was on TV at the bar," Gus mumbled. "Didn't say a damn word about Duluth. I'll bet he's never seen iron ore, or a paper mill. Damn. Look at that moon."

The man waited for the boy to acknowledge him. Gus didn't buy that innocent posture. He knew exactly what Chris had tried to do to his daughter. Gus had done it to many fathers' daughters. "That's a hell of a moon," he mumbled.

The boy awkwardly extended his hand. "Hi. I'm —"

Pixie spoke for him. "Christopher's been getting some playing time on the varsity squad."

Gus scoffed. "I'll bet he's been getting some *playing time.*"

"Daddy!"

He shrugged. "Does this one play hockey?"

The boy shook his head. "Just football. And I also like to watch nature."

"You watch nature?"

"Chris is poetic, daddy. He's my soul-mate."

"That's stupid."

"Daddy!"

"Well, it's been a helluva night," Gus said. He yawned, and scratched himself. "Did the poet touch you?"

"Daddy!"

Gus raised his voice and threatened, "If your soul-mate touched you, you're going to confession."

As if avoiding eleven attackers, Chris rushed around the drunken man, and then pivoted down the stairs. "Bye, Pixie."

chapter forty-five

A YELLOW LEAF fell from an elm tree . . . and returned to the sky like a bird. A gust of wind sent a whole flock of leaves flying toward the dark, beautiful clouds.

Chris tried to focus on football practice, but his soul was being called to the festival of molecules all over the place. The quarterback handed him the ball, and Chris immediately fumbled. He tried to scoop it up, but the ball bounced wildly as if invisibly kicked. The star running back tripped, and rolled in the grass, and lay motionless on the ground, staring into the clouds. The other players and coaches must have thought he was injured, or at least dazed, the way the gravity was holding him.

"Sacramento!" Moosehead bellowed. "Get up! Let's run another play!"

Chris stayed down, watching and listening as if for the wings of angels.

A concert of choral thunder was rolling in from the lake, crossing the shoreline and playing for the field. Whistles blew, voices commanded, and football practice was destroyed by larger forces. Lightning began to burn the air in branching flashes. The lightning struck everywhere, making Chris wonder if all of creation were a form of fire. From the molten center of the earth to the incendiary heavens . . . it seemed to be all aflame.

"Lagorio!" the coach called out. "Move it! I don't want a lawsuit because a lightning bolt takes a liking to you!"

The young knight stayed on the ground for a few more minutes, drenched in more light than he'd ever seen before.

chapter forty-six

A SUN-YELLOW Volkswagen Beetle was Chris's first car.

On a bright fall Sunday, he exchanged four hundred dollars for the 1969 rustbucket and drove it home, backfiring and sparking.

"You have to pay for your own insurance," his father said, standing in the driveway. He was wearing his lecturing face, but was obviously proud of the purchase.

"Yeah, I'll rake more leaves."

Chris's mother beamed and patted the Bug. "This is a very proud moment, Topher. You bought a car — a really cool car!"

His father warned, "You'll need to shovel extra snow this winter."

"Yeah, I will."

Joe pointed at the sky. "What if it doesn't snow?"

Chris laughed. "This is Duluth. I can make a million dollars by shoveling."

Val jumped up and down, her thyroid gushing happily, her pink sari billowing. "C'mon! Let's go for a ride!"

She started to open the passenger-side door, but was stopped by her husband's words. "Let him go alone."

"Oh, it's such a fun little car. Topher, sweetie, you'll take us for a ride later, right?"

"Of course."

His father ordered, "Stay within the city limits. And remember everything you learned in driver's training class."

Chris was ecstatic. "Here I go!" And away he flew, grinding the gears and ascending the hill. *Pitter-patter-spark-bang!*

Driving the sun-yellow car was like flying and made Chris maneuver his vision to include more of the miraculous. His eyes were everywhere at once — ahead, behind, to the sides, and above. He ascended the hill to Skyline Drive, seeing the sights more like a pilgrim than a visitor.

Lifting into the wind, the wings of a sparrow were full of earth's physics and the metaphysics of angels. Every flutter of the bird was a reminder to the boy: "Lift up your heart." And he noticed smoke from leaf-barrels whispering into a sky of autumn prayers. And down in the harbor, bodies of mist were arising from the great lake as if Superior were giving up its dead.

Sputter-putter-spark-bang!

Music, more in motion than ever before, filled the boy's soul: O life, life, in locomotion; life eternal on the road!

Sputter-putter-spark-bang!

And with a swerve in time, he gasped at the last moment to avoid plunging over the cliff and rolling down in flaming glory to the water.

"Yikes — for God's sake, be careful," he told himself, refocusing on the center line.

Chris drove Majestic around Mount Royal, peeked quickly in the windows of the library and Caribou Coffee, and then lit out for the farms. The land above Duluth reminded him of the landscape of Sacramento, the same striving of the trees to reach the clouds, and the artistic tangling of a thousand kinds of shrubs, bushes, weeds, and grasses all making their life's journey together as if in perfect stillness.

Chris almost hit the brakes, but instead shifted into neutral and coasted quietly, hoping he would not be noticed.

The Mudgett family was in their front yard, gathered beneath an oak tree. Grant was about to leap into a mountain of fire-colored leaves. Mrs. Mudgett was singing. Her husband was in a chair, whittling. Chastity was giving milk to the baby. And Mary Joan, in a dress the color of a harvest moon, was just being beautiful.

Grant leapt into the fiery leaves while Chris rolled past, gritting his teeth. Nobody seemed to notice his sputter-puttering car, except for a few roaming chickens and Miss America the goat; she goggled at Majestic as if laughing, and continued to chew on the fence.

The boy turned east and began his descent; and he clicked on the radio. There was no stereo but he found a Golden Oldies station that filled the rustbucket with more than enough sounds of nostalgia. Chris made himself nod-dance to the forced rhythm of "Teen Angel" and wound his way down through the farms and woods toward Lake Superior. Accelerating and decelerating, shifting and downshifting, he rolled through the fall colors and looked ahead, behind, to the sides, and above.

The boy knew that his parents were waiting for him back at the house. His father wanted to talk about insurance, and his mother wanted to go for a ride. So it was selfish to continue this journey.

"Just a little further," he whispered.

The radio began to play "The Wanderer." Chris refused to hum along with the bravado-voice that enjoyed exploiting the whole world of women. However, the young knight could not help but join the refrain, feeling that maybe he, too, should get around, and around. No more of this "just friends" and "soulmates" nonsense. Why not be a wanderer? Especially now that he was hot on wheels.

A sign appeared.

TWO HARBORS.

Waves of adrenaline pounded his heart as he contemplated what was beyond the far border of the town: the cathedral-house.

Terra Corwin danced into Chris's mind and made him panic for the brakes — he forgot what he'd learned in driver's safety class — and Majestic skidded across the center line. Had there been an oncoming vehicle, the boy would have met death again. This time it would have been bone-crushing, not a dream.

"The Wanderer" and all of its bravado faded into A.M. oblivion, and the weak voice of Bob Dylan began scratching out of the dashboard. Chris turned Majestic around, and slowly, very slowly, accelerated into "Knockin' on Heaven's Door."

chapter forty-seven

PIXIE GAVE Chris a call — he had finally gotten a cell phone — but he did not answer. "Hey," she said in her message, "have you ever been to Sunshine Laundromat? It's the best place in the world to escape from the parents. They have birds in here. Really. Birds in a laundromat. A big aviary above the washing machines. People wash their clothes while tropical birds fly back and forth across the building. It's awesome. Whoever thought of this is a freaking genius. Seriously, how many people on earth are capable of opening a business that includes laundry and parakeets? Chris, I wish you were here. Bye."

On a foggy Sunday afternoon, Chris met Pixie at Sunshine Laundromat. The two friends reclined in the old stuffed chairs and viewed the tropical birds in their huge cage.

"This is amazing," Pixie said. "It's like we're not even in Duluth."

"Oh, we're in Duluth," Chris said, gesturing toward a lady a few feet away.

The barrel-chested woman in a flannel shirt took a towel out of the dryer and gave it a mighty shake. *SNAP!* She took out another towel. *SNAP!* She took out a pair of overalls. *SNAP!*

Chris pretended to get injured by the snapping. He acted like his ear had been cut off, and also his arm, and he contorted into feigned agony. Pixie got the giggles and whispered, "Stop it.

Stop it! You're killing me." And Snappy Lu Bunyan, as they later called her, said to the teenagers, "You seem like a nice young couple. Remember to invite me to your wedding."

The teens blushed and went over to the dryer where the cheerleader's clothes were still wet. Chris plunked some more quarters into the machine. "This is cheaper than dinner and a movie."

"Oh, Lagorio, you're so romantic."

"I am?"

She shook her head. "Not really. I mean, yeah, you have your moments."

"Is that why you like me? For my romance?"

As a joke, she eyed him up and down; and then blushed for real.

"Fair enough," he said. "I guess our relationship is a mystery."

The girl gave him a flirty look. "Why do you want to be friends with me instead of some other cheerleader?"

The boy's nerve endings tried to move some poetry from his heart to his brain to his mouth. Several lovely phrases were caught up in the queue, including something about the swan-like elegance of her neck.

"You rock, um, my world," he stammered. "Wanna drive, um, up to Skyline Drive?"

"Hmm. My clothes will be done in thirty minutes."

He motioned to the shadowy hill out the window. "Can you think of a better way to spend half an hour?"

"Hmm. I don't know . . ."

"The view will be inspiring. And then we'll come back and tell the birds all about it."

Laughing and taking his hand, she said, "Okay. Let's go."

In twilight, Duluth appeared to be in another time, medieval in the mist. The boy drove the girl dangerously to Skyline for another tryst in the sun-colored car. They eased into the back seat and moved skinward slowly, not making much of the kisses for half an hour. Chris almost told Pixie that he loved her. "You're beautiful," he said, groping for more. "You're really exquisite."

The mist disappeared into the night, and the growing darkness accelerated the passion. Beneath the migrating constellations, with the Southern Cross holding steady in the mirror, the football star was fallen and falling, all swooned out for the swan-like. The neck of Pixie led him down in quickening kisses from skin as if to feathers. If they became one, the boy was sure he and Pixie would burst through the roof.

The girl seemed both gravity-bound and ascendant. The celestial in her skin was warm as tears for the boy, and torrid for Heaven. "Chris, Chris, oh God, please stop."

"Okay," he said, kissing her again . . . and again.

"Chris, listen. Stop. I want to talk about our souls."

chapter forty-eight

COACH LUNDBLAT chomped his gum and yelled at his assistant coach, "Call a damn play that works!"

The offensive coordinator, Mr. Heitilla, sent the signal to the quarterback. "Thirty-three power." That was a tailback play for Lagorio to find light between the left guard and tackle. Shifting through the line of scrimmage, leaving the defenders grasping for air, Chris and his lawnmower legs whirled down the field and into the end zone.

Pixie cheered, her voice spiraling over the hundreds of exclamations in the stadium. Coach Lundblat chomped his gum and barked to his assistants. "Call that play all night!" And scouts from several colleges scribbled enthusiastic notes about the sophomore sensation, the God-gifted kid who'd never played football in his life.

Number 33 politely tossed the ball to the stunned ref, who spit out his whistle in disbelief. He'd never seen a kid score a touchdown so easily.

After the game, Chris and Pixie went parking again on Skyline Drive.

The great lake sparkled with hazy starlight. The temperature was dropping and the steam between the kisses began to fog the windshield. Occasionally, a car rounded the bend and flashed its brights. Diffused through the misted glass, the lights made soft haloes around the boy and girl in their self-created agony.

"Stop, oh God, stop," Pixie said.

The boy had just been cheered by a whole stadium for not stopping, so the command made no sense to his flesh.

The girl leaned away and rolled down the passenger-side window. The end-of-October chill rushed in, along with a swath of burning sky.

"Chris."

"Yeah?"

"Do you ever want to leave?"

"Leave what?"

Pixie craned her neck toward the stars. "I'd like to leave, and go someplace like Sunshine."

"Huh? You want to go to the laundromat?"

She sighed to the heavens. "You don't understand."

He said under his breath, "That's for sure."

She eyed a constellation as if it were her future home. "I'd like to live someplace warm, with tropical birds. Like Rio de Janeiro. Or Belize."

The boy stroked her shiny hair. "So far away? You could at least stay in the country. Florida has flamingoes."

Pixie continued to look at the heavens while rolling up the window. "Can we go to the laundromat?"

"Symbolically, or for real?"

"Don't be a goof. I always talk for real."

While Chris drove Majestic around the deadly bends of Skyline Drive, and then descended the hill, Pixie talked about how she was not born to live in Duluth. She enumerated its negatives, including the weather, poverty, depression, alcoholism, fake niceness, and lack of real community. "People need more festivals," she said. "Festivals for the soul."

"That's a good idea," Chris said, pausing at an intersection. He allowed two flannel-wearing jaywalkers to have their way, despite the green light.

Pixie asked, "Don't you think Duluth is plain and boring?"

"Nope," he said, revving up Majestic again.

"Aren't you bored all the time? There isn't much to do here."

Chris laughed, turning on to Fourth Street. "There's plenty to do here."

"Are you serious?"

"Yeah."

She stared at the boy as if awaiting further explanation. When he failed to speak, she said, "California must have been exciting. You probably miss it like mad."

"Not really. Duluth isn't that different from Sacramento. Trees, water, and fish."

"You have trees, water, and fish in your head."

"Maybe."

"And snow on your brain."

Chris grinned. "I love snow. I can't wait."

The girl stared out the window. "Don't you want to fly away to some exotic place?"

Chris flicked the turn signal and eased to the side of the road. "Duluth is exotic, in its own way. And right around here is everything that I love."

Pixie faced him with sad, soulful eyes, and whispered, "Do you know what I love?"

Me, he almost said.

"I love . . . birds. I love birds more than anything."

"Um, that's good. Here we are."

The teenagers went into Sunshine Laundromat. The girl hurried toward the aviary and began chirping at her favorite parrots. The birds chirped back at Pixie through the wire cage, as if they were all planning an escape to Rio and Belize.

Spit!

Dip was seated in one of the cushy chairs. He slurred, "Word on the street is that you scored, Lagorio."

Chris waved awkwardly. "Hey, Dip. What are you doing in Sunshine?"

The spitter gestured toward the cheerleader. "Scored during and after the game, eh?"

While the birds made a fluttering commotion, Chris scampered around the cushy chair, pivoted, and lowered his shoulder. The muscles in his legs sprang with such anger that the chair and Dip went crashing into a washing machine. The slime in the drool-can spilled all over Dip's face and sweatshirt. A trickle of blood ran out of his mouth.

The sight of the blood made Chris's wrath turn to contrition. "Sorry, Duane."

Pixie reached into her pocket for a tissue. She dabbed at the drooler's mouth, and scolded him. "You shouldn't have baited Chris. Why do you keep stalking him?"

Dip smiled, revealing a bloody gap between his teeth. "Lagorio's done playing football. He's finished."

Eyes flashing, Pixie questioned, "You did this on purpose? To get him kicked off the team?"

Dip grinned, ghoulish and pathetic, and spit a tooth into the garbage can. "Finished. Both of you."

chapter forty-nine

THE FOLLOWING Sunday, after Chris had raked and bagged some colorless leaves, the last of the season, he and Pixie met again at Sunshine. They cooed and chirped at the tropical birds, and then went for a walk in the last of the light. A rugged trail in the middle of town ascended the Duluth hill. The teenagers braved a clay path riddled with roots, rocks, and boulders above a dangerous gorge.

"Be careful," Chris said. "Just because there are no railings doesn't mean you can go where you want."

Pixie traipsed near the edge, lost in her own thoughts.

The boy reached over, put his arm around the girl's waist, and pulled her away from the roaring waters below.

"You're such a demanding boyfriend," Pixie joked.

He thought: did she just say *boyfriend*?

Chris leaned over to kiss her on the cheek, and the girl broke out of his grasp and traipsed on ahead of him.

Near Skyline Drive, the roots of old-growth pine trees arose from the earth in patterns that seemed like a code. A code that Chris suddenly wanted to break. Some of the roots formed obvious letters, and sometimes a partial word could be deciphered. The boy knelt on the ground and brushed away some pine needles and dead leaves. "Hey Pixie, look at this."

"What did you find?"

"I'm not sure."

The cheerleader knelt beside him and studied the roots. "Oh my gosh."

"Yeah. It's like a word, right?"

She nodded. "The roots say *l.o.* And they're low to the ground. That's really cool."

The boy wiped away more needles and leaves. "Look again. See the *v*?"

"No."

"You can't see the *v*?"

"Hmm. Oh, that little ridge! It *is* a *v*."

The boy traced his finger along the cursive roots. "*l . . . o . . . v.*"

"Love," she said, shaking her head. "That's unreal. Did you plant that?"

He laughed. "How could I have planted it? This tree is much older than us."

"*Love* just appeared . . . like that?"

"Yeah. Well, without the *e*."

Pixie traced her finger along the roots. "This is how I text *love*. Without the *e*. How would the earth know to do this?"

Chris was busy finding another word. "Look here."

She looked. "What? I don't see any letters."

He pointed. "There's the *s*. And there's the *x*. Now if we could just find that elusive *e*."

Pixie punched his arm. "Don't make me have to tackle you."

"Please do."

The girl lowered her shoulder and charged. She'd meant to pull up before hitting him, but was a little late, and nearly sent him into the gorge. "Christopher!"

He wobbled, arms upraised.

She reached out and grabbed his shirt.

"Geez," he said, staggering forward. "You almost killed me."

"Sorry. I didn't think I could move you."

"Let's sit down for a minute."

"Good idea."

They sat on a large smooth stone, several feet from the rushing water, and caught their breaths. Eventually, twilight began to descend over the Skyline bridge, but the river stayed lit and shimmering. Pixie rested her head on the boy's shoulder. He enjoyed looking through the locks of redness that gave extra color to his world. And he loved the feel of her softness on his face. "You feel like springtime in autumn," he said.

"Your shoulder feels like rock," she answered.

"Is that a bad thing?"

"It is if I'm trying to sleep." And she pretended to fluff his shoulder like a pillow.

"Don't get too comfy. We need to climb down before it's totally dark."

A few minutes later, Pixie spoke in a dreamy voice, "If the tree roots say *l-o-v*, then what does the water say?"

Chris liked the question. He thought it over, watching the twilit water descend toward the great lake. He answered, barely audible: "Love."

Pixie immediately stood and shook her head in disagreement. She pointed down at the gorge. "I think the water says *freedom*."

chapter fifty

ON MONDAY MORNING, Chris was called into Coach Lund-blat's office.

Chomp, chomp, chomp. "Turn in your stuff, Lagorio. You're off the team for fighting."

"What about my side of the story?"

Lundblat sighed. He slouched back in his chair, and then leaned forward and pounded his desk. "I invested a whole season in you! A sophomore. I let you have the ball while juniors and seniors sat on the bench. Do you know how many angry phone calls I've gotten, complaining about you and your showboating?"

"Showboating?"

"Kicking up your legs like some sort of half-assed dancer. I never said anything, because you were gaining a lot of yards." *Chomp, chomp.* "But I never liked it."

Chris wasn't sure what to say. He shuffled his feet. "Hmm . . . I never meant to make anyone angry. I just ran as best I could. Maybe you should have coached me a little more."

Lundblat stood and stomped around the desk. "If you want to challenge me, then just punch me in the face."

"Huh?"

The coach chomped and offered his chin to the boy's fist. "Hit me hard, Lagorio."

The boy curled his fingers. "And if I do, will you put me back on the team?"

Lundblat chomped and tried to think. "No, but I'll give you ten dollars."

"What?"

Chomp, chomp. "Yeah. I'll give you ten dollars if you punch me."

The worst thing Chris could do at the moment was laugh. And that's exactly what he did. And he also spoke a dangerous truth. "I heard that Dip's father threatened you."

Lundblat raised his hand. "That's a lie, Lagorio!"

"Then what's the real reason for dismissing me?"

Chomp, chomp. "For fighting."

"For fighting?"

"Yeah."

"But coach," the boy said, trying to keep a straight face, "you're trying to fight me now."

"What? Exactly. That's why you're being cut from the team."

"Because you started a fight with me?"

"Yeah. I mean . . . wait a second. Get out of here, Lagorio. You don't want to listen to reason. You're gonna believe what you want to believe." *Chomp, chomp, chomp.* "Go on. I have playoffs to prepare for." *Chomp, chomp . . .* swallow. "Oh, crap."

chapter fifty-one

AFTER THANKSGIVING, Chris picked up Pixie in the Bug, gave her a little kiss, and said, "Where do you want to go?"

"Away. Anywhere."

The girl was out of sorts. It was the first time Chris had seen her without makeup and lip gloss, and she wore a rumpled gray sweatshirt with the hood hiding her beautiful hair. "Drive me downtown. Or up the shoreline. It doesn't matter."

"Okay. Be sure to fasten your seatbelt."

"No, I don't think I will."

"Why not?"

"I don't feel like it."

Chris leaned across her body, and fastened the seat belt for her. "There. We're good to go."

Majestic sputtered away. A hint of snow was in the air, and yet the air seemed to be holding its breath. It was the in-between season of no-longer fall and not-quite winter. The Bug descended a few blocks, and Chris turned onto Superior Street.

"Slow down," Pixie said, "there's a deer on your right."

"I see it."

"Slower. Another deer on your left."

The boy hit the brakes. "A buck and a doe."

Pixie reached over and honked the horn. "The hunters chase them into town. It happens every year."

"Don't worry," Chris said. "Nature will take its course. It will be all right."

Rolling down her window, the girl shouted, "Go back to the woods!"

The two deer trotted into the yard of a large brick house.

"Go back to the woods!"

The deer paused near the porch, and turned to look at the Bug. They stood like decorative statues, their ears pointed forward. The deer didn't want to return to the woods. They liked Duluth. There was plenty of food to eat — natural and unnatural — and life was good and easy when they weren't getting hit by cars and trucks.

Chris turned on the headlights, revved the engine, and rolled away. Further down Superior Street, the Goth kids were gathered, as they always were, at the entrance of the Holiday Inn. Wearing black skirts and shorts, they shivered in the Advent chill, as if they realized, perhaps, that death was not their friend.

Honking, Chris gave them a friendly wave.

Several Goths waved back. One flashed the sign of the devil with his fingers. The horns.

"Do you know these evil kids?" Pixie asked. "They seem to know you."

"I've had lunch with them in the caf."

"By the Emo window?"

"Yeah. The kids by the Emo window are all pretty cool. You'd be surprised how many of them are A students. They're just going through some stuff at home."

The Goth who flashed the horns now approached the car.

Pixie's face grew tense, and she said, "Let's get out of here."

"What?"

"Drive!"

"Where?"

"Anywhere!"

Chris drove away from the Goth, who called out, "Sacramento! Don't you want to hang with us?"

Sputter-sputter-put-put. Majestic crossed over to Canal Park.

The boy glanced at Pixie's face and noticed that she was very pale. Her hands were folded, or rather clenched, in her lap. He asked, "Are you okay? Did Billy scare you?"

"Park here," she said in a shaky voice. "I want to walk on the lift-bridge."

The wind was whipping down from the north, with large waves rolling and crashing into the canal. Mist flew in the air and turned to ice, slicking the concrete walls and the steel bridge. The boy stopped. "Hey, the weather's getting rough. You wanna just go to the Seitz Building? Grab something warm at the bakery?"

Pixie stopped walking, slid a little, and then turned. Her eyelids were livid, squeezing out angry tears. "You think all I need is a pastry? Give the girl some flour and sugar, and everything will be sweetness and light? What's wrong with you? Can't you see that my whole life has gone down the toilet? First I get kicked off the cheerleading squad because you fought with Duane. I was considered guilty by association, because of you. Now the other cheerleaders won't speak to me, as if it's my fault that we lost the first playoff game. And then while you and I were messing around on Skyline, my mother moves to Missouri and leaves me with my drunken father. He's been having an affair with a waitress who just turned twenty-one. I heard him on the phone today saying something about an abortion. And then you take me on a date to meet up with some devil-worshipers. How can you be so stupid?"

What could he possibly say to all that?

"I'm sorry. I didn't know things were that bad. I'm really sorry."

She batted her eyelashes, tears flying. "Whatever. It's okay."

Chris put his arm around her, wondering if they had just broken up. Had they even been together? Regardless, he silently vowed to find a good Christmas present for her.

The boy and girl stood shivering on the lift-bridge, facing Lake Superior. The icy mist coated their hair like years and years of aging, until the bells began to ring, warning them that a ship was coming in . . . and the bridge would be going up to the sky.

chapter fifty-two

ON CHRISTMAS EVE, the clustered lights of the Duluth harbor were like bulbs that had fallen from a tree the size of the sky.

Chris and Pixie stood in the downtown Skywalk, suspended above Superior Street. The glass windows made the Skywalk seem like a long hollow icicle connecting the buildings. Snowflakes fell to the street and sidewalks, swirling around the feet of window shoppers as if the whole world were about to become frozen.

"I hate it here," Pixie said.

She was dressed in a red coat and green pants, a surface of holiday festivity. "Everything sucks," she muttered.

Everything was so beautiful. Chris put his arm around her. "Want to go to Mass?"

Her eyes filled with tears and then flashed with anger. "My parents always went to Mass on Christmas Eve. And look where it got them. No, Chris, I don't want to merely go to Mass. I want to kill myself. Or else get married to God."

"Oh," the boy said.

Chris wanted to give her all of the hope in the world. But what he had was much less than that. "We could go to my house. My parents will drive us crazy, but not insane."

Pixie wiped away a tear and laughed. "I guess crazy is good enough for tonight."

Chris led her through the Skywalk and down the stairwell to the fresh snowy air. Majestic was beginning to resemble an igloo, and the boy drove with the windows rolled down, because the defroster wasn't working.

"Pixie, are you freezing to death?"

She nodded, the wind and snow swirling around her face. Her teeth were chattering when they reached the Ruins. Chris turned into his driveway, sliding toward the embankment, almost losing control of the igloo-mobile. He joked, "I hope Santa drives his sleigh better than this."

A horrible thought came to the girl, but she kept it locked behind the chattering teeth. She almost said, "I wish we'd crashed and burned."

"Happy Solstice!"

Val Lagorio, wearing every color of the hippie rainbow, stood in the open door of the glowing house and encouraged the kids to hurry inside. "I have steaming hot chai, and Turkish coffee, and ginseng tea. Whatever you want to warm you up!"

Pixie gave Val a brave cheerleader smile. "Merry Christmas, Mrs. Lagorio."

"Come in where it's cozy. We have the fireplace stoked."

Chris whispered in the girl's ear, "My parents might actually be stoked. But they won't hurt us."

Pixie stomped the snow from her furry boots, and ventured into the strange Lagorio cheer. It was fun to sample the various hot drinks, and the candied octopus pieces were surprisingly edible. The sitar music was like nothing the girl had ever heard before, and it created an otherworldly ambience that was better than most of the pop-Christmas songs on the radio.

TWA-WANNGG . . . ZEE-WEENNGG . . .

"This is nice," she said, gesturing at the whole scene. "Thank you for letting me be here tonight."

Joe had turned off his computers and cell phones and was making himself completely available to the flesh and blood in the room. He made eye contact with everyone, smiled, listened, and made interesting conversation. Toward the end of the evening, he said, "Young lady, I've heard that you have an interest in birds. Especially tropical ones."

Pixie beamed. "That's true."

"So. You'll be able to take care of them."

"What do you mean, take care of them?"

Val slipped out of the room, obviously on a mission.

"What's going on?" Pixie asked. She had an inkling that something really wonderful was about to happen.

"We have a present for you," Joe said. "It was Topher's idea, and we sort of helped him."

The girl grabbed the boy's arm. "I thought we agreed not to buy any presents."

He shrugged. "I didn't buy anything."

Val returned with a golden cage full of chirping.

"Birds!" the cheerleader cheered.

"For you," Chris said. "From Sunshine."

Val placed the golden present on the girl's knees, and she cooed at the two plum-headed parakeets. "Ohh, you're so beautiful. Ohh, I love you, I love you."

"Merry Christmas," Chris said.

Hugging the cage, Pixie tried not to cry, but there was no stopping the joyful tears. "This is the best gift. Thank you, everyone. I can't believe you did this for me."

The Lagorios gave each other happy, satisfied looks, and that was the best gift they'd shared in a long while. The sitar music played itself out, and the night became silent, except for the raucous birds. "Your name is Rio," Pixie said to the female. "And your name is Belize, buddy."

The light of the fireplace illuminated the girl's wet face, making her resemble an angel in a church painting. There were other presents in the house, but nobody made a move to distribute them.

"What's better than birds?" Pixie whispered.

chapter fifty-three

CHRIS RECEIVED a Gibson guitar. Glossy body and six strings shimmering. After a quick glance at the instruction book, the teenager spent Christmas Day in his room, strumming chords and humming melodies like a troubadour in the making. He glanced out the window at the snowy trees. Flashes of silver appeared between the branches — glimpses of Lake Superior — and the boy knew there was a perfect love song out there. He'd try to give voice to that greatness. But first he had to master the notes, chords, and progressions.

His cell phone rang, and he answered. "Hey, birdie girl."

"Chris, the birds are amazing. I've just been sitting here watching them. I love how they drink water. It's so cute. And Rio is such a little flirt. She chirps whenever Belize is looking away. Check this out — when my dad left the house today, I let the birds out of the cage to stretch their wings. A few swoops over the living room and then Rio roosted on the kitchen table and Belize claimed the top of the fridge. There was only one small accident, and they were good about going back into the cage. I'm looking at them right now. And it makes me want to kiss you."

The guitar was resting on the boy's knees. He plucked random strings while listening to the rhapsody.

"I walked down to Sunshine Laundromat this morning to thank the owner for letting you buy the birds, but the manager wasn't there. Do you know who was working? Can you guess who was cleaning the aviary?"

Uh oh, he thought. "Was it Dip?"

"No, don't be silly."

"Moosehead and Skunk?"

"Guess again."

He plucked a few strings. "I don't know. Was it an angel?"

"Don't be sacrilegious."

"Sorry. I was just imagining that the angels must clean up a lot of things. If they really exist."

"Whatever. Try to control your imagination."

Pluck, pluck. "If I control my imagination, then I can't guess who you saw in Sunshine."

The girl sighed, giving up the game. "It was Trevor."

Pluck, pluck. "Who's Trevor?"

"He's a senior. Sort of thin and serious. Kind of cute."

"You mean the preachy kid?"

"He wants to be a priest."

"God save us."

"He's nice."

"Yeah, I broke his glasses a few years back. Now he wears contacts and the chicks dig him. Including my chick."

"Your chick? Ha ha. Listen. Are you listening?"

Pluck, pluck. "I'm all ears."

"Chris, I want to ask you out on a date."

"Cool."

"There's going to be a party at Sacred Heart on New Year's Eve."

Rio and Belize began singing in the background. The boy imagined the lyrics: *Trevor, Trevor, we love Trevor.*

"Pixie, how did you hear about the party? Did the cute senior invite you?"

"Well, umm, yeah."

"So this is a date with you and me — and Trevor Nelson?"

Pixie didn't answer. The plum-headed parakeets chirped happily.

"I'll talk to you later," Chris said.

The boy tossed the phone aside and began strumming wildly on the guitar. And he accidentally found a fresh chord. A sound that wasn't in the instruction book.

chapter fifty-four

JOE AND VAL LAGORIO had mountains and mountains of vinyl records, and Chris explored them all, searching for the Music of the Spheres and tunes for an aspiring troubadour in the works of Muddy Waters, The Who, The Beatles, Manfred Mann, Neil Young, Van Morrison, Carlos Santana, Deep Purple, The Moody Blues, King Crimson, Pink Floyd . . .

The boy visualized the seemingly magical fingers that could create such sounds. How did the guitarists play with such power? Where did it originate? Was it God-given?

"Turn that crap down!" Joe shouted from his office. He pounded the wall, protesting his own music, the very sounds that he once believed had set him free. "I'm trying to get some work done!"

"Sorry."

Chris put on the headphones and considered The Rolling Stones, Led Zeppelin, Jefferson Airplane, Jimi Hendrix, The Grateful Dead, Jethro Tull, The Yardbirds . . . and settled on Bach.

His parents had one classical album: *Four Lute Suites*.

At first Chris was bored with the progressions. The lute player seemed talented enough, but where was the passion? Where was the love? No wonder the world had turned against that sort of music. The boy was about to grab the needle in disgust and remove the disk from the turntable and put on Kiss, when a series of quiet notes, simplicity upon simplicity, gave him pause. His heart began to pound. The music was like a contemplative prayer, and it began to sound perfect.

Were human beings capable of perfection?

It made no sense. Human beings, including himself, were a complete mess. The closest thing to perfection that Chris believed he'd ever encountered was Lake Superior. However, even that had its problems, with its tendencies to kill and destroy. As much as the boy loved Superior, he realized it was an Old Testament god, demanding ancient sacrifices that were no longer helpful.

The lute called to Chris's soul with a perfection that was both alluring and demanding. The strings were simply played, and yet full of the wings of the world, and beyond the world. The heavenly muses were in the music of Bach. And even if the composer had not been perfect, the gift was.

The boy listened to the lute and played along as if in prayer, for days and nights, as if finally receiving his spiritual calling.

And he could not help but think: this guitar thing, if I can master it, will really impress the girls!

chapter fifty-five

ON NEW YEAR'S EVE, Chris pulled up to the Johnson house, and Pixie literally ran out of the door. Her father had been celebrating all day, swilling beer, foam spilling all over the place. He slurred at his daughter, "If Lagorio tries anything, I'll cut it off! Understand?"

The girl climbed into the car with tears in her eyes. She did not let them fall, however, because she was wearing new mascara. Chris knew she wasn't wearing it for him, but he said, "Hey. You look exquisite."

"Thanks."

The boy revved the engine and ground the gears, and Majestic carried them away to Sacred Heart. The former cathedral, a desacrilized Gothic Revival, had been saved from demolition by an organist. The brick and brownstone majesty, with its great spire rising into the mist, now served as the center of the local arts scene.

Festoons of lights were strung around the entrance, suggesting another world of festivity. Pixie got out of the car and hurried toward the old cathedral as if to a new lover. And Trevor Nelson appeared at the door as if by magic.

"Hey, girl," Trevor said, grinning.

She gave him a big hug. "Tonight's the big night."

"Yes, indeed. Everything's arranged."

Chris trailed behind, wondering why the hell he'd accepted this invitation.

New Year's Eve in Sacred Heart was a flurry of spiritual activity, with a live band playing praise music. "*Your love is alpha and omega. Yesterday and now. Your love created galaxies. Only You know how. Your love creates, and recreates, and every knee shall bow.*"

Slouched in the back pew, Chris watched the party. Happy young Catholics, inspired by John Paul II, were singing, dancing, and lifting their hands toward the ceiling. Pixie was elated — seemingly walking on air. Trevor introduced her to a new circle of friends. The girl was hugged into a realm of Catholicism that she did not know existed. And she was whisked away to the sanctuary where the lights were paradisal green and rosy hued. Pixie joined the dance of the multiple heavens that were singing into her soul. She joined hands with shining strangers and exchanged smiles that signified beyond flesh. The light show exploded an hour before midnight, bulbs of all blooms, and laser beams that shattered the stained glass and yet left it unbroken. All was crystalline and molten, and the ex-cheerleader could not help herself — she laughed and shouted and praised.

And she made her confession to an old priest who had agreed to help chaperone the party.

Chris watched the ancient priest raise a glowing hand — blessed all the way back to the Apostles — and mouth the incendiary words of love as if burning the girl's sins to ashes.

"Huh. She looks really happy," Chris said, and went out for a smoke.

Chris thought cigars would be appropriate for the evening's celebration. So he'd brought a pack of *Swisher Sweets*, thinking some of the guys at Sacred Heart would join him in making a contemplative cloud. The sky had cleared and the galaxies seemed to be lowering. He lit up, staring into the dazzling North, and blocked his view with his own breath, and wondered if he were really missing out on most of the universe.

A minute before midnight, shivering, he snuffed out another cigar in the snow and returned to the party. Boys and girls had paired up in the musical lights, licking their lips for the New Year's ritual kiss. The ex-football star stood alone in the back of the old cathedral, squinting and searching. Pixie was leaping up and down, calling out, "Ten, nine, eight . . ."

Chris thought about rushing up and claiming her. ". . . five, four, three . . ."

His muscles tensed, recalling the touchdowns and the cheers, and the fleshy rewards that came after.

Too late.

Trevor and God had already beaten him.

"HAPPY NEW YEAR!"

chapter fifty-six

UNCLE LOUIE'S CAFÉ was noisy at brunch-time, with fuzz-brained partiers returning to their senses. The café boasted a long counter with shiny chrome stools, several roomy booths, and a large bright window looking out upon Fourth Street.

Chris was intrigued by the human nature of Fourth Street, the strange mix of everything from Floyd's Hair Choppers to a belly-dancing studio to Loiselle's Liquor (open at 8 a.m.) to Sacred Heart.

Trevor Nelson considered himself the "Father of Fourth Street" because he loved to discuss theology in the café. He often invited "seekers" to enjoy a deep conversation, a cup of coffee, and Louie's addictive pancakes.

On New Year's Day, Trevor and Chris found an open booth by the window.

"You can have the view," Trevor said, feeling beneficent after Mass. He sat with his back to the belly-dancing studio.

"Thanks," Chris said with a smile.

"You better pray about it."

"Pray about what?"

"Lust."

"Don't worry, Trev. It's going to snow. That should smother everyone's lust."

"Actually, the blizzard will make everything worse. People will think God can't see them, and they'll act like God doesn't exist."

Chris tried to change the subject. "You gonna watch the football game?"

The priest-to-be ignored the question, concentrating on lust. "Up in the Arctic, the Eskimos fool around like crazy. Their sexual practices include —"

"Trev, you really think about these things?"

"Yeah."

"Well, you shouldn't."

"Somebody has to worry about this world."

"Hmm." Chris stared across the street at the red building that housed Eman's Belly-Dancing. He imagined the clinking of hip chains and the sway of a dark-skinned enchantress.

The Greek waitress leaned over and placed two coffees on the table, her shirt opening slightly. "I'll be back to take your orders in a second."

"Thank you," the boys said in unison.

Chris gulped some coffee and felt the dark warmth work its way into his belly. He glanced over at Eman's again and realized he hadn't danced in ages, not since the polka. He tried to imagine Terra Corwin in the role of enchantress, hip chains clinking and arms and legs hypnotic in their allurement; but all Terra would do in his imagination was what she would do in real life.

The waitress reappeared and said to Trevor, "The usual?"

"Yeah. And bring more syrup."

She scribbled on her order pad. "And what about the other gentleman? A gyro? The lamb just came in yesterday. It's fresh as fresh."

Chris ran a hand through his unruly hair. He sighed, and shook his head. "Nothing for me. In fact, I'm ready for the check."

"The gentleman isn't hungry?"

"Oh, I'm starving. But I don't feel like eating."

Trevor gave Chris a disappointed look. "Didn't you want to sit for a while and discuss the Church?"

"Nah. I just want a smoke. See you later."

chapter fifty-seven

WHEN VAL LAGORIO smelled tobacco on her son's clothing, she wept for hours.

Joe eventually noticed the weeping and asked his wife, "What's wrong?"

"Topher is what's wrong. He's bent on destroying his thyroid. With *Swisher Sweets*! I can't bear it. After everything that I've taught him about mind-body balance, he's lurching toward the abyss. Why are you laughing?"

"Because. Umm, we smoked a hell of a lot ourselves. Worse things than cigars. And we turned out fine."

"Well, I may have to face menopause early."

Joe gave his wife a hug. "Topher is just going through a phase. He'll be a good, healthy man. Don't you worry."

She sniffled. "And will he give me healthy grandchildren?"

He held her tight. "I don't think he'll be a Tibetan monk."

Val nodded. "I've been feeding him a ton of cabbage. He'll have an ocean of testosterone."

Joe laughed. "Is that a good thing?"

She sniffled and thought about it. "Uh oh."

chapter fifty-eight

CHRIS SPENT the remainder of his sophomore year as a recluse, daydreaming during school, smoking in the woods after school, and practicing chords all night. Descending chords, and ascending.

In order to pass his English class, he had to write an extra-credit paper, which he wrote while listening to Bach's lute suites.

A FANTASY THAT COULD BE TRUE

There are whales in Lake Superior. The great leviathans lurk and frolic a thousand feet down. Larger than woolly mammoths and more powerful than icebergs, the whales of Superior are warmer-blooded than most creatures. They are able to absorb the most invisible rays of sunlight, moonlight, starlight, and especially the Northern Lights. That's their favorite meal.

Full of light in the depths, the Superior whales guard the sunken ships and all of the treasures. And they sing for our souls and leap out of the lake. Their tails swishing through the air. You should see the colorful droplets fall like a special rain into the harbor, upon the town, and over the hill.

Lake Superior whales rise deep into the night. They swim toward the moon that always turns blue at the sight of such things. And captains of ships on the verge of becoming ghosts get all trembly, because it's time to sink, swim, or sing.

The end.

Mr. Kendall wrote on the paper, in blotchy blue ink, "Not a bad vision, Lagorio. Strong imagery and good sense of motion. The story swims nicely. I wish you'd written the full three pages of the assignment. D+"

chapter fifty-nine

BY THE BEGINNING of the summer, Chris had shot up to almost six feet tall, and his whiskers were appearing. He sported dark sunglasses, inside and outside, and on a warm June night he felt old enough to enter a bar to hear some live music. He avoided eye contact with the bartender and sat in a chair in the back corner. The tall teen made himself at home and observed the performer on the stage. The jaded old musician plowed through covers of Dylan ("Blowin' in the Wind") followed by a huge gulp of frothless Budweiser, and then James Taylor ("I've Seen Fire and I've Seen Rain"), followed by chugging, and then a mumbled Glen Campbell ("Ever Gentle on my Mind"), followed by a stagger toward the bathroom.

Of the handful of people in the bar, the only one to applaud was the underage kid in the back. "Bravo! Bravo!"

The bathroom door slammed shut.

Chris stood and strode over to the bartender. "Excuse me, sir —"

The burly guy flung a dirty towel over his shoulder. "Sir? I don't think so. Let me see your ID."

Several schemes appeared in the boy's mind, and he was sure he could fool the man behind the counter. However, he confessed, "I'm not quite seventeen, sir."

The bartender sighed and shook his head.

"All I want is a pen, sir."

The guy kept shaking his head, frowning, and eventually laughing. He handed over a black ballpoint.

"Thanks."

"If you cause any trouble, I'll rip out your guts and fry 'em up in the fryer."

"I'll be good."

Chris returned to his seat while the performer returned from the toilet. Another song ensued, with no sense of artfulness or the holy calling of the troubadour, and Chris free-associated his own lyrics, scribbling them on a *Twin Ports Reader*. He wrote a song about a mountain lion. A love song. It was all mixed up with the heavenly and the worldly, with clean abstractions and crazy images. And at the end of the night, he tossed the *Reader* and the lion into the garbage.

During the rest of the summer, the whiskered kid in shades became a pub crawler, charming his way across the music scene — from Lakeview Castle to the Buffalo House. He'd reached the point at which he could simply say to his parents, "I'm going out," and they let it happen without any questions. As long as he returned by midnight.

"Or else your Bug will turn into a pumpkin," his mother warned.

Chris drove Majestic from haunt to haunt. He sought out the hidden, unsung singer-songwriters who lurked in the dives and mused on the dangers and delights of adventuresome love. The aspiring troubadour thought that perhaps he would end up like them. Most nights, the performers were forgettable hacks whose ramblings never rose above "Puff the Magic Dragon." Chris always applauded, and tipped the bartender several dollars for the water. And he always fantasized that he would be called to the stage, so his Gibson was always ready in the back seat of Majestic.

One night at the Lakeview Castle, Chris sat in the back of the bar, doodling on a napkin and yawning to the music of a somnambulant songster. All of a sudden he was struck by a beam of light that found him from the stage. Chris took off his sunglasses and stared into the light, thinking this was it; this was inspiration; this was the moment to write his song. The aspiring troubadour searched the light for the words worthy of a muse. The spirit was willing, but the flesh was weak as ever. Chris knew what he wanted: a love song that would make the syllables blush, and not blush. He knew how to do it. There was no gnostic trick or magic turn of phrase that would make the words radiant. If only he would consider the given world.

Chris imagined a grain of pollen floating on its journey in the light . . . a grain of pollen that had seen it all, from the days of Noah to the Resurrection . . . the near-invisible traveler filled the air with enough creative force to inspire a billion bibles of love-psalms.

The light from the stage blinked out. Nobody applauded.

The aspiring troubadour squinted into thin air, and sighed. "I got nothing."

chapter sixty

THE NEXT evening, at the Amazing Café, near the aerial lift-bridge, a woman with an electric cello seemed to have all of Minnesota's lakes and rivers in her strings. There were schools of fish in the music, swim-flying beneath and above every blue surface, and seagulls ghosting through the mist, and relentless waves from Superior storming the coastline, and the lakeside houses sliding down hills into the graveyard of ships.

Chris wept when the music was over, and stumbled outside to the shore. The fog was rolling in, waves roaring. The fog and mist swallowed up the aspiring musician, and Chris felt as if he were gone, drowned in the cloud. "What do you want from me?" he whispered. "What more do you want?"

The boy wiped his tears and found his way to the parking lot. He fired up Majestic and sped into the disappearing city, up the hill and over to his neighborhood of mansions. He parked beside the Ruins, reached into the back seat and grabbed his guitar. He knew that he could never find Superior, or something even greater, in those strings. And so Chris placed his present beneath a crumbling archway, paused for a moment where a prayer of sacrifice should have been, and hoped that the gift would be carried off by morning.

It was.

chapter sixty-one

IN THE FALL, eleventh-grade English class became a sort of holy hour for Chris. It all started with "Ode on a Grecian Urn" by Keats. When Mrs. Lindstrum uttered the magic phrase "Beauty is truth, truth beauty," Chris felt like dying. And it made him wildly happy.

Poetry was like dragon fire on the tongue, and when Mrs. Lindstrum asked the class to comment on Frost's "Stopping by Woods on a Snowy Evening," he waited for the others to have their say.

Moosehead: "I hate poetry. I hate this poem."

Mrs. Lindstrum: "Okay, class. That's a start. Now, can we feel anything other than hatred?"

Skunk: "The poem made me feel cold."

Mrs. Lindstrum: "Good. Anything else?"

Skunk: "The author's name is Frost. And he wrote a cold poem. Does that mean anything?"

Mrs. Lindstrum: "Maybe."

Emo Girl: "I think it bodes."

Mrs. Lindstrum: "Bodes ill or well?"

Emo Girl: "It just bodes."

Mrs. Lindstrum: "Oh."

Pixie: "I don't understand why the owner of the land lives in town. I thought people were either farmers or city folk back then. Why does someone in the city own the land?"

Mrs. Lindstrum: "That's a good question. Anyone have an answer?"

Pause.

Long pause.

Moosehead: "See? Poetry is stupid. Nobody knows what it means. Not even the teacher."

Mrs. Lindstrum: "I could give a lecture about the history of land ownership in New England and the Puritan work ethic and how those ideas are embedded in the poem. I wrote my Master's Thesis on Robert Frost."

Pause.

Long Pause.

Mrs. Lindstrum (opens a drawer and begins searching for her faded Master's Thesis): "Now where did it go? Oh, here it is."

Pixie: "I think . . ."

Mrs. Lindstrum: "Yes?"

Pixie: "I'm probably way off, but . . ."

Mrs. Lindstrum: "Go ahead. Tell us your theory. My Thesis can wait."

Pixie: "I think the narrator is a doctor. He's on his way to check on a person who's been hurt. Or maybe he's going to deliver a baby."

Skunk: "What are you talking about? Did we read the same poem?"

Moosehead: "Doctors don't sit around and stare at the falling snow. That's how people die."

Mrs. Lindstrum: "Pixie, I like your theory. Tell us why you think the narrator is a doctor."

Pixie: "Who else would be out in the countryside at night?"

Pause.

Long pause.

Dip (*spit!*): "A killer."

Emo Girl: "Man, that bodes."

Mrs. Lindstrum: "In the context of the poem, Duane, where do you see evidence for the killer theory?"

Dip: "I don't know about evidence, but I just had a bad feeling about the guy."

Emo Girl: "See? It bodes like crazy."

Dip: "Maybe the guy robbed a bank or something. He's an outlaw, looking for a place to hide in the woods."

Pixie (looking closely at the textbook): "But he doesn't go into the woods. He's tempted, because the woods are 'lovely, dark, and deep,' but he doesn't go into them."

Mrs. Lindstrum: "Why doesn't he?"

Skunk: "Because he's Santa Claus!"

Moosehead (laughing): "That's ridiculous."

Abercrombie Girl: Like, I don't know if I really know what I'm talking about, but like, maybe, he's not really Santa Claus, because he has a horse instead of a reindeer. But, like, maybe he is like Santa. It's Christmastime, and like, there are bells, and he has promises to keep, like delivering presents."

Moosehead: "You're just making stuff up."

Mrs. Lindstrum: "Shush."

Moosehead: "I don't understand why this class is required. Literature is so stupid. Just a bunch of made-up garbage that doesn't mean anything. Who cares if the guy is a doctor or a killer or Santa Claus? What difference does it make?"

Boy on Drugs: "Yo, bro. Just write a letter directly to Santa if you want your stuff. No need for a snow-poem. That's what I say."

Pause.

Long pause.

Mrs. Lindstrum (opens her Master's Thesis as if to read it to the class): "Ahem."

Chris: "It's about God."

Moosehead (snorts his anger): "Ridiculous. You should have stuck with football, Lagorio."

Pixie: "Where do you see God?"

Chris: "God is not in the poem, but the whole poem is about God. The narrator is the Angel of Death. That answers the question of who would be out in the countryside at night. The woods belong to God whose house is the church in the village. The Angel of Death stops by the woods because he's struck by the beauty of God's creation. The woods are lovely, dark, and deep. It's like a wintry Garden of Eden. The Angel of Death would like to enter that place, but he has promises to keep and miles to go before he sleeps. His work is never done. Not until we stop dying."

Pixie: "Wow. That's a cool interpretation."

Abercrombie Girl: "Like, hello, depressing."

Dip: "I knew he was a killer."

Pixie (under her breath): "Holy Mary, Mother of God, pray for him."

Moosehead: "That's the dumbest thing I've heard in my life."

Skunk (lisp-whispering): "Let's get some beer tonight and go into the woods."

Boy on Drugs: "Life is short. Go straight to Santa."

Emo Girl: "The Angel of Death. That really, really bodes."

chapter sixty-two

AFTER SCHOOL, Pixie asked Chris to go for a walk. It was a colorful September afternoon with sunshine tempered by a cool breeze, perfect for football and cheerleading.

"Do you miss it?" she asked.

The boy knew what she meant, but acted confused. "Miss what?"

Pixie gestured toward the practice field. "You know, the blood and the glory."

Chris laughed. "I never bled. And I wouldn't call scoring a touchdown a form of glory. I might have believed that before, but not now."

The girl, her red hair glowing like autumn scarlet, smiled and asked, "Can you walk a mile with me?"

Chris touched her hand, but did not hold it. "Where are we going?"

"It's a surprise. C'mon."

Through corridors of bright leaves, Pixie led him to the Green Mercantile, a sort of hardware store for artistic types. She traipsed inside and bought him a Second Nature notebook and a pen made of pine.

"What is this for?" he asked.

"Happy birthday, Chris. Sweet seventeen."

"You remembered."

"Of course I remembered."

"This is an excellent present. Thank you."

She grinned at him proudly as if at a brother. "I think you might have a gift. You might be a real writer. You're amazing at interpreting things."

Chris shrugged. "Whether or not I have a gift, I do love words."

They left the Green Mercantile, hand in hand. And the birthday boy kissed Pixie on the cheek. "Existential delight," he said, as if asking for more.

She pulled away. "I wish you'd join the Bible study. There's still time."

Chris put on his sunglasses. "Trevor's Bible study? No thanks. Didn't the seminary turn him down?"

"The Director of Vocations said to apply again in a year or two. Anyway, I think you'd like the Bible study. Trevor is really good at pointing out passages that support the teachings of the Church. I think it would feed your soul."

Chris gestured toward the lake. "Do you hear that? I believe I'm being called."

Pixie pouted. "I guess I'll talk to you tomorrow."

"For sure. Thanks again. And give my highest regards to Saint Trevor."

"Whatever. Go write."

Notebook in hand, Chris descended the hill to the shore to consider the inscape of Superior. Reclining near the waves, he wanted to reveal something about the shivering stones in the shallow water, how they awaited the next storm to carry them in to the beach or way out to the depths. And he nearly dropped his notebook at the sound of the invisibly wild, a wailing that seemed to want his heart. A pair of loons were nearby, but where? The wailing echoed between the water and the sky, and Chris tried to spell out the emotive sounds, combining vowels in the most imaginative ways, attempting to render a perfect sound. He filled a whole page with failed attempts to capture a song that was beyond human language.

The boy scribbled and suffered, already feeling the madness of all poets — the bliss of inspiration scourged by the pen's losing it on paper. He needed at least three more vowels to capture the ecstatic mourning.

He began thinking about Terra. And Mary Joan. And Pixie.

And Chris wondered if love was nothing but animal affection. That's what he'd learned in science class. So if the scientists were right, and human beings were merely soulless beasts, then what sort of soulless beasts? Apes? Dogs? Pigs? Birds? Fish?

The boy laughed, and considered Superior again. Had no scientist ever witnessed how even a pair of loons will arise from the cold, inner darkness of the lake and swim side by side, reflecting light on each other? Light from this world and light from another world. Chris knew: within instinct there was a great shimmer of spirit. Loons were full of all sorts of that treasure. And even the seagulls on the shore, in their own fluttering and flickering ways, reflected something like Holy Fire.

And every man and woman knew it.

No matter how sad it made them feel.

The aspiring writer ripped out the page, crumpled it into a tiny ball and cast it upon the water. The whiteness bobbed in the shallows for a few moments, and then began to drift out, expanding like a piece of bread.

That was quickly devoured by a descending bird.

chapter sixty-three

LATE OCTOBER brooded crystalline over Duluth, a snowfall that did not fall but filled the air with color, a cloud of rainbow enlightening the whole city.

Chris and Trevor sat by the window in Uncle Louie's Café, arguing about the Church.

"Are you bigger than the Church, Lagorio?"

"Nope."

"Smarter than the Church?"

"Nope."

"More spiritual?"

"Hell no."

Trevor took a swig of tea. "Then why won't you submit to something that's bigger, smarter, and more spiritual than you?"

Chris gulped his coffee, and stared at the belly-dancing studio. "You took my girl."

The priest-to-be was incredulous. "You won't submit to the Church of Christ Almighty because I catechized Pixie?"

"Catechized? Is that the word the Church uses to claim every soul and body on earth?"

Trevor sipped. "*Catechized* simply means 'properly educated.' "

Properly educated. The words sounded so pompous, so full of pride. And yet Chris wanted to know everything that was true.

He looked Trevor in the eyes. "You really believe the Catholic Church has it all?"

"As far as the Faith revealed by God, yes."

"It doesn't seem likely."

"That's reality. Like it or not."

"And all of the sins of the Church? The scandals?"

"Those are sins against the Church."

Chris stood up to leave. "You're playing with language."

Trevor smiled. "And you're playing with fire."

"Yep. I know."

chapter sixty-four

BEANER'S CENTRAL, one of the best coffee-and-music houses in the North, hosted a New Year's Eve party. The event was an open mic that began with an Emo Girl, wearing a black dress and fishnet stockings, moaning *Me and Bobby McGee*. Her tongue was so into the *la-la-la* of the final chorus that Chris, sitting near the front, blushed and stared down at his notebook.

Next up at the mic was a clean-cut boy in a gray sweatshirt. "Hey. I'm Kyle." He sat on a stool, and crooned a sweet song about deer hunting with his grandpa. After the lyrical deer had been shot and gutted, and the meat packed away in a freezer in the basement, the song trailed off. Kyle smiled at the confused but polite crowd. "Hey. I have a few CDs for sale. Well, I have lots of CDs left over. Boxes and boxes. So, if you want to buy one, or something. Yeah. Maybe for Christmas next year. Or if someone is having a birthday, and they like to hunt, give me a holler."

Chris wrote in his notebook: "*A dead deer cannot be led to water. Let it leap.*"

A long-haired guy in his fifties meandered up to the microphone. He had a harmonica attached to his guitar and performed a wailing song about hopping freight trains. The chorus was, "*I'm just a piece of iron ore, an unrefined hobo, rolling up the North Shore.*"

Chris scribbled: "*A comic metaphor can still carry weight.*"

Next on stage was a Nordic young man wearing a blue parka. He took off his mittens and his pale fingers were truly gifted. He played the twangy banjo with joyous passion, and earned some praise in the notebook: "*If Bach had traded his lute for a banjo, he would have played it like the guy with pale fingers — with a fiery sublime.*"

After that, a lullaby-girl swayed at the mic like a lost soul at the prom. Her lilting voice searched, verse after painful verse, for an everlasting harmony.

"*I'm searching . . . for an everlasting harmony. I want more than roses and money.*"

Chris gave her some free-verse:

> *She swoons for romance*
> *but what she really wants*
> *is the unfathomable*
> *song a thousand feet down*
> *rising in the harvest moon.*

"No, that's not it," he muttered, and ripped out the sheet of paper. He sipped some coffee and tried again:

> *Her melancholy is an open invitation*
> *to her own heart, the original songbook*
> *buried deeper than desired seduction.*

He ripped out the page and crumpled it, and didn't notice the new performer ascending the stage. Chris began scribbling a poem about music and romance and the woods, feeling good about it until the fourth line, when he looked up from the failed words and saw a familiar face and heard a familiar voice, accompanied by the guitar he'd sacrificed to the Ruins.

Mary Joan Mudgett, more voluptuous than ever at seventeen, was playing her first-ever gig, strumming and singing like a pro.

"*The lion of the northland sleeps among the strawberries. The roar of dreaming rises and carries. The dream becomes the doorway to many acres. Fields and forests within the fields. The lion of the northland sleeps among the strawberries. Don't go there, boy. Don't go there, boy. Don't go there. Unless you bring your roar of dreaming, too.*"

At the end of the song, Mary Joan received a polite round of applause. Grant, in a Santa hat, yelled from the back of the room, "Encore! Encore!" The girl took a bow, saw Chris in the middle of the audience, and began to blush. She descended the stage and tried to whisk past her former non-date, but he stopped her with a compliment. "You play my guitar better than I ever did."

"Your guitar?"

He pointed. "That's my Gibson."

"No, it isn't."

He grinned. "I'll bet you another guitar that my name is on that one."

Mary Joan shook her head. "You're as crazy and selfish as ever."

"Is it a bet?"

She held out her hand. "Sure. It's a bet."

Chris took the Gibson and held the bottom to the light.

Nothing was there.

"Pay up," the girl said. "I want a Stratocaster."

Chris angled the guitar, this way and that way, trying to catch the light just right.

"There. Look."

Mary Joan did not want to, but she glanced. And in the shine, very faint, was a slight scratch. The boy's name.

"Christopher!" Grant said, sliding into the table. "I thought that was the back of your head. There was a goat in your hair. How the hell are you?"

chapter **sixty-five**

THE CELLIST with the water-music in her strings appeared and began to play toward midnight. The audience all stood and danced to the cascading and rising sound. Chris slowly moved to the music and said to Mary Joan, "I was only joking about the bet. You can keep the guitar."

She danced closer to him. "You won the bet fair and square. The guitar was yours all along."

The cellist kept finding new depths in the strings, and Chris danced to within a heartbeat of Mary Joan. He wondered if perhaps they were meant to be together. She smiled warmly at him, and soon they were dancing more together than apart.

"I missed you," she said.

"I missed you, too."

At the approach of midnight, while the crowd was counting down, Chris tried to figure out what to do about the impending New Year's kiss. He had ten seconds to make a decision, and his mind was a mess of romantic confusion. He thought: the last time I kissed her, all hell broke loose. Yet that was all lust in the woods. This is something better. Maybe I should just kiss her on the cheek. Hmm. What if that makes her think I don't find her exquisitely beautiful? I could kiss her on the lips without being a wild man.

"HAPPY NEW YEAR!"

Mary Joan leaned over . . . and kissed her brother on the cheek. Then she turned back to Chris and shook his hand. "I hope you have a great year. Many blessings."

"Umm. Same to you."

Grant gave Chris a punch on the shoulder. "We'd like to stay and hit you some more, but we promised the folks we'd be home just after twelve."

"Oh, see you later, Grant. See you later, Mary Joan."

And they were gone.

When the sun came up later in the morning, Chris, who hadn't slept all night, looked out through the frost-glowing window and whispered, "I should call her today."

He waited until almost noon, when he knew the Mudgetts would be home from Mass. He picked up his phone and found Mary Joan's number buried deep in the memory. And Chris couldn't make the call.

He tried again the next day. And the next. The phone would tremble in his hand, and the boy had no idea if his nervousness was due to love or a sign that he was on the verge of a great mistake.

The New Year's dance had inflamed a thousand good memories of Mary Joan and the farm. He imagined a world of fecund possibilities. Perhaps he and she were meant to have their own farm, with life all over the place. "God," he said, "what's the deal with this girl? What should I do?"

"Talk to your mother," Val said, having sneaked into his room. "Topher, dear, you seem to be in agony. What's wrong? Is it physical? Too much cabbage? Tell your mother everything."

"I'm fine, Mom. And I'd like to be alone."

"Okay," Val said, leaving the room. "But I don't believe you."

Confused as ever, but tired of not taking action, Chris finally called Mary Joan the day after Valentine's. She was very quiet while he stammered on and on about the weather and the prospects of an early spring. The conversation was going nowhere until he asked Mary Joan about her family. She spoke glowingly about Chastity and the baby, and how the farm was as perfect as ever. Mary Joan's voice filled with excitement, and she hinted that Chris should drive out and visit. "We haven't played the Face Game in ages. Everyone would love to see you."

Chris wanted to see all of the Mudgetts, too, except he wondered if Mr. Mudgett would greet him with an axe. So the nervous boy suggested they meet at a neutral location. "Can I buy you lunch or dinner at the Amazing Café?"

"Sure. I'm playing there on Sunday night. We can eat first, and then maybe you can stay and listen to my music. Does that sound good?"

"Are you going to sing the lion song?"

"Yeah, I think it's my signature."

"Sounds great. Meet you there."

"Meet you there, Christopher."

"Oh, umm, Mary Joan?"

"Yes?"

"Well, you know I like Grant. He's a great kid and all —"

She laughed. "He's a jerk. With a good heart. But no, he won't be there. He's been grounded."

"What did he do?"

"During Mass, he told a sweet old lady that he'd like to bring her hair to a taxidermist."

"How long is he grounded for?"

"To the end of his natural-born life."

"Yikes."

For the rest of the winter, Chris met Mary Joan at her gigs. They enjoyed good comfort food and conversation, taking it slow with the relationship. He watched admiringly while she sang and played his guitar. The farm girl filled every venue with an artsy, Christian vibe that went over the heads of most people. Yet she was too talented to dismiss easily and always got respectful applause.

At Sir Benedict's Tavern, on a melting Saturday afternoon in April, the whole Mudgett family appeared, including Chastity with her baby.

"Hello, stranger," the young mother said. "I'd like you to meet Francis."

A tiny smile graced the baby's lips.

Mrs. Mudgett laughed. "Oh, I think Francis blessed you, Christopher!"

Chris grinned, until he noticed that Mr. Mudgett was carrying a knife, a frown, and a chunk of wood.

A voice announced, "Please welcome an up-and-coming singer-songwriter to the stage! Mary Joan Mudgett!"

A decent crowd welcomed her, and the girl took them on a musical pilgrimage to meet the lion of the northland.

Mrs. Mudgett was as theatrical as ever, singing harmony at the top of her lungs during several of Mary Joan's songs. Mr. Mudgett occasionally looked up from his whittling and nodded approvingly. And because it was a special occasion, Grant was allowed a leave of absence from the farm. He sat quietly in his seat, munching beer nuts. Chastity tapped her feet and cooed at the baby, and Francis cooed back.

Mary Joan sang her songs as if they were psalms. Chris got lost in them, especially the ones that were about him. Or about someone who was almost him. It seemed that the girl had created a character in his image and likeness, and set him free to roam the lyrical realms.

"Don't go there, boy. Don't go there. Unless you bring your roar of dreaming, too."

chapter sixty-six

IN EARLY JUNE, Chris looked out of the window of Amazing Café and considered the crabapple trees. Their branches were fully bloomed, with thousands of small white petals fluttering in the wind like warm snowflakes.

"Hey," Mary Joan said, swishing up behind him.

He pulled out a chair for her. "Hey there, girl."

She nodded at the window. "Check out the blooms."

"Yeah."

Chris leaned over and kissed her gently on the cheek.

She said, "Why did you do that?"

He shrugged. "I like you."

Mary Joan turned away, not rudely or shyly, but with the strength of someone who knew who she was. And she spoke at Chris's reflection in the window. "You're not a real Catholic."

He tried to play it cool. "I don't know about that."

She smiled sadly. "You've never received Communion."

He met her eyes in the reflection. "So?"

"So, we wouldn't have a future."

"That's ridiculous. Of course we can have a future."

Mary Joan turned from the window and told him to his face. "We'd be unequally yoked."

He laughed. "Yoked? What are you talking about? We're not oxen."

She took his hand. "No," she said. "We're not oxen. We're human beings. Spiritual as much as physical. And I can only marry someone who shares that reality."

"Marry? I'm not getting married until I'm at least in my twenties."

"And in your twenties, will you be a good, practicing Catholic?"

He joked, "I'll probably be a bad, practicing Duluther."

"Not funny."

Chris's hand trembled, and he was about to suggest that he meet her at Holy Spirit on Sunday, as in the old days, for Mass and then a breaking of bread with her family. He was about to suggest that they belonged together — on earth as in Heaven — when she let go.

"We're not meant to be," Mary Joan said, "anything except who we are."

"Then who are we?"

"Friends," she said. "Just friends."

The boy stared numbly out the window. The tree blossoms were falling in a joyful cloud . . . as if there had just been a wedding.

chapter sixty-seven

THAT SUMMER, Duluth was not a northern paradise.

The city smoldered.

The young man tossed and turned in the swelter, unable to sleep.

His father did not believe in air conditioning. "We live near a melted glacier," Joe said. "That should be cool enough."

"It feels like a furnace in my room. And I'm sunburned from mowing."

"Just imagine yourself in Lake Superior. Mind over matter. Suck it up."

Hours later, Chris was sure that he was going to die from suffocation, despite the open windows. His flesh enflamed, the last thing he needed was a vision of Pixie. She flew in through the window in her cheerleading outfit. "Is this good for your soul?" she asked.

Chris groaned, and Pixie flew away.

And Mary Joan appeared. Wearing nothing except his guitar. "We could harmonize if you joined the choir," she said and disappeared.

The boy groaned again. "Why am I being haunted by Catholic girls?"

And Terra Corwin appeared, all grown up, tall and lovely. She made Chris feel very biblical, as if he could be fruitful and populate the whole earth.

"O God, have mercy."

The heat was just too much. At three in the morning, Chris rolled out of bed and trudged down to the lake for a swim. The stars, bright as streetlights, burned ancient images in the sky, and the reflections flickered on Superior like embers.

The boy disrobed and entered the frigid water. He thought about shipwrecks and the many people who had drowned. Submerging all the way into the enduring chill, he thought about the three girls who had haunted him, and the Three Persons they were in love with, and he stayed beneath the surface of Superior for as long as possible, his flesh tightening and transforming and yet still remaining flesh.

Chris arose from the water, shivering, and began to sing, *"C'mon girls, light my fire! C'mon, girls, light my fire! Try to set this lake on . . . FIRE!"*

chapter sixty-eight

FATHER HANK, who helped with special events at the former cathedral, had a sinus infection that tormented him like the plague. Some days he couldn't speak. The syllables felt like migraines. The low vowels hurt the most, and the poor priest couldn't even say, "God's love is like a dove coming down from above" without nearly fainting. He was in such a weakened state, he wasn't able to say no to Trevor. The rejected seminarian wanted to give a talk at Sacred Heart, and Father Hank nodded his congested consent.

Trevor's speech was expected to draw a small crowd. However, his advertising went viral on email, and he got a pre-event story in the *Twin Ports Reader*. "GLOBAL WARMING: A SUPERIOR UPDATE."

The story went on to pose the question: "What happens if Minnesota warms up?"

Sacred Heart was filled to overflowing on a Friday night.

Trevor appeared in the lights at center stage, holding in his hands the entire world.

Chris and Pixie watched from the back row.

The girl nervously twirled her hair. "Will he do good?"

"God only knows."

In the former sanctuary stood the confident young man, holding a globe.

The audience, an assorted mix of liberal tree-huggers, conservative fishermen, and regular folks who simply loved the Northland, offered their complete attention.

Trevor's arms began to shake beneath the uplifted world. The globe had real weight, filled with something heavy, and it was getting difficult to keep the thing airborne. Some people in the audience, including Pixie, whispered apprehensions. Father Hank rubbed his sinuses, and a bearded guy shouted, "Hey sonny! What's the news about global warming? The earth's not getting any cooler while you stand there."

The crowd laughed gently, as if among friends and family. Pixie took Chris's hand. "He's going to be great."

Trevor seemed strengthened by the laughter. His arms steadied, and he began his talk. "Thank you for visiting Sacred Heart today. Considering all of the things that you could be doing, we are honored to be graced by your presence."

Father Hank removed his hand from his forehead, the pain subsiding. He loved the phrase, "honored to be graced by your presence." It was much more welcoming than he'd expected.

Trevor continued. "The Good Lord gave us this planet to cherish, the whole expanse of beauty — from family gardens to wildflowers in the woods, and from cultivated fields to great lakes — it's all glorious."

Heads nodded.

Chris could hardly believe it. Trevor was actually moving the crowd. He had a strong voice, slightly musical, and his eye contact was all-embracing. Now if he could only maintain that level of connection. Who knows, maybe he could become a priest.

The globe began to shake. "Everyone in this building is worried about the world. We love this little planet, the greens of spring and summer, the sun-colored reds and oranges of fall, and even the grays and whites of winter. God is the ultimate artist, and we can find inspiration in everything on earth. An ant is a speck of sunshine. An eagle is a ray of light. The forests are great beams. The lakes are pools of blue that God uses to dip his brush and paint the sky. The bright heavens drip down into the Great Lakes."

Trevor held out the shiny globe as if offering it to the crowd.

The audience gave each other knowing looks. A few clapped.

"He's doing good," Pixie whispered. "He's really doing good."

"Yep. So far."

Had the sermon ended right there, all manner of thing would have been well. And then Trevor opened his mouth again. "Global warming, as you imagine it, is nothing to be feared. Don't worry about the polar ice caps melting. Don't worry about the polar bears running out of food. Don't worry about Texas becoming one big desert, or Florida sinking into the Everglades. None of that matters in the slightest."

The audience leaned forward. Father Hank rubbed his forehead again, the pain returning.

Sweat dripped from Trevor's face onto the globe, which he now held tightly to his chest. He shouted, "There is only one warming to fear! In the center of the earth is a molten, flesh-melting hell!"

Pixie's face turned ashen. "What is he doing up there?"

Trevor began to poke a finger into the globe where earlier he'd drilled out a hole and filled the planet with warm, red gelatin. However, there was too much glue on the patch, so it was difficult to re-puncture the world. Trevor had wanted to create a dripping of something like blood, and catch the drops in the palm of his hand. He'd wanted to say something about the Blood of Jesus being food for the saved. And liquid fire for the lost.

Poking and poking, with nothing happening, the rejected seminarian stood in the lights, drenched and trembling like a kid with a failed science project.

Father Hank felt the Spirit moving him to call the whole thing off.

Chris also felt moved to act, his football legs rushing up to the former sanctuary. He was worried that Trevor would be upset and possibly throw a tantrum, but Trev nodded with appreciation and handed Chris the globe.

Some in the audience interpreted that as a sign of Big Oil grabbing the whole planet. They playfully booed the interloper, while Trevor again tried to poke his way into the Gulf of Mexico. The playful booing turned into a more negative energy when Trevor let fly a few curses. The audience was well practiced in their own foul language and didn't think it was usually a sin, but even the lapsed Catholics thought it was wrong to swear in Sacred Heart.

Chris whispered, "Chill, Trev. Give it up."

The rejected seminarian was furious. Gritting his teeth, he began throwing punches at the globe. *Smack! Smack! Smack!*

Among the murmurings, Pixie called out, "Trev, move on with the message!"

He pretended not to hear and continued punching like a crazed boxer, until the outer crust gave way and a fourth of the world caved in. There was an eerie pause, followed by a sudden expulsion of the entire core of scarlet gelatin.

PLOP.

The goo sludged all over the floor.

THUD.

Father Hank fainted.

The audience stopped booing, but didn't know what to do next. The old cathedral was filled with confusion. Pixie burst into tears and waved her hands over Father Hank, trying to revive him. "Wake up, wake up. We need you."

Trevor hadn't planned on the gelatin hardening so quickly. He'd wanted it to stay warm as blood, so it would slowly drip when he punctured the globe. He took a deep breath to continue his sermon, but Chris cut him off. "Ladies and gentlemen," he said, not sure what to say. "Umm, what we have here, with this, umm, mess, is, well, a perfect example of what's happening to some of our lakes, rivers, and oceans."

Heads nodded vigorously.

Chris pointed at the sludge around his feet. "We need to protect the perfect ecosystems that God ingeniously invented. Whatever else we believe about God, we all agree that the Creator loves creation."

The audience piped up.

"Yeah, that's right."

"Darn tootin'."

Father Hank regained consciousness in time to hear the words, "the Creator loves creation." The woozy priest stood up to see who'd spoken those words, and he exchanged a surprised look with Christopher Lagorio.

"Bless you," Father Hank said in a benediction voice. "Bless everyone here for visiting Sacred Heart tonight." The old priest hoped to end this thing without further surprises. "We all love the earth, and especially Lake Superior, and we need to work together to make sure that God's greatest lake is protected — for your children and grandchildren."

The audience agreed.

"You betcha."

"Sounds good to me."

"Amen."

chapter sixty-nine

UNCLE LOUIE'S CAFÉ was a whirlwind of strong aromas and passionate conversations.

"It's pronounced 'yee-row.' It's not that difficult to say, Trev."

Swallowing the lamb-beef, Trevor shook his head. He licked the cucumber sauce from his lips and proclaimed, "You're wrong, Lagorio. Haven't you heard of a gyroscope? It's not a yee-ro-scope."

"So, the Greeks are wrong about their own food?"

"The Greeks are fallible," the rejected seminarian said and took another bite.

Chris knew better than to argue, but he said, "Listen, Trev. The Greeks gave us philosophy. Can't we at least pronounce their food correctly?"

Trevor shrugged. "The Apostle Paul said the Greeks didn't know what they were talking about."

Pixie didn't want the Apostle Paul to cause them any trouble, so she spoke romantically, "I'd love to go to Greece. And to Rome. I wonder how much it costs to fly over there."

Chris glanced across the street at the belly-dancing studio. He just couldn't help himself. A woman dancing, especially like that, was one of the world's most powerful motions. He thought: if that energy could be harnessed, it could power the whole earth.

A tall Indian man came stumbling into the café, capturing everyone's attention. Chris turned and waved at the homeless guy. "Hey, Stephen. You doin' all right?"

The Indian nodded without emotion and shuffled toward the table.

"Here, take this," Chris said, offering up his toast.

Stephen gladly accepted. "Buttered on both sides. Thanks." Munching the toast, he headed toward the bathroom.

"Poor thing," Pixie whispered.

Trevor stole a piece of her waffle. "Listen. These homeless guys come in here all the time. They don't buy anything, and they befoul the bathroom."

Chris narrowed his eyes. "Befoul?"

"Yeah. Befoul."

"Dude. They're making use of the restroom. They aren't befouling anything. They're just being human."

"That's not how humans should live."

Leaning across the table, Chris sniffed Trevor's shirt. "You reek, dude."

Trevor nosed at his armpits, and smiled. "Old Spice. It's all good."

"All right," Pixie said, changing the subject. "Listen to this, you guys. I'm starting to take a yoga class. It's so relaxing, and I've already gotten more limber."

Shaking his head, Trevor said, "You aren't."

Pixie nodded. "I am too getting more limber."

"You can't do any more yoga," the rejected seminarian said, chomping his gyro.

"What do you mean? The class just started. It goes for six weeks. And by then I'll have overcome the laws of gravity."

"Sorry. We don't do yoga."

"I know we don't," Pixie said, lifting her bare leg above the table, "but I do."

Chris stared in lusty amazement.

"Put your leg down," Trevor said. "And please stop going to that yoga class."

Laughing, Pixie lifted her leg higher, almost parallel to her ear. "I couldn't do this a week ago. It's amazing what the body can do with the proper training."

"Put it down."

"Why? Muscle stretching is good for you. I mean, good for me. You'd probably pull a hamstring, Trev, you silly ham."

He frowned proudly. "It's so easy to become spiritually blind."

Pixie winced as if she'd been slapped. Her leg fell and scraped the side of the table.

"You okay?" Chris asked.

Trevor cleared his throat. "Yoga is not about stretching muscles. It's a religious ritual, and it's not the religion of our Lord."

A tear trickled down Pixie's cheek. Chris reached out to wipe it away.

"I'm fine," she whispered.

Trevor continued, "Yoga is pagan. It's about stretching muscles for other gods. It contorts the soul. In fact, yoga will twist your soul into a New Age pretzel."

"Actually, the pretzel is a medieval symbol," Chris said.

Trevor sighed. "This conversation is going nowhere. Anyway, I have to get going. I'm meeting with the bishop's assistant to figure out my latest seminary application." He stood and reached into his pocket for a twenty-dollar bill, and placed it next to the salt shaker. "This should cover just about everything, if Lagorio gets the tip. I'll call you later, Pixie. We'll pray the Rosary."

She nodded. "Sounds good."

There was a near collision at the door when Trevor and Stephen arrived at the glass at the same time.

"Excuse me," Trevor said, rushing ahead.

The homeless guy held the door for him, and then said to Chris, "Thanks for the toast. I love double-buttered."

"You're welcome, Stephen. See ya later."

"See ya."

The Indian shuffled outside into the summer sun, his long black hair flying in the wind.

"How do you know him?" Pixie asked.

"I know almost everyone on Fourth Street."

"Isn't that depressing?"

"Why?"

"You know what I mean. Getting close to some people, if they're on the wrong path, can be really depressing."

"Do I make you depressed?"

Pixie slapped his wrist playfully. "Don't be silly."

"Speaking of silly, you and Trev seem to be getting serious."

She laughed. "He'll get into seminary, eventually."

"And you'll join a convent?"

"Ha ha."

A large family bustled into the café, including twin girls with matching purple skirts.

"This way," the Greek waitress said. "I have a good table in the back."

The whole family marched — the twin girls whirling and twirling — and disappeared into the party atmosphere on the other side.

Pixie began to climb out of the booth, and then leaned back and gave Chris a kiss on the forehead. "See you at Mass tomorrow?"

"Hmm. No, I think I'll go fishing."

chapter seventy

DAPPLED WITH plated bones, the prehistoric sturgeon was once considered a net-ripping monster, a fisherman's dragon. The whiskered bottom-feeder was seen as a haunting, an undead dinosaur. Nobody knows who first took up the knife and transformed the fossil into a sacrifice of gold.

Caviar.

And oil.

The Lake Superior sturgeon became a northern god, worthy of slaughter to the point of near extinction.

When Chris walked into an empty church — Saint Mary Star of the Sea — just to look around one afternoon, a length of sunlight swam through a blue window like an uncaught, ghostly fish.

The young man instinctively opened his mouth.

And for forty nights, Chris was haunted by a swimming glow-shadow, the prehistoric fins gliding through his dreams like fiery lights through isinglass.

chapter seventy-one

IN HIS SENIOR year in high school, Chris decided it was time to make some real money.

He approached his father with a business plan. They met in Joe's office in the house, surrounded by computers, with financial news blaring from a large-screen TV. Joe wore a headset as if he were an air-traffic controller for the powers and principalities of trade.

"I don't like these numbers, Topher. You've overpriced the product, and underpriced the cost of producing the things."

"So, it's not a good business plan?"

Joe pulled off the headset as if ripping thorns from his scalp. "Give me a break. Mugs? You want to sell mugs? In this economy? How did you come up with that idea? Have you started drinking? Switched from cigars to pot? Don't be like me, son. Just think how successful I'd be if I had preserved my brain cells. Just think. Can you imagine?"

The young man thought: *why are my parents so strange?*

"Help me out here, son. I can't catch the vision if you can't paint me a picture. Hurry up, I'm expecting a call."

Shuffling his feet, standing before his father's cluttered desk, the young man tried to remember how he'd gotten the idea for the mugs. He mumbled, "I saw a kid slobbering."

"Your business plan began with slobbering?"

"There's a kid at school, Duane Schmidt —"

"The kid you fought at the laundromat?"

"I didn't fight him. I tackled him. Anyway, he's always drooling into a pop can. Often the spit slides into his lap, onto his desk, or down to the floor. It's sort of gross."

"Sort of? It's really gross. C'mon, help me out here."

"Every time I see him making a mess, I feel sorry for him."

"You feel sorry for the kid who got you kicked off the football team?"

"I forgave him and moved on. Anyway, he needs a big coffee mug or something to collect his slime."

"Like a spittoon."

"What?"

Joe laughed. "In the old days, when millions of people were spitting all over the country, they had spittoons. They were shaped like open-mouthed trophies, made of brass, real nice and decorative. They'd be in lobbies and hotel rooms, train cars, mansions, everywhere."

"You think a spittoon would solve Duane's problem?"

"You tell me, son. You're the visionary here."

"A spittoon isn't what I'm envisioning. I mean, yeah, Duane needs something like that. But my mugs are not for spitters. My mugs are for clean entertainment. And social satire."

Chris's father was losing his little patience. "What exactly are we talking about here?"

"I'm talking about Mug Shot Mugs."

"I don't get it. What do mugs have to do with spittoons?"

"Nothing. Just look at the last page of the prospectus. See the sample that I Photoshopped?"

Flipping through the pages, acting as if it was a very difficult task, Joe muttered, "Where is the image? Where is it? Oh, way back here. Hmm. Hmm. Well. Maybe. Okay, I think I get it. Hey, that's pretty funny. It's a mug shot . . . on a mug."

"Yep."

"I like it, Topher."

"Thanks. And notice the smaller image."

"Mug Shot Shot Glass. That's really clever."

"You think?"

Joe stood and shook his son's hand. "We've got a deal here."

Chris grinned. "We do?"

"Darn right. Seventy-thirty."

"You should get more than thirty percent, dad. You're putting up all of the capital."

The old hippie nodded. "I'm getting the seventy."

"Oh."

chapter seventy-two

THE MUGS and shot glasses, featuring the faces of celebrity criminals, sold like crazy. Along with Nick Nolte, other bestsellers included Jane Fonda, Hugh Grant, Paris Hilton, James Brown, and Pee-wee Herman. All of the sales happened in cyberspace, with the shipments sent out from a clearing house in Indiana. The Lagorios didn't have to do a thing except watch their sales figures double and triple and quadruple. With thirty percent of the net earnings, Chris found himself swimming in cash.

"You should buy a house," his mother said, handing him a celebrity mug of green tea.

The young entrepreneur took Jane Fonda into his hands. "Trying to get rid of me?"

She sipped her own brew from Pee-wee. "Not yet."

"So, what would I do with a house?"

"We'd decorate it."

"Yeah? You and me, Mom?"

Val smoothed a wrinkle on her fuchsia sari. "You're growing up so fast, Topher. I'd like a chance to work on a project with you, before you journey into the world to achieve more fame and fortune. Your father says you're some kind of genius."

Chris laughed. "Are you serious?"

Val sipped her tea and gave him a loving smile. "I'm thinking about seeing fewer patients. I want to spend more time with you. We'll revitalize an old house, like that stone cottage down on Third Street. I'd paint the walls and ceilings, and put up new crown molding and colorful drapes. You can do the dirty work, Topher, like putting in new toilets and finding renters."

"Gee, thanks, Mom."

Val helped her son buy the stone cottage, co-signing all of the documents. The eighteen-year-old had plenty of money for a down payment, insurance, and closing costs. And by the middle of October, he was a property owner. The next thirty days were some of the happiest of his life, working on the renovations with his creative mother. Val had agreed to keep the style of the house less modern and more medieval, and was overjoyed to discover, upon doing research, that some of the same bright colors of the '60s were also enjoyed in the 1360s. Mother and child laughed while painting the formal dining room a royal red with sun-orange trim. And they found gold-yellow chairs at an auction, high-backed and worthy to support the banquets of lords and ladies.

The day the chandelier was hung in gleaming light, Val said, "Topher, you should keep this place forever."

The boy grinned at the festive dining room and then at his mother. "This really is awesome. Thanks for all of your help. Hey, let's have dinner here tonight. I'll cook. Okay?"

"You got it, dude. Should we invite your father?"

"Sure."

"I think he'll be very happy, and proud."

chapter seventy-three

"SELL, SELL, SELL," his father said.

The housing market had taken a good turn in November, and Joe calculated that Chris could make a net profit of between ten and twenty thousand dollars. "And, if you keep making good decisions, you'll have a million dollars by the time you're twenty. And twenty million by the time you're thirty."

Sadly, but thinking his father knew best, Chris planted a "For Sale by Owner" sign in the front yard of the stone cottage. Then he turned away from his latest business venture, and slunk up the hill to Skyline Drive.

His head hung low, he stared at his feet scuffing over the shoulder of the narrow road. He kicked pebbles over the side of the cliff and listened to them clack from boulder to boulder, until they eventually rustled snugly into the undergrowth. One pebble traveled farther than expected, ricocheting off a house. Chris stopped guiltily in his tracks, and then peered over the ledge. Many houses were scattered down the hillside, all the way to where his own cottage was standing like one shiny stone. It would be impossible to figure out which roof had taken the hit. Nobody was outside in a yard, cursing and shaking a fist at the sky.

Walking more carefully, lifting his feet as if marching, Chris traveled another mile or so, and then stood in the partial shade beneath a large oak where he had a perfect view of everything — hill, city, harbor, lake, and beyond. He turned and scanned Mount Royal and could barely believe what he saw. The trees all around Duluth were already bare. Chris wondered: how did I miss the colors? When was the peak of the season?

Brow furrowed, he lamented, "The beautiful death of the season . . . How could I have missed it?"

chapter seventy-four

THE FIRST snowfall, even for the grimmest of Minnesotans, is glorious. The whirling crystals fill the wilderness world with a childlike hope, despite what is coming next.

Chris was depressed on Thanksgiving Day, and while the snow piled up and buried the last of autumn, he slouched in his room in his parents' house, staring at a computer screen. His father had convinced him to sell the mug company to a novelty chain in Los Angeles. Thirty percent of the transaction resulted in nearly a hundred thousand dollars. Chris squinted at the balance. Even with the mortgage payment on the unsold cottage, he somehow had more money than ambition to spend it.

Sigh.

Sigh.

Click.

The computer screen faded into its darkness, and Val called happily up the stairs, "Time to eat! Wash up and come down!"

Not bothering to wash, Chris plodded down the stairs and took his place heavily at the table.

Val had made her traditional Thanksgiving meal: turkey-tofu. She'd carved little fowl legs out of blocks of fermented beans, and placed them neatly on flowered plates from Tibet.

"Beautiful!" Joe exclaimed. He was in high spirits because of the sale of the mugs.

Chris muttered, "Why can't we have real meat today? And mashed potatoes and gravy, and cornbread and strawberry jam?"

"Don't be such a downer," his mother said joyfully. "Don't you know what the Dalai Lama said?"

"The Chinese are killing me?"

"That's not funny."

Joe laughed. "Yes, it is. The Chinese are going to destroy our economy. Do you think they bought any of our mugs? Hell no."

"The Dalai Lama has reminded us," Val said, bowing over her leg of tofu, "to always and everywhere be grateful. That is the core of our souls. No matter what else you believe, the key to life is to give thanks."

Chris's eyes filled with tears. "I wanted real meat."

Val thought her son was on the brink of an illness. "I have some pills that could help you."

"I'll bet you do."

"What?"

"You have lots of pills, Mom. You too, Dad."

Joe warned, "Watch yourself, now."

"This food looks absolutely delicious!" Val lifted a pale little leg to her mouth. "Everyone at once, now. C'mon. No more talking. Eat up."

Joe's phone rang out. "Sorry, but I have to take this." He hurried away to the next room.

Chris buried his head in the flowery plate, sucked in the tasteless tofu, and swallowed each of the fake legs whole. And then, rising from the table, he let out a loud burp. "For the Dalai Lama."

His mother said, "You call that gratitude?"

He picked up her plate. "You call that food?"

"Put it down."

The plate shattered and the shards of colorful petals scattered across the table.

The next day, Chris ordered a new set of plates off the Internet and apologized to his parents. They accepted his apology, but suggested that he move out of their house.

"Before the winter solstice," his mother said. "That's a good time to begin a new life."

"No problem. I'll go live in the stone cottage. It doesn't seem to be selling."

"You should advertise for some renters," his father said. "But then again, renters are destroyers. They can ruin your whole investment. However, if you pay rent to yourself, and stop breaking things, then you'll build some good equity. And what about college? Have you applied to UMD or Saint Scholastica?"

Val chimed in. "I know a nun at Scholastica who practices natural healing. I think they have a good mix up there of ancient and modern thinking. It would be a good education, especially if you decide to become a teacher."

"A teacher? Me?"

She nodded. "Yeah, you. A teacher."

"Or a professor," Joe said, messing the boy's hair. "I can totally see it. Professor Lagorio."

"Hmm. What would I teach?"

"Business," Joe said.

"Art," Val said. "Or literature. You have a very expressive soul."

"Hmm." Chris thought about it. "Well, if I were to become a teacher, I would probably teach earth science or biology. Trees. Rocks. Water. Fish. You know, the things that make sense."

"There's good money in science," Joe said.

The rich young man looked his father in the eye. "To be honest, I don't really care about the money."

"Good boy," Val said. "Just be grateful for everything."

"Okay, Mom."

"And never take less than market value."

"Okay, Dad."

chapter seventy-five

CHRIS DISAPPEARED into a world of snow. Majestic was an igloo, hulking in the driveway, growing larger by the moment. The young man used his bare hands to brush snow from the windshield, and then climbed in and turned the key. *Sputter-putter-spark-bang*... and away he rolled. *I love this old wreck,* he thought.

The heater was broken, the steering wheel was sluggish, and the radio received only one station. The Catholic station.

"You've got to be kidding me."

Chris reached out to turn it off, and hesitated. "Who is that singing?" The voice was familiar. In fact, there were two familiar voices, ringing out in stereo on the AM dial.

"Trevor and Pixie," he whispered, his breath shrouding the words.

There had been an email about this. Trevor and Pixie had been given a radio show by the diocese, a one-time deal that could become weekly if all went well. The concept was experimental, and yet followed a traditional pattern: they'd simply read a whole letter of Saint Paul or several chapters of the Gospels, with no commercials or commentary.

Chris cranked up the volume and veered toward the lake. "*Love is patient, Love is kind* ..." His friends read the First Letter to the Corinthians as if they were in love with the words and with each other.

Driving with his attention on the voices, Chris plowed through a snowdrift, nearly overturning Majestic at the entrance of Brighton Beach. The engine died. "You've got to be kidding me." And the rich young man sat trembling at the wheel, facing the silence of Superior. The water was dark as the clouds above, and the lake took it all in, forcing everything to enter the funereal depths.

Chris turned the key, and Majestic sparked to life. The beautiful voices poured out of the radio and seemed to fill the killer lake, and the whole dark world, proclaiming the three remaining things.

"... *the greatest of these is love*," Chris said, joining the voices.

The show was suddenly over. Trevor and Pixie said, "Thank you for joining us today."

And then music. Guitar strings lifted the melody like a harp, yet electric. And the singer . . . who was that? Her voice was the blues, crying out of "the heart the North," telling Chris the story of his life. Sad, hopeful, solemn, and wild, the song seemed to know things about the poor boy that were impossible to know.

"That was Mary Joan Mudgett," the announcer said, "with her latest single called 'The Christ-Bearer's Tale.' "

chapter seventy-six

AT THE BEGINNING of December, amid the swirling snow, Chris moved out of his parents' house and into the cold medieval cottage. The small structure was mostly unfurnished and felt like a mansion in his soul. All of his worldly possessions fit in one room; and the young knight purchased one additional item for his personal housewarming party: a suit of armor. It was shiny, and fit him, but like most things found in cyberspace, it was not exactly real. It was made of aluminum, as if the seller in London had tinkered the thing out of ale cans.

Chris hid the suit of armor in a closet, away from any windows that would reveal its thinness.

Two weeks before Christmas, Trevor in a Santa hat and Pixie and Mary Joan in green coats came caroling at Chris's door, fa-la-la-ing with faithful enthusiasm. They stood on the snowy steps and tried to get their old friend into the holiday spirit. When they sang, "*Bring me flesh and bring me wine,*" Chris closed the door on them.

As the dark days continued, Val Lagorio became worried sick. She tried to get her son to move back home, and when that didn't work, she brought some healthful food to his door. Chris thanked her with a weak hug, and then, after his mother had driven away, he tossed the cabbage soup into the backyard. Birds, deer, and skunks arrived before the soup was frozen, and stayed when the slop was gone, and the yard became a sort of zoo for the neighborhood children.

The angry father of one young girl strode over and said, "You're a terrible neighbor. What's wrong with you?"

Shrugging his bony shoulders, Chris replied, "I need Holy Communion. But I just can't accept it."

The father wanted to slug him in the stomach. "My kid almost gets mauled and gassed by a rabid skunk, and all you can do is talk philosophy?"

"Technically, sir, it's theology."

The father slugged him. "There. We're technically even."

Chris felt the adrenaline fueling his fists. He could easily knock out the guy, but restrained himself. "O . . . kay. We're . . . even."

The father's face was rage-red. "Now shovel your damn sidewalk. We try to keep up appearances around here."

"O . . . kay. I'll try."

"Try? That's your whole problem. It's not about trying. It's about doing."

Chris retreated to his small stone abode. He sat on the floor in the living room, and sighed, and waited, monk-like. He considered the long hours of loneliness, the silence of the grave in his house. He stayed away from school, but tried to keep up with his homework, reading the textbooks until his eyes drooped and he nodded off.

The light seemed ancient and ever-new, visiting from above the hill, shimmer-ghosting through the windows and dancing in the chandelier as if it were a crystal fireplace. And the young man was troubled in spirit, the aching melancholy always returning, especially at night. Born of earth and haunted by the heavenly, Chris reconsidered the star fields. His prodigal soul knew — had always known — the heroic path. There was the way . . .

And yet he hesitated.

Was that a dragon in the sky? Or a lion?

Falling to the snowy earth was a low growl, soft as starlight . . . and wilder than fire.

On the twenty-third, snow fluttered like ashes from the heaped clouds that grew darker as the day burned through the bitter cold. Chris did his homework at the window, shivering through his literature anthology. With one eye on blurry Superior, and the other on Robert Frost, he considered the untaken roads all over the place . . . the highways that were plowed and salted, and beyond them, the buried roads in the woods that glowed like *camino reals* to the deeper places. The bad student with the good soul let the anthology fall to the floor, where it stuck fast like a ship in the ice.

chapter seventy-seven

"WAKE UP! Wake up!"

The party started with Moosehead and Skunk walking in on Chris's seemingly lifeless body and presenting him with a half-empty bottle of whiskey. The lit-up boys tracked snow into the living room and plopped down on the floor next to their friend. Moosehead bellowed, "You bought a freaking house! Congrats!"

Skunk lisped, "This is fantastic. I should buy a house myself. I've saved a few hundred dollars."

"Hey, guys. Welcome. You didn't have to bring me a gift." Chris sniffed the whiskey, made a funny face, and took a good gulp. He choked and coughed as if he would barf. However, that first swig did wonders to his mood, the booze oozing into his brain as if it belonged there. "Whoa! My goodness!" he exclaimed and took another drink.

The party accelerated when several hockey players arrived. They had a case of beer, and girlfriends. One of the girls said, "Man, this place really bodes." Jokes and boasts and laughter filled the cottage; and the vampires arrived, amazed to find out that the rumor was true: Sacramento owned his own house! And emo music began to wail, and the whiskey and beer ran out, but only for a few minutes, because Chris let Moosehead and Skunk borrow his wallet to "buy more supplies" and that meant a sixteen-gallon keg; and the party went wilder, with dozens of teens arriving with booze and smokes and hormones, the stone walls had never seen such kissing, in all corners, and scraps of conversations tidbitted into Chris's ears. "Do you know Sacramento?" "No." "Some people call him the Christ-bearer." "That's a lot to bear." "Yeah, better give him another beer." And a neighbor showed up — the guy who had punched Chris — and this time his face was not rage-red but happy as holly, swigging beer from a big cup and telling stories about glory days of drinking in ice-fishing houses; and the cottage filled to bursting with a hundred uninvited guests, and Moosehead and Skunk ordered pizzas with Chris's credit card, and wings and ribs and spaghetti and moo goo gai pan; and sometime around midnight, the young knight squeezed into his suit of armor and began dancing, clink-staggering from room to room while the partiers cheered and roared and the aurora borealis colored the windows like enlivened stained-glass.

Chris stood on a high-back chair, took off his knight's helmet as if to give a speech, perhaps something pleasant about Christmas, to inspire his fellow lords and ladies . . . and filled the helmet with his sick.

chapter seventy-eight

GRUNTING AND groaning on his hands and knees, the rich young man spent the day wallowing in filth. Not only his own filth, but the garbage of his guests. Rib sauce was everywhere, and the pasta on the walls resembled stringy intestines. Moo goo gai pan was like animal poo all over the place. And spilled beer yellowed the floors as if the partiers had sprung leaks as they pleased.

"Yuck," Chris said in the adventing light of Christmas Eve day. "This place is a sty."

He had no cleaning supplies, so he used bath towels and T-shirts to mop up the various messes. His head pounded with the after-curse of whiskey mixed with beer, wine, and whatever else had been offered to him. Chris recalled something about a police officer and a call to his parents — it was all a buzzing, painful blur — and he would have to clean up that mess, too.

By late afternoon, the stone cottage looked respectable again, despite some stains that seemed permanent, and the last thing to get put in its place was the fake suit of armor. Chris's inclination was to throw it away with the rest of the garbage. But he had soaked the helmet in hot water and Irish Spring, and washed away all of his sick, and for some reason, perhaps because his heart was still full of *Holy Grail Adventures*, he decided to keep the suit. He carried it to the closet and propped it up in the corner, and was closing the door on the fake shininess when he noticed another glow.

It was the box of books that were given to him by Professor Corwin. And on the top was the *Book of Kells*, shimmering as if the closet were kin to the sun. Tearing up, not quite knowing why, the young knight hefted the great book from the box and carried it to the living room. He sat beneath a window letting in the last light of the day, and took it all in.

Perusing the illuminated manuscript, with its fiery iconography, was like looking through a thousand windows into Heaven. The Latin was mostly a mystery, although Chris recognized a dozen or so words representing grace, faith, hope, and love. Gilded with gold as if the letters were taken up from the pavement of Paradise, the *Book of Kells* seemed to be the *alpha* and *omega* of art and literature.

"Good God," Chris said, holding the exemplar to his heart. "Good God," he whispered again, opening the pages by the fireplace . . . "Good God . . ." and the young knight fell asleep with the greatest of books on his chest, heavy as treasure and lighter than a feather.

chapter seventy-nine

ON CHRISTMAS morning, Chris arose early, eager to attend Christ's Mass.

The young man shaved, took a good-cleaning shower, and dressed in his white-linen suit. He joked at his reflection in the mirror. "Looks like I'm going on a date."

The smiling young man hurried out of the stone cottage and scampered through the snow to where his car had become an igloo again. He brushed and scraped the windshield and hoped the car wasn't dead. Chris climbed in and turned the key.

Sputter-putter-spark-bang!

Chris rolled down a window to keep the windshield from fogging, and plowed his way to the road.

Majestic maneuvered safely around the icy potholes, and Chris began humming while watching out for patrol cars. The cops sometimes thought people were drunk because of their swerving, but most of the time it was just the potholes causing the bad driving. Brisk wind in his hair, bright sun in his eyes, the young man was revved up to be alive. He began to sing the Christ-Bearer song, "*You can take the boy out of Sacramento, but you can never take Sacramento out of the boy.*"

Oh, how he wanted to witness the Mass again, and rethink his doubts and perhaps get beyond the thinking . . . and beyond the dragons. However, Chris did not immediately drive up to

Holy Spirit but instead accelerated downtown, waving at the other drivers as if in solidarity with everyone. "Merry Christ's Mass," he said, grinning like a child who knows the whole world is a present. And while looking for a turn toward Skyline, hoping he hadn't missed it, Chris ran a red light. He panicked and slammed on the brakes, skidding to the side of the road and through a snow bank, nearly crashing into a building. Saint Mary Star of the Sea.

He tried to back up, wheels spinning. Majestic was stuck near the stairway, and the young knight knew it was impolite to keep revving when people were inside tending to the Christ Child. So Chris killed the engine and thought: *I'd better find a tow truck.* He sighed, said a quick prayer, and then decided to forgo the towing.

The stairs leading up to Star of the Sea were salty and steep, and Chris had to pause at the entrance to catch his breath. He was still sickly from the accidental kegger, and wondered if perhaps he should return to Majestic, get it unstuck, and go home and rest.

With all of his strength, he opened the door to the church.

Shuffling through the entryway, past a bulletin board with posters that included "RESPECT LIFE" and "SUPPORT MISSIONS," the sickly young man was greeted by an angel. Standing between him and the pews, the angel cradled a large seashell, offering holy water that sparkled like ice. Chris wondered if the water was from Lake Superior. He dipped a trembling finger, made the Sign of the Cross, and crept into a back pew.

The Faithful were mostly older folks, dressed in dark winter clothes, with a few red and green scarves to suggest festivity. The people seemed like peasants in a medieval church, and Christopher loved them. Their voices were somewhat heavy with the sorrows of the world, even in the midst of Christmas. And yet gold and purple lights from the stained-glass windows crowned the heads of the worshippers as if everyone were royal in the liturgy. The knight in shining linen wanted to serve the Faithful in some way, to offer up his life to make them merrier. It was a delusion of grandeur, perhaps, and yet beautiful and appropriate for the day.

Giving his voice to the cause, Chris began to feel stronger. He sang the hymns and responded to the Scriptures with reverence and verve. "Thanks be to God!" and "Praise to you, Lord Jesus Christ!"

The Incarnation was the focus of the homily. The gray and wrinkled priest tried to make sense out of the Mystery, talking about the Flesh of Heaven appearing in the manger. "It was a feeding trough," the priest said. "And so you see, from the first moment, the Savior appeared as food. Not for the animals, however, but for us."

During Communion, Christopher knelt and watched everyone else go forward to receive their Christmas Gifts. His heart felt blessed and cursed with sensations of feast and famine. Why, he wondered, was it so easy for others to accept the Gifts?

The young knight watched a lovely peasant girl, or maybe she was a princess, return from the altar. Her face was radiant; and the boy blinked his eyes.

"Terra?"

She knelt and disappeared. Chris lurched into the aisle and strode to the center of the church.

"Terra?"

Her eyes brimmed with tears. She whispered, "Christopher?"

He scooted into the pew and knelt beside her. "Long time, no see."

"Christopher, you look like a ghost. Is it really you?"

He nodded. "It's really me."

Terra wept, and kept kneeling for the remainder of the Mass, and Chris stayed at her side. When the church was empty, the boy put his arm around his favorite girl in the world. "I've missed you."

"I've missed you, too," Terra replied, her face glistening. She rested her head upon his shoulder and sobbed. "My mother is dying. She has pancreatic cancer."

"Oh, I'm sorry. I'm sorry."

"The doctors have given up. And she refuses pain medication. All she does is suffer. I can't bear it. Christopher, my mother was always the strongest person in the world. Now she can't eat or drink. She can barely speak. Every breath seems to be killing her. And my father is nowhere to be found."

Chris gently touched the girl's face, brushing away the tears. The young knight looked up and glared at the artwork on the ceiling. The images portrayed the Savior as being capable of everything. So why were so many things in the world left undone, unfixed, unhealed?

Terra stayed kneeling for another hour, begging for her mother to be cured. Her prayers became wordless — groans and sighs — and then nothing but the tears.

Chris agonized at her side. And finally, he could not take it any more.

"I have an idea," he whispered.

Terra made no response.

"I believe my mother might be able to help."

"Your mother? How?"

"She knows about alternative remedies."

The silence in the church presaged the answer.

"No, Christopher."

The young knight kept trying. "Many people have been healed from cancer. There are herbs and supplements, other approaches to —"

"No. It's in the final stage. She's already received Last Rites."

chapter eighty

EYES HALF-OPEN, Mrs. Corwin turned slightly in the bed, the movement causing her to wince. "Is that . . ." she rasped, "who I hope . . . it is?"

Chris approached the bed shyly, waving like a little kid.

Mrs. Corwin tried to lift her skeletal hand to wave back. She could not lift it, but smiled anyway. "Christopher . . . the great . . . reader. *Holy Grail . . . Adventures . . .* Remember?"

Stepping closer to the bed, Chris wanted to say the right thing. His mind searched for the appropriate words, for something soothing or profound. Fumbling forward, he instinctively bowed and kissed Mrs. Corwin lightly on the forehead.

"Old . . . romantic," she rasped. Joy filled her bloodshot eyes, and a lone tear dribbled down to her thin, white lips. The dying woman closed her eyes with a sense of finality.

Chris was sure that Mrs. Corwin had passed away and gone on to whatever was next. The boy turned to Terra and looked imploringly, as if to suggest they call for help.

"She's just resting, catching her breath. It's okay."

Backing away from the bed, Chris swiped at the tears rolling down his face. This was not how he wanted Terra to see him after so many years. When he'd recognized her in Star of the Sea, it seemed like a sign that was also a promise, a future full of happiness. Not a future full of death, the most bastard of dragons.

Chris took another step back. He paused and looked out the window. There was great Superior, with its bright coils of mist, undulating like a fire-breathing serpent, approaching the hillside as if laying claim to the whole city. So much for Christmas Day, Chris thought angrily.

So much for Mrs. Corwin passing away with a sunny kiss on her cheek. God! Why bother to be so brave, strong, and Catholic? Here comes the earthly reward, the burning of the dragon.

"No," Chris whispered to the window, "you can't have her. Not yet."

The young knight returned to Mrs. Corwin's side. "Is there anything I can get for you? Just say the word, and I'll get it. I'll go to any store. Do you want chocolates? Gourmet coffee? A bouquet of roses?"

Terra reminded him, "The stores are all closed."

"I don't care. I'll break in if I have to."

Mrs. Corwin opened her eyes. "I do want . . . something."

"Name it," Chris said. "Anything."

The once-powerful woman lifted her skeletal hand. She reached out, trembling, for Chris's hand, and held it warmly.

"I want," she said, "to apologize."

"Apologize? What for?"

"At the dance . . . long ago . . . I said you would . . . hurt us."

"Oh, Mrs. Corwin. You were just being a protective mom. It's okay."

The dying woman's eyes were sunken, but soft and glistening as a newborn's. "I was . . . wrong," she said. "You are . . . a help . . . to us."

Approaching the other side of the bed, Terra was all tears. She broke down and held the bony body as if she could hug another year of life into her mom.

Mrs. Corwin whispered, "Shush . . . now . . . Terra . . . sweetheart . . . remember . . . the dance . . . with Christopher . . . good life . . ."

All that day and night, Chris stayed in the hospital as if he were part of the family. He sat silently most of the time, allowing Terra and her mother to have most of the conversations, because it was so hard for Mrs. Corwin to speak, and it took all of her energy; every word was precious and almost killed her. But when the dying woman was sleeping, Chris spoke in hushed tones with the girl he'd always loved.

"How is your grandfather? Wise and funny as ever?"

She smiled mournfully. "He passed away last year."

"Oh, Terra. I'm so sorry."

"It was a good death. His heart was clean, and there were angels at the bedside."

"I wish I'd known. I always wanted to contact you and keep up with your life, but something always made me stay away."

A hint of happiness filled the girl's eyes. "He mentioned you, Christopher."

"Your grandfather?"

"Yes. The day before he died. He was wired to some horrible machines in Intensive Care, just up the hall from this room. All of a sudden he chuckled, and said, 'I will go to Saint Louis . . . with Silvenshine. And we shall slay a dragon.'"

Chris's eyes grew wide. "He said that?"

"Yes. He said that."

"Really? For real?"

Terra reached over and punched him on the shoulder. "Really, you dork."

For the next two weeks, Chris stayed with Mrs. Corwin, never leaving the hospital room. He encouraged Terra to go to Mass, and run whatever errands she needed to do. And through the hours, while falling snow whitened the bleakness outside the window, Chris read from a book that made the dying woman smile. *Canterbury Tales*. The first few tales he read very quickly, thinking that Mrs. Corwin wouldn't make it to the end. However, her attention seemed to increase after a few days, and she was able to sit up in bed. Chris slowed his cadence for the last chapters, and wondered if perhaps a miracle was occurring.

Mrs. Corwin hung on, and hung on, making it all the way to the end of the final tale, with the Parson telling of Heaven and hoping for the best on the day of doom.

"Great . . . book," she said. "I loved . . . all of it."

Chris leaned over and kissed her on the cheek. "I loved reading it to you."

Mrs. Corwin smiled, and winced at the same time. She struggled for breath. "Dearest . . . Christ— . . . opher . . . join . . . us."

It was a rather obscure request, but Chris knew exactly what she meant. During the past several days, she had overheard many conversations in which Terra had tried to convince him to make a good confession and receive Holy Communion.

"Join . . . us," Mrs. Corwin said again.

The idea of having the fullness of God enter his body was always terrifying to Chris. Wouldn't a communicant literally explode with energy? Who could bear a God that was wilder and more powerful than all of the congregated suns in the universe? A mere drop of His Blood would drown a human heart with unquenchable flame. Chris knew that he could not live with that Communion.

And he could not live without it.

"Someday," he said.

"Do you . . . promise?"

Chris started to say no, and the dying woman pleaded with her sunken eyes as if making a final request.

"Okay," the young knight said. "I promise."

chapter eighty-one

WHEN MRS. CORWIN entered a coma on the sixth of January, Terra stroked her mother's hair and quietly prayed. Chris stood at Terra's side, trying to be a strong presence, although his knees were shaking at the sight of the impending death.

Terra sighed heavily, her legs going weak as well, and leaned on Chris for support. "Today is the Feast of the Epiphany," she said, "and I have to start thinking about funeral arrangements."

"I'll help you. Don't worry."

She buried her head on Chris's shoulder. "There's so much to do, and I don't feel like talking to anybody."

"If you want, I'll call your father for you. Maybe he can return before the funeral. It would be good if he could say farewell to his wife."

Terra wept. "Yes, that would be good. But there's no way to contact him. He doesn't carry a phone, and I have no idea where he is."

"There must be a way to find him," Chris said, holding her more tightly. "The world has become such a small place."

Terra shook her head, rubbing her wet eyes on the boy's shoulder. "He's missed so much of my mother's life. And now he's going to miss her death. And her funeral."

Chris struggled to breathe, on the verge of a panic attack. Seeing his beloved Terra in the writhes of agony made him burst out with an impossible boast. "I'll find your father!"

Terra raised her head and searched the young knight's eyes. "We don't even know what country he's in. It could be Ireland. Or Ethiopia. Or the Ukraine. Wherever there is a holy place, that's where he could be."

"Even if he's in New Zealand, in some hobbit monastery, I'll find him."

A smile crossed the girl's mournful face. "A hobbit monastery?"

"Yeah, or wherever. I'll find him."

Terra couldn't help but laugh. "There are no hobbit monasteries, you dork."

"Yeah, but I'm just saying. Even if there were such a place, and your father were there, I'd find him."

The boy was saying both the exact wrong thing, and the exact right thing. His words made Terra feel both hopeless and full of hope.

She gave him a hug. "I love you, you dork."

Before he could reply, Mrs. Corwin quivered slightly in the bed, and there was a gurgling in her chest. It was not quite the end, but almost.

Chris whispered, "Do you carry a photograph of your father?"

"In my purse, yes, always."

"Give it to me."

Terra seemed to know his plan. "There just isn't enough time. Mother will be gone any moment."

"Let me have the picture. Please."

"Okay. Here it is, Chris. But you can't carry it all over the world."

The young knight admired Victor Corwin's wild face, and said, "With some help, I can."

chapter eighty-two

CHRIS RUSHED into his father's office. "Dad, can I rent all of your computers?" The rich young man pulled out his wallet. "Name your price, Dad. I need your office to help the Corwins."

"Topher, sweetheart!" Val cried, entering the room. "Is that you? How are things going at the hospital?"

"Not good."

"Oh, sweetie. I'm sorry."

Chris took all of the money from his wallet and slapped it on his father's desk. "If you need more, I'll go to the ATM."

Picking up the money and counting it, Joe scoffed at the offer. "A thousand dollars? Don't be foolish. If you're trying to help people, son, then my office and everything I have is yours — for free."

"Thanks, Dad. I appreciate it."

"Here, son. Take your cash. And don't carry so much around. Invest it in municipalities."

"Okay, Dad."

Val gave Chris a hug. "Sweetie, are you hungry? I made a fruitcake. A vegetable fruitcake. You'll love it."

"Maybe later, Mom," Chris said. He sat and fired up a computer and dialed his cell.

"Okay," Val said. "Just let me know if you need anything."

Chris nodded, and spoke urgently into the phone. "Pixie? Hey. I need your help. And can you get hold of Trevor? Yeah, it's urgent. Come over to my parents' house right away. And bring your laptop. Thanks!"

The young knight also called Moosehead and Skunk, and they soon arrived in an ice-covered Blazer. The football players stomped into the Lagorio house, politely took off their boots and coats, and said, "What's there to eat?"

"Be careful what you ask for," Chris said. "Thanks for coming over. Let's get to work."

The whole group gathered in Joe's office. With posters of the Grateful Dead looking down on them, and a cadaverous winter wind rattling at the windows, the young people sent a scanned attachment of Victor Corwin's photograph to every holy place they could find. Trevor was extremely helpful in locating links of pilgrimage sites and corresponding hostels. From Jerusalem to Lourdes to Fatima to Canterbury to Patmos, and a thousand other places that a pilgrim might be, the group sent out their plea for help.

HAVE YOU SEEN THIS MAN? HIS WIFE IS DYING AND HE NEEDS TO RETURN HOME. PLEASE RESPOND TO THIS EMAIL OR CALL THE NUMBER BELOW FOR CHRISTOPHER LAGORIO. $50,000 REWARD.

Trevor, who had been studying Greek and Latin to improve his seminary application, knew about a website that would translate the email into any language. While Pixie snuggled at his side and gave suggestions for where she would go if she were to make a pilgrimage, Trevor presided over the whole project. And around the globe the message flew. Within a few minutes, responses began to flood their computers.

"Here's one from Croatia!" Moosehead bellowed. "It says they saw Victor about a year ago, down in a crypt. I guess that's a cave."

"That's a good sign," Chris said. "We're on the right track."

"I just got a message from Wales," Skunk lisped. "They said we won a lottery!"

"Delete that one," Chris said.

Val entered the room with a tray of sliced veggie-fruitcake, and a special tea she called "The Wide-Eyed Special."

The young people all imbibed, and Moosehead ate four slices of the strange cake. "Mrs., um, Doctor Lagorio," he said, flirting nervously, "you're the best. I wish you were my mom."

Skunk poured himself another cup of tea and lisped, "This is delicious, Mrs. L. I wish you were my doctor."

Val reached out and touched the front of his neck. "Your little butterfly gland seems to be in perfect flight."

"Butterfly gland?"

"Your thyroid."

Turning bright red, Skunk gulped his tea, and choked on it. *Cough, cough.* "I just swallowed . . . my thyroid." *Cough, cough.* "Is that bad?"

The room exploded with laughter.

"Quiet, everyone," Trevor said. "Listen to this. Victor was seen at Chartres Cathedral two weeks ago. We're getting close."

Chris ran over to the rejected seminarian and enthusiastically shook his hand. "Great work, Trev! Keep sending out emails to that part of France. And take a good look at the satellite images. Try to figure out the best walking routes to the nearest holy places, including the border countries."

"If you let go of my hand, I can press the keyboard, Lagorio. Sheesh. You must really love this Corwin guy."

Pixie smiled knowingly. "I think Victor Corwin has a daughter."

"I got dibs on the daughter!" Moosehead bellowed.

"The girl's all mine!" Skunk lisped.

Everyone laughed. And the group had more cake and tea, and went back to work for several more hours. They listened to Bach, Dylan, Joni Mitchell, and the Moody Blues, and sent their cry for help to the four holy corners of the earth.

A few minutes before midnight, Chris's telephone rang.

chapter **eighty-three**

A BEARDED MAN with a sorrowful countenance entered the hospital room. He wore simple, woven clothes in the style of a medieval peasant.

"My love," he said to the dying woman.

She opened her eyes. "My . . . love."

"I'm sorry I've been away again."

She began to cry. "The angels . . . brought you . . . back."

Victor leaned down close to his wife. He brushed away her tears and gently stroked her hair. "My beautiful, beautiful. I never wanted to be away from you. Never for a moment. When I was returning over the deep this time, wishing the airplane was quicker than light, I began thinking about our wedding."

"You . . . handsome."

Victor shook his head. "I was nothing. And you were radiant. I was all nerves and confusion, and you stood calmly at the altar as if you were already taking your place in the forever of Heaven. In the forever of love."

"Sweet . . . talker." Mrs. Corwin smiled. And her eyes told Victor that this was the final smile.

He stroked her thin, gray, radiant hair and looked with love deeper than he had ever looked into her eyes. And then he gave his beautiful wife a last kiss, soft and passionate and perfectly sad.

"Angels . . . brought you . . ." she said, trailing off. "And . . . now . . ."

"Mom," Terra pleaded, "don't leave us. Not yet. Dad promises to stay this time."

". . . love . . ." and she was gone.

The bearded man held his wife's limp hand. He wept as if his sobs could travel through time and place and fill every chapel, church, and cathedral ever known to the world. And then he composed himself, and whispered, "My lady, I wish I had served you better. Now all I can do is pray for you. May your journey not end until you reach the very heart and castle of our Lord."

chapter eighty-four

AT THE FUNERAL Mass, in the upper room of the Corwin house, Chris sat in the back and watched Terra's boyfriend comfort her with smothering hugs. What a snake, he thought. He's taking advantage of her suffering.

The liturgy was lovely as any sorrow, the incense and Latin rising toward the descent of the Cross.

And Chris the young knight could not see the Holy Grail on the altar. He could not see the Blood, the Body, or the Fire. His eyes were blotched with grief and rage, and he entered the Dark Ages of his own creation, the machinations of his mind gearing up for a hundred years of war, or more, however long it would take to defeat his enemy. No, not defeat. Kill. Kill the hugging and kissing serpent. It would be a good riddance, Chris thought.

Where had Terra's boyfriend been during the long days in the hospital? The snake had made a few phone calls, and when Terra had said, "Love ya" at the end of the conversations, Chris didn't believe it. She would never proclaim love to such a dragon.

During the funeral Mass, in the upper room where God was supposed to be, the place where Grace was lifted above every form of magic, all Chris could do was conjure up revenge.

I'll kill him, he thought, while the liturgy lavished love on the deceased.

I'll kill him, he thought, while the mourners mourned the body in their midst, the foreshadow of every life's journey.

"I'll slay the son of a —" Chris hissed, and a powerful woman sitting in front of him turned and gave him such a scolding look that his conscience was scalded. He stood and slunk out of the service while everyone else knelt for the Consecration.

The young knight stumbled down the stairs from the upper room, paused for a moment at the sign that warned of dragons, looked sadly at the library and its thousands of beckoning volumes, and dashed down the remaining flights of stairs as if fleeing for his life. Out the back door, he was confronted by memories of spring flowers, summer birds, and walks with a lovely girl in perfectly fallen nature; and he immediately buried those memories in the glacial cold. Chris stood where he had known the depths of spiritual friendship, and he glared at Lake Superior, newly covered with ice. "You're not so great after all," he said. "You can be buried, too."

Chris staggered through the snow, circling the cathedral-house as if to perform a frigid ritual, a final goodbye. He muttered to the three storeys, "God be with you." And he was startled when the echo muttered back, "God be with you."

The young knight staggered away from the startling echo and the last ascending notes of the Mass. He climbed into Majestic and sputtered toward the highway and turned sharply, nearly plummeting into the ditch. "Ha ha, nice try," he said, as if boasting to fate. Windows open, the winter air kissed his face, making his image ruddy and radiant. Chris struck the mirror aside, not wanting to see himself as anything nice while he swerved along the icy North Shore cliffs, speeding home to make preparations for war.

In the closet of the stone cottage was the suit of armor, propped up like a sick joke. The seller on the Internet had lied, in capital letters, "THIS SUIT HELPED TO WIN A CRUSADE." Chris could have paid an additional thousand dollars to purchase the silver sword, "SLIGHTLY STAINED WITH ENEMY BLOOD" but he could see that the discoloration was not blood; it was rust. Deep inside, he'd known the suit of armor was not really armor. It was a charade. However, it was a game for which he was willing to suspend his disbelief and play along. He wanted to have a Holy Grail Adventure, and by God, he was going to have one.

"I'll kill him," he said, writhing to fit into the fake suit. The young knight took a few clinking, tinny steps into the living room. "I'll kill him, and I'll set my lady free."

Weaponless, Chris stumbled from the living room toward the dining room. The large window by the table was without a curtain — it had been pulled down at the party — and now winter light was pouring in and filling the room like a feast. Chris stared through his helmet to see the chandelier all wild and shimmering. There was a whole army reflected in the crystals, the knights all looking up at the ceiling, or through to the sky, or into the higher places. The fiery army was focused as one, and moved as a single body, the slightest movement a hundred sparks of synchronicity.

"I'll kill him, I'll kill him . . ."

A flash of reflection caused Chris to look down, and he saw the army of light shining on his false armor. He punched himself in the chest, making a good dent and fragmenting the increasing number of knights. "I'll kill him," he said, breathing hard; and he punched himself again. "I'll kill . . ." and he punched and punched until dents gave way, and the façade of armor broke apart, and the white linen beneath revealed a glistening red, just a drop bleeding through, and that was enough.

"I forgive . . . I forgive," the young knight said, giving up.

chapter eighty-five

THE BOY WENT back to East High and slouched in the corners of the classrooms, unmoved by the poets, bored by math and science, irritated by humanities, and, finding nothing in his soul for art, he became the worst student in the school. Worse than Moosehead and Skunk. Worse than the vampires. Worse than the girl who knows what bodes. And even worse than Dip.

Every night in the gloomy cottage, he sat beneath the unlit glass of the chandelier, and waited for the phone to ring. Waited for a chance to say what was singing so painfully in his heart. Waited for Terra to call so he could say in his most knighted voice, "I am sorry. I love you. And I will never see you again."

The times when the phone did ring, it was Pixie. Followed by his mother. Followed by Mary Joan Mudgett.

He gave the same speech to all of them. "I'm fine. Don't worry about me. I'm just suffering a little from the winter season. That's all."

Mary Joan knew better. She made some small talk about farming and music, and then said, "Maybe you're sick because you're in love."

"Out of love," he countered.

"Well, sometimes it's the same thing. Like with Mr. and Mrs. Corwin."

"How do you know about them?"

"Everyone's been talking about them. It's like an epic love story."

Chris lamented into the phone. "It was almost tragic."

"And it ended up perfect."

He paused, remembering the final kiss. He wouldn't agree that it was perfect. The real perfect thing was Mrs. Corwin's final word. How many people in the history of the world have ended with *love*?

Mary Joan sighed. "Christopher, I must say I'm mad at you."

"Why?"

"You never invited me to the Internet search party for Victor Corwin."

"You hate computers."

"I thought you hated them, too."

The boy shrugged. "Yeah, but sometimes they can be useful."

"Like for passing your classes? I heard you're flunking out of school."

"Who told you that?"

"Everyone's been talking about you."

"Oh? What are they saying?"

"They're saying you spent all of your money to find Victor Corwin, and that you're moving back to your parents' house, and that you're suicidal about . . . some girl."

"I'm fine, Mary Joan. And I'll be fine. Don't worry about me. Just keep making your music."

"Well, you need to make something, too. At least make yourself a high-school graduate."

"Yeah, yeah, whatever."

"Chris, don't sell yourself short. Everyone has a vocation."

"A vocation?"

"Yes, a holy calling."

He sighed. "Whatever that's worth."

chapter eighty-six

WINTER, WINTER, wide-open treasury of the North. A keeper of snow had a whole January of accumulated wealth, and a generous February in which most of the glittering heavens seemed to have fallen. Around the stone cottage and on the roof, great banks were piled — as if the silvenshine could be returned to the sky.

Inside the dark house, on the homeowner's mantle, was a growing mound of envelopes: unpaid bills and overdue notices. Depression had paralyzed Chris's will to write checks, and with no current income, he was becoming less than rich. He lived as simply as possible, frugal as a monk, not even buying shaving cream to tame his wilding whiskers. Money, and all of its manifestations, obsessed him the rest of the winter. Even his dreams were battles to gain gold from hording dragons and investment brokers. However, instead of simply shoveling his neighbors' sidewalks for cold, hard cash, the young man ventured into abstraction, reading online back-issues of the *Wall Street Journal*, *Barron's*, *Fortune Magazine*, and *Investor's Weekly*.

At East, Chris started paying attention in economics class; and when the bell rang, he went tromping downtown, all bundled up in a second-hand parka, to make the rounds of the coffee shops. Chris studied the leftover business sections of the national and international newspapers. And his favorite activity became eavesdropping on the conversations of the local business owners and bankers. Between the worthless small talk about the underperforming Minnesota sports teams, Chris, by the end of winter, had acquired a lucrative education about the florist industry, candy stores, nightclubs, art galleries, farmers' markets, commodities exchanges, restaurants, consignments, real estate, fisheries, bakeries, and banks.

He was ready for every world of gold.

chapter eighty-seven

IT WAS A morning fit for a world of faith, the lamb-like end of March, having seen the last of the roaring snowstorms. Green grass was springing up and down the hillside; and Chris walked barefoot in his own backyard, enthralled by a black-capped sparrow that was chirping psalms in a pine spire. The early-rising bird seemed full of earth's physics and the metaphysics of angels, wings gleaming and suddenly in the air.

Chris surveyed the ground, his proud investment. Duluth in spring was still wintry, and when he strolled down the slope through the frosted grass, his feet and toes were both numb and tickled. Grinning, Chris bent down, almost to his knees as if to pray. There were glimmers of the infinite in the frozen clover, in the crystalline cathedrals of triune green. Considering it all, the young man almost burst out with his own psalm. And then it was gone. The elevating sun had lifted the earth to the degree of melt water, turning the mini-cathedrals into plain old clover.

And Chris knew it was time.

It was time to sell, sell, sell.

And invest in more glory.

chapter eighty-eight

BY GRACE and good brains, Christopher Lagorio managed to pass enough tests and write enough papers to graduate.

He purchased a cap and gown, but the day of graduation was so perfect, he decided to skip the ceremony. As if being called, Chris marched up to Skyline Drive while cars and trucks honked at his appearance of pomp and circumstance. Feeling as strong as when he played football, he leap-climbed the winding stairs to the top of Enger Tower. The structure was the most ancient-looking in Duluth. Built of bluestone, like Stonehenge, the tower entered the sky above the harbor and offered a panoramic view that any eyes would consider visionary.

The graduate brushed the fluttering tassel away from his face, and contemplated the great lake and the Zenith City. The homes and churches on the hillside shimmered down to the water, where the ships were buoyed up by waves of sunlight. Mist arose from further out on Superior, giving rise to seagulls whirling in their ghostly dance. Chris looked north to the cathedral, and through the spires he thought he could see the Lakeview Castle.

The graduate's black robe, a remnant of the Middle Ages, was all sheen and sparkle in the bluestone tower, absorbing the sun the way others had absorbed God's lights of theology, philosophy, and art. Chris hovered above Duluth and thought of

Chaucer and Canterbury, the tales of fallen human beings on quests to rise higher.

"Everything is here. Duluth could become a holy site, with pilgrims from all over the world spiriting to this shore. They could pray in the cathedral, climb this tower, dance in the Lakeview Castle, go on quests in the wilderness, and find their fill of the goods of the world at the festival market. The festival market . . . We need something like a medieval marketplace where lords, ladies, knights, peasants, and pilgrims celebrate the holiness of days."

Footsteps began pounding up the tower staircase, with laughter and shouts of excitement, a large family climbing toward the view.

"Saint Francis Market," Chris whispered. "I'll open it . . . for them."

chapter **eighty-nine**

THAT EVENING, Joe and Val invited their son over for dinner, even though they were upset that he'd skipped the graduation. To make it up to them, Chris made himself handsome, shaving his wild whiskers and getting his hair cut short. His parents rewarded him with hugs and kisses, and then gave him broccoli, cauliflower, spinach, and green apples.

"Yum yum," the graduate said. "May I have some more?"

After a dessert of vegetable fruitcake, Joe and Val asked what else he wanted for a graduation present.

"Do you want a new computer?"

"No thanks, Dad."

Val made a sewing motion. "I could put up new curtains in the cottage."

Chris smiled with a slight look of mischief. "What I want, believe it or not, are more fruits and vegetables."

His mother knew about the hotdogs and tater tots that he'd ingested at school — it had caused her many sleepless nights — and now she was delighted by her son's change of heart and palate. "Sweetheart, we'll give you plenty of great food! Let's go to the Co-op and fill a whole cart."

The graduate shook his head. "I'm afraid one cart won't be enough."

"Okay," Joe said, feeling generous, "we'll fill up two carts."

Still shaking his head, Chris said, "I'll need more produce than that."

"My goodness," his mom said, gasping. "Is your colon superhuman?"

"Listen, folks. I'm gonna need a whole truckload of fruits, vegetables, nuts, and berries. Understand?"

Val was incredulous, unable to speak

Joe laughed. "Ha! Aha! I do understand! I know the entrepreneurial spirit when I see it. This is very interesting. You're starting another business."

"Yep."

Val clapped her hands. "A health-food store?"

"Something even better."

After dinner, Chris drove his car to an empty storefront in downtown Duluth and began to formulate a plan to help people get healthy. Body and soul.

Saint Francis Market.

It would be an ever-renewing farmers' market and arts and crafts festival.

The graduate's first task was to get the stone cottage sold. He accomplished that in forty days. And then, with his modest profit, he rented the empty store and transformed it into a little paradise of commerce.

Saint Francis Market opened its doors on the weekend of the Fourth of July. It had been difficult pulling permits and getting everything situated; but with the help of his parents and the Mudgetts, the shelves were stacked with a splendorous array of local foods and handmade goods. Many farmers and artisans in the area were eager to support the endeavor, including parishioners from all sorts of churches. Everyone loved the joyful saint from Assisi and felt at home in the healthy, festive atmosphere.

Mary Joan played her guitar and sang on the sidewalk, enticing the downtown crowd to give Saint Francis a try. Duluthians and tourists poured through the doors. They bought everything from fresh flowers to blueberries to goat cheese to unique arts and crafts — including "Chastity's Belts." The young mother had created a fashion line of beaded suede and could not keep up with the demand.

Pixie bought one, and Chris was intrigued to catch a glimpse of her and Mary Joan having an animated conversation near the smoked fish. He thought they were talking about him, but he was too busy helping customers to catch the details.

Saint Francis Market did enough business during July to pay for most of the start-up expenses. Chris's vision, idea, hard work, and help was transformed into a positive part of the local culture. He had proven that a Christian-oriented marketplace could be just as good as, if not better than, the pagan places. And he was delighted to see many of the old Co-op patrons, with their piercings, tattoos, and goatees, hanging out at the coffee bar and leafing through the books, including *Holy Grail Adventures*, *The Lives of the Saints*, and the poetry of Gerard Manley Hopkins. It warmed his heart to hear a pierced tongue recite, *"The world is charged with the grandeur of God . . ."*

A dozen or so customers were in the store at all times, and the conversations were the best in town, and perhaps some of the best in the world, enlivened by the ever-lit fireplace, the colorful art like Kells on the walls, and the inspired books. The eclectic patrons of Saint Francis, when not shopping, reclined in the comfy chairs overlooking Superior and explored the depths of knowledge with a discourse approaching the soulfulness for which the tongue was formed. And sometimes the patrons just sat and laughed, feasting on sweet-potato scones, or triple-chocolate muffins, washing them down with a daily bold.

Among the various suppliers for the store were monks and nuns, experts for centuries at roasting coffee beans and making sweets. Chris, when he wasn't busy doing everything from taking inventory to working the register, loved to lounge as if he were not the owner but just another partaker of the soulful community.

Saint Francis Market was more of a dance than a store, with an old piano and a lute at the ready in the reading room. Music, made by whoever had the gift, blessed the aisles and made the shoppers hum and want to linger among the vegetables, fruits, and whole grains of the earth. A customer might buy a small amount organic spelt and yet feel as if she had partaken of a great harvest festival.

Because of Chris's devotion to local farmers, and his disdain for corporate agribusiness, he suffered during the winter months. He refused to stock his shelves with so-called "fresh" food that had to be trucked from Florida and California. Without many fruits or vegetables, the store survived the burial of snow by selling paintings, photographs, wood carvings, icons, candles, stained glass, books, eggs, smoked fish, milk, cheese, chocolate, baked goods, coffee, and live music. Mary Joan Mudgett was becoming more and more famous in the Northland, so Chris restructured the layout of the building in order to expand the stage area. Mary Joan's shows, especially on weekends, brought in crowds and kept the cash register ringing.

Saint Francis made it through the precarious winter.

In fact, after the first full year of operation, the store returned a net profit of more than thirty-thousand dollars.

Several other businesses had failed downtown, but Chris was very fortunate, and careful with his money. He lived in the apartment above the store, ate the unsold food, and bought second-hand clothes. He liked his little car, but he needed a pickup, so Chris traded in Majestic for what he called a car-up: a 1979 El Camino. It was the color of an iron-ore mine — like a shaft of rusted sunlight — and its payload was always packed with one good thing after another for Saint Francis.

The young entrepreneur worked sixteen hours a day for his success, and was featured in the *Tribune*, on the front page of the business section, as the "Miracle Kid of Superior Street."

chapter **ninety**

JOE LAGORIO sat at the coffee bar, beaming over the newspaper. "You've made a great start, Topher."

Chris stood behind the counter, smiling appreciatively. "Thanks for your help, Dad."

"You're welcome," Joe said. "Now, this is your business, and I don't want to say too much. But think about the possibilities. You could open a store in Minneapolis. And another store on the West Coast. C'mon, son. Think about it. Saint Francis in San Francisco. You should probably open two stores there."

Rubbing down the coffee bar with a towel, Chris thought about it. "That's a brilliant idea. But, truth be told, I'm happy with what I have."

"C'mon, son, have more ambition," Joe urged. "With your magic touch, you could own a hundred stores. You could really be somebody."

The Miracle Kid shuffled around the coffee bar and settled into a big cushy chair. "I love Duluth, and I can't imagine not seeing Lake Superior every morning. I'm not going to trademark Saint Francis or turn it into a chain. In fact, I hope people take my idea and make it incarnate in their own communities."

Joe shook his head in disbelief. "Why would you let others profit from your vision?"

Chris shrugged. "I have my reasons."

To give away ideas that would spring up gardens for others. That was the way of Saint Francis. While worldly greed shrivels *caritas* to the size of a credit card, Chris was more economically fecund. He had scribbled in one of his notebooks: *The marriage of spiritual and human graces is the only revolution that can turn mammon into milk and honey.*

"Are you sure, Topher?"

"Yeah, Dad."

The old hippie stared out the window at the richly graying water. "Son . . ."

"Yeah? What is it?"

Joe turned to consider the interior of Saint Francis again, his eyes brimming at all of the goods. "I want to say that I'm proud of you. I'm proud of everything about you. And your mother feels the same way."

The Miracle Kid grinned, and tossed his father a whole-grain biscuit. "You're not so bad yourself."

Joe caught the biscuit and took a big chomp. "Mmm. This is good. Really good."

"Yep. It's all good."

The Grateful Dead wailed from Joe's phone. It seemed to be an important call by the way he stared at the screen, but the old hippie turned the phone off. He gazed at his son's face and noticed a dreamy look in his eyes.

"Oh, don't tell me, Topher. Don't tell me."

The boy laughed. "Is it obvious?"

"Oh, don't tell me. Don't tell me. God help you, son. God help you. You're in love."

"Yep."

"With that redhead?"

"Pixie? No, we're just friends. She moved to Steubenville, Ohio, to study God and birds. She has a boyfriend there, and is doing really well."

"What about that girl who plays guitar?"

"Mary Joan? She's too busy becoming famous to have a boyfriend."

"Huh. Then who are you in love with? Is it someone new?"

chapter ninety-one

A YOUNG WOMAN dressed in light blue walked like water music into Saint Francis and ordered a caramel latte.

Chris had been dreamily watching the waves on Superior, and asked the visitor, "Extra foamy?"

"Yes, please."

"Good choice. And would you like a triple-chocolate muffin?

The young woman smiled. "Do you sell them by the dozen?"

"Of course. I can sell everything here by the dozen. Would you like twelve welcome mats?"

She laughed. "Maybe. Did you make them?"

He grinned, hoping the visitor would become a regular. "I'd make a welcome mat for you."

"You're sweet."

"Well, I'm no triple-chocolate muffin."

"Maybe triple-vanilla," she teased.

Chris held up his pale arms. "Yeah, I need to take some time off and get outside. I've been spending all of the light here in the store."

The visitor gestured toward the icons and stained glass. "This is more than a store. It's like a chapel."

"I love beauty," Chris said, "beauty and truth."

"Exactly."

While the Miracle Kid made the lattes and plopped the muffins into a box, the young woman leafed through one of the many books scattered about. "*Feasts and Festivals of the Middle Ages,*" she said. "This is wonderful. Exactly what the world needs. And I love the music you're playing."

Chris nodded toward the speaker above the lakeside window. "This song is the "Sailor's Jig" — it's very old — fifteenth century."

"Sounds like the sailor is walking on water."

"Well, after the ship sank, it was the only way home to his beloved."

The young woman laughed.

Blushing, Chris asked, "What's so funny?"

"Nothing."

"What? Tell me."

"It's nothing, really."

"What?"

She gave him a smile as if giving him a birthday present. "You said the word *beloved*. Not many guys today would say that word. And I think it's adorable of you."

While Chris blushed more than ever, the beautiful visitor reached into her purse for cash and handed him two twenties for the lattes and muffins.

"That's too much," he said. "A dollar tip is about the most we ever get."

Terra grinned. "I'm going to do everything I can to keep Saint Francis in business."

chapter ninety-two

THERE WAS only one full-time employee who helped Chris keep the store a step ahead of the Second Law of Thermodynamics. This person always came to work several minutes early, considered cleanliness next to godliness, lived to keep things in order, and had the special knowledge to engage in the theological conversations that occurred every day in Saint Francis. He never stole merchandise, or wasted time texting, or went outside for a smoke. He was worthy of being Employee of the Month twelve times a year. And his name was Trevor Nelson.

Trevor acted like a high priest, or higher, pontificating about the Church as if he held the Very Keys in his unwrinkled khaki pocket. One could imagine how bad he was for business, how he'd drive away the masses with his spiritual pride. However, like a chess master or a juggler in a city square, Trevor was the life of the party. The tattooed philosophers, shoulder-chipped agnostics, battlesome vampires, and spaced-out hippies loved to visit the failed seminarian and challenge his ideas to the pain, to the death, and just for fun.

The Goths, especially, were frequent customers and big spenders, with an almost insatiable appetite for French roast and goat-milk truffles. And Trevor, as if he were Albertus Magnus mentoring the medieval young at the University of Paris, quoted from the Holy Scriptures, the Fathers of the Church and the

Code of Canon Law, hoping to lead everyone to the straight and narrow path of everlasting bliss. Chris made him clean the toilets, mop the floors, wash the windows, and distribute leftover food to the poor. And when the failed seminarian asked for a raise, the Miracle Kid gladly gave it. After all, with Trevor watching the store along with a few trustworthy part-timers, Chris could get away to be with Terra.

She had returned to the Northland for summer vacation, having completed her first year of the Great Books program at Thomas Aquinas College. All of her reading of the deepest minds made her come home, or at least close to home, to live and work at a hospice for dying nuns. And to be with her beloved dork.

Their first date was a morning walk through the fog around the cathedral-house and up near the purgatory cave.

Terra apologized for not telling Chris about the nasty boyfriend. "He was a consummate liar, and I bought it for a while."

Chris apologized for not kicking his ass. "I wanted to kill him, but then I had a sort of vision about my own problems."

"Look at that," Terra said, pointing.

The fog was like a river above the lake, flowing north and becoming lighted with sunrise. At the shoreline, a heron's beak pierced the mist as if daggering an invisible fish.

"This is the best place on earth," Chris said.

Terra nodded, tears streaming down her face. And she took his hand.

The young lovers made their way to the purgatory, and sat in the dark on the cold stone ledge. Superior was like a great ghost, the waves whispering. Chris and Terra said nothing for nearly an hour, their bodies softly touching, the good haunting of a hundred memories making them shiver in their shared warmth.

"My father sold the house," Terra said.

Chris noticed that she did not rub her eyes. She let the tears fall as a matter of course.

"He sold it dirt-cheap to the Historic Preservation, and moved to Europe."

"To England?"

Terra tried not to laugh, but could not help herself. "To England . . . Wales . . . Scotland . . . Ireland . . . Spain . . . France . . . Germany . . . Lichtenstein . . . Vatican City . . . you know my father, still doing his penance, still saying his prayers."

The boy shifted his weight a little closer, as if giving himself to the girl. She smiled, and moved slightly away. Terra leaned forward, her eyes on Superior, watching the veil of fog lift while the sunrise star burned in the water like a chalice of golden fire. Her body language was leading the boy to consider the holy sight, and take the whole thing in.

And the young knight, trembling with a familiar chill of doubt, closed his eyes in hopes of fighting the dragons another day.

chapter ninety-three

TERRA RETURNED to Duluth the next three summers, ministering to ever-new groups of the dying. And when she wasn't at the hospice, she was at Saint Francis, lounging at the coffee bar and going for walks with Chris during his breaks. The old friends were more than serious, although the words of love and the attendant promises remained unspoken.

"What a perfect couple," everyone else said. And some bleary-eyed romantics would add, "When is the wedding?"

Chris began attending Mass with Terra at Star of the Sea, beginning each day with the deep-water music of the liturgy and the great cloud of incense offered by an elderly priest who seemed to have one foot in the grave and the other foot in 1940. His homilies never lasted more than five minutes, and were always about the overwhelming love of God. "He is going to get you," he said one morning, as if directly confronting Chris.

The young knight was the only person at daily Mass who did not go up for Communion. He stayed kneeling with his eyes closed, praying for the well-being of the whole world and especially for Terra. She always went up for Communion. Yet before she did, she leaned down and kissed her earthly beloved on the top of his head. Chris felt as if the kisses filled him with light.

While Terra braved the aisle to accept the Divinity, Chris recalled his conversations with the professor in the cathedral-house library. Unlike when Trevor Nelson preached at him and did more harm than good, the words of Professor Corwin were like gardens in a park that kept on growing.

"Medieval," the professor had said, his eyes lighting up with his favorite lecture. "The word *medieval* is spoken by some as if cursing. But when I taste the word *medieval,* my soul is feasted, and I am satiated by epic poems of pageantry, chivalry, romance, devotion, and miracles. The Middle Ages made Europe immortal, because the Body and Blood of Christ immortalized every aspect of culture. It was the Age of the Eucharist, and it inspired the most glorious works of art, intellect, and faith, producing the most luminous people on earth."

Chris raised his hand. "And there was darkness as well, right?"

"Yes, that is true. There was much war and illness. The world was fallen then, as it is now. However, our age has fallen further away from the Light."

"Do you think this is the Dark Ages?"

Looking out the window to the cobalt lake, the professor said, "There is no need to speak of the unspeakable. If we were to quantify the sins of the current Culture of Death, it would require a long and agonizing list of atrocities."

Just a kid, Chris already knew about the daily murders, rapes, porn, abortions, greed, thefts, and blasphemies. He whispered, "Are we doomed?"

"Silvenshine," the professor sighed, staring at the numinous lake. He turned to the boy as if recruiting him. "This dark world needs shining knights again, in the full armor of the Faith. This dark world needs to remember the real mission of the hero."

Chris leaned forward. "Real mission? What does that mean?"

The professor glanced at the stairs to the upper room, and he pointed at the dragon sign. "It means you have some work to do."

chapter ninety-four

ON THE NIGHT before Summer Christmas, Terra sent an email from the hospice.

Dear Christopher,

Despite all the damage done by sinners in the Church, the Mass is the hope of civilization.

The Mass is the pinnacle of philosophy. Our minds approach the Holy Gifts in fear of God, the beginning of wisdom. Our hearts accept the Holy Gifts in love of God, the end of wisdom.

The Divine Liturgy is the epitome of language and poetry. It is the most powerful form of drama, a play that appears to descend into tragedy, yet ends in the height of heavenly bliss.

The Mass is housed in the most glorious architecture ever constructed. Not all churches are grand, but the world has been given the supreme cathedrals to remind us of the majesty of the Maker, who appears on the altars.

The Divine Liturgy is the grand unified theory of physics. Beyond all of the quarks, multiple dimensions, and dark matter is the greatest gift to science: Transubstantiation.

The Mass is the quintessence of agriculture — the simple fruits of the earth transformed into spiritual nutrition.

The Mass is the bloodline of the best art. From icons to stained glass to mosaics to statuary to all of the variations of paintings, the Sacrifice enlivens creativity.

The Divine Liturgy is a perfect education. It is reality. We kneel. We bow. We give up our rebellions and embrace the hierarchy of the created order. We submit to every demand of Love.

The Mass gives voice to the music of angels, the chant of nine choirs and seven heavens. It culminates in the most noble act of physicality. We accept into our bodies the Creator of all flesh, in whom we live and dance and have our being.

The Mass is the most personal relationship that one can have with God.

The Mass is the most heavenly occurrence on earth, and the most viciously attacked — from within the Church and without.

The Mass has produced the humble, superhuman saints, multitudes of heroic men and women, from the beginning of the Church to the end, miracle workers from every walk of life — patrons for every holy passion.

The Divine Liturgy of Heaven gathers the most purposeful community in the world, the assembly of Communicants. Beyond the goodness of human friendship, the friends of Heaven are perfected in the Feast.

The Mass makes life worth living. It is the gateway out of our self-inflicted pain, to fully enter into the death and resurrection of Christ.

Will you, in the name of Love, become a Communicant?

chapter ninety-five

ON THE DAY of Summer Christmas, Chris, with his clothes freshly washed at the Sunshine Laundromat, was between wild and radiant in his white-linen shirt and pants. And in his pocket was a stellar ring. Singing a silent version of hallelujah, he drove the El Camino up the hill to the hospice, believing this would be the day, and the night, that would forever be marked on the calendar as the "Feast of the Engagement."

Terra, taking the afternoon off from the dying, appeared on the sidewalk as if she had already said yes. Her whole face was a smile, and she wore a bright coordination of green blouse, tan slacks, and good leather hiking boots that could make any journey.

"Looks like you're ready," Chris said.

She was holding a large picnic basket. "We have everything we need, good sir. Now, do you mind telling me where we are going?"

"It's a secret."

Without hesitation, she climbed in the car, the basket on her lap. "Oh, you and your secrets. It's just one surprise after another."

He nodded, trying not to grin.

Chris drove the El Camino over the hill and into the woods and toward the headwaters of perhaps the greatest river in the world. The Mississippi, so powerful that it seemed it could move the whole world with its current and ancient song, had so enamored the European explorers that they named it Holy Spirit River.

"Mississippi has a nice ring," the boy said, hinting. "The word Mississippi has a ring of romance."

Terra nodded, bubbling with enthusiasm. "I love the Ojibwe language. After Latin, Greek, Hebrew, French, and Spanish, it's my favorite."

Chris laughed, amazed that she had missed the hint and yet pleased by her seemingly never-ending knowledge. "What other Ojibwe words do you know?"

She reached over and tapped his rib cage. "*Odayin.* Isn't that wonderful? O-day-in."

"Heart full of light," Chris said, turning the wheel and driving deeper into the forest.

Terra had graduated first in her class, having written her senior thesis on theological philology. "I love it when words need no translation," she said, innocently holding her hand to his chest. "By some linguistic miracle, sometimes the words convey across languages."

"Tell-tell me more," Chris stammered.

"With pleasure," she said. "*Babamadizwin.*"

"Hmm . . . the first part sounds like a baby, or a sheep, or a baby sheep . . . and the last part is *win.* I'm not sure about the middle. What does it all mean together?"

She pointed at the tree-lined road and the birthplace of the invisible river beyond. "*Babamadizwin* means 'journey.' "

Chris was so happy, he could not think of much to say. "Far out . . . far out."

"Like, right on, dude," Terra said with a playful laugh.

A mile or so from the headwaters, the Mississippi appeared in a clearing like a holy form, silver-splashing as if with infinite raindrops. Without a cloud in the sky, the splashing was a trick of light or ingenuity of grace.

Terra said, "*Geesis.*"

Chris was confused. "Jesus?"

"The Ojibwe word for 'sun.' *Geesis.*"

"For real?"

"Yes, for real."

The river disappeared again, swallowed up by the insatiable forest, and Chris turned the wheel of the El Camino and drove up a power-line road that was not really a road. When his family had first moved from Sacramento, and were spending their Sundays discovering the known and hidden landscapes that made Minnesota a day-tripper's dream, they had happened upon what appeared to be an ancient campsite. Joe had theorized, "The first Europeans to reach the headwaters probably believed it was more than a mystical place. They thought the land around here would be swimming in gold."

The path to the campsite could not be reached by Chris's El Camino, so he parked beneath the power line near a small meadow. "Here we are. Almost."

Terra raised an eyebrow. "Are you sure that last turn was the correct one? I don't see Lake Itasca."

"Follow me," he said, reaching over to open her door. "You're going to love this place."

She grabbed the picnic basket, and away they went to seek their engagement.

Among the meadow grasses were butterfly weeds, flowering with yellow-orange blossoms. And above the meadow, a flicker bird flew — red flame on its head, as if lit by a finger of Sinai.

"I already like this place," Terra said. "And it gets better?"

"Better and better," the boy said.

At the edge of the meadow, just before reaching the shimmer of birch and the shade of pine, they were confronted by a seven-foot fireweed, burning with other-worldly, earthy light.

Terra whispered, "It's like the angel at the gate of Eden."

"It's just a weed," Chris said.

Terra handed him the picnic basket, and then slowly approached the fiery giant. "We have to say the secret word to get past. Just as in *The Lord of the Rings* — when they were stopped at the entrance to a cave."

Chris rolled his eyes. "Oh, please."

The fireweed leaned over in a gust of wind, as if allowing the lovers to pass.

"Let's go!" Terra said gleefully. And Chris played along, running at her side and whooping like a young Adam in Paradise.

The forest floor was an illusion of calm and sturdiness. In fact, it was a roiling mess of bacteria, algae, and fungi. The moiling earth, and the countless micro-creatures in the soil, were all playing their invisible graces, fusing the green fertility. The pine needles and leaves glowered as if photosynthesizing the shade, and Chris noticed that some of the leaves were heart-shaped. He paused, and plucked one for Terra, and then realized the heart was jagged, surrounded by fiery teeth.

Damn, he thought. Were the dragons into everything?

"That's beautiful," Terra said, and took the heart shape from Chris's hand. "All right, lead the way."

There was a sort of path to the ancient campsite, and the way twisted and turned, allowing for many pauses and opportunities to listen to the lyrical wilderness.

A vesper sparrow sang, "*Here here! There there!*"

A song sparrow answered, "*Sweet-sweet-sweet!*"

A cardinal announced, "*What cheer! What cheer! Birdy-birdy-birdy . . . what cheer!*"

As if unafraid of the birdies, a monarch butterfly fluttered into the territory, wings like stained glass. The resurrection bug lighted for a moment on the crown of Chris's head, and then flitted like a happy drunk, stagger-flying and disappearing into the deep sweetness of the forest.

Along the sort of path were starflowers, far from the sky, just a half-foot above the ground. Terra seemed to gather them up with her gaze. "*Trientalis borealis*," she said in a lilt of Latin that made the boy bow his head. "Christopher, do you know this flower?"

He nodded. "I've seen it before. What is it?"

"It's a starflower, but people call it the honeymoon flower."

"Why do they call it that?"

"Because it blooms during the wedding season of June."

Was she hinting? Did she know the ring was in his pocket? "Honeymoon flower," he said. "That has a nice ring to it."

"Lead on," she said. "I want to see the ancient campsite."

"Okay. It's just a little bit further. But I have to warn you. There isn't much there to see. It's more about the feel of the place."

Terra tossed her head, the gold hair rivering across her shoulders. "I know I'll like it. Lead on, good sir."

He liked being called sir. Should he call her lady? Or would that be too much? "Right this way, Miss Trientalis Borealis."

Her smile told him that she loved that. The young knight turned and led his lady to the place of the proposal. It was a grassy hill with a circle of boulders near the top where countless fires had burned through the centuries, with a slight but perfect view of the headwaters through the trees. There was also a stone table at the site, a volcanic gift, and two petrified logs that served as seating.

"I love it, I love it," Terra said.

Chris picked up a fallen pine branch and swept debris from the table. Then he placed the picnic basket in the middle and gestured for his lady to sit. "Shall we?"

"Indeed, we shall," Terra answered. "Christopher, my goodness. This is the best Summer Christmas I could imagine."

A ladybug was shining on a page of birch, shining as if part of an illuminated manuscript, like a fiery speck of Kells. The young knight thought: okay, okay, the signs are all perfect. I should ask Terra now. No need to wait until sunset. Ask her now. Hmm, what is that over there?

He was distracted by a tiger swallowtail that was prowling the campsite, nipping at the starflowers. Chris noticed that the tiger had been wounded — a bite taken out of a wing — a whole stripe removed by the chomp of a bird.

"Let's eat," Terra said. "Are you hungry?"

"Umm . . . yeah. Starving."

Terra reached into the picnic basket and, like magic, brought out honey-glazed salmon, cheddar cheese, bread, and two bottles of Deep North Water.

That's another sign, Chris thought. I should propose to her. Now, now, now.

"I have chocolate and coffee, too," Terra said, "for dessert. Hey, Christopher."

His hand was halfway down his pocket, reaching for the diamond that had been given to his grandmother in Sacramento, and given to his mother, and given to him that morning by a teary-eyed, joyous Val.

Terra pulled the red thermos from the basket and held it for Chris to take. "Do you know the Ojibwe word for 'coffee'?"

"No," he said, his hand abandoning the ring for the thermos. "What is it?"

"*Muckadaymashkeekiwabu.*"

"Did you just make that up?"

"Ha. I wish. *Muckadaymashkeekiwabu.* Isn't that one of the tastiest words in the world?'

Chris wasn't sure. "It starts with *muck.*"

"Well, we're talking about black coffee."

"Yeah, I guess that makes sense."

"Maybe you could name one of your daily brews *muckaday-mashkeekiwabu.*"

"Or shorten it to *muckadaymash.* Even I can say that."

The young lovers laughed and enjoyed their feast, not saying much while the sun turned the headwaters into many colors, ending with scarlet in the last of the light. It was time to propose, Chris thought, and at that very moment, the phone rang. He had meant to set it on vibrate, and he had made Trevor promise not to call unless it was an emergency.

"It's an emergency," Trevor said, not even waiting for a hello. "We've got tobacco juice all over the produce. It's on the lettuce, the cabbage, man, he spit all over this time."

"Dip Schmidt?"

"Yeah, who else? And this time I called the cops."

Chris believed in solving problems without bringing in the authorities, and he was not happy with Trevor's decision. "You shouldn't have called the cops."

Terra leaned forward. "What happened? Is everyone okay?"

"They're taking Dip in for more questioning," Trevor said. "I filled out a report itemizing everything that has happened the past several years. The shoplifting, the vandalism, everything. Sacramento, you can't simply put up with the abuse. It's time to put a stop to it. We're talking about crimes here, not fun and games."

"Trev, I wish you'd called me before calling the police."

"You said not to bug you."

"Well, you bugged me anyway, didn't you? And now the problem is worse."

Terra wanted to know. "What problem? Is everyone okay?"

Covering the phone, Chris said, "There's a guy who hates me, and he hates Saint Francis, and he's always causing damage. Trevor wants to have him arrested."

"He's right," Terra said. "The person should be arrested."

Chris uncovered the phone. "All right, Trev. We'll talk about this tomorrow."

"Bright and early, bro. So. Are you and Terra getting engaged or something? This is the first day you've taken off in ages."

"Talk to you tomorrow, Trev."

"Pardon me for saying this, but . . ."

"What?"

"Well, I think she's a little out of your league, bro."

"What?"

"Yeah. Everyone's been saying it. But I'm the only one honest enough to tell you."

Hanging up, Chris let out an angry sigh. "I hate this freaking cell phone. And I'm not thrilled with my employee, either."

Terra took a piece of dark chocolate out of the picnic basket and held it to Chris's lips. "Here. This will get the bad taste out of your mouth."

"Thanks. Yum. Wow. Really yum."

She took a piece of chocolate for herself. "You said it."

Chris pushed the thermos cup toward his beloved. "Now wash it down with some delicious *muckadaymash*."

Giggling as if they were kids, the nearly engaged couple nibbled more chocolate and sipped more coffee . . . until the falling darkness and the rising mosquitoes required a fire. Chris gathered some thick branches and thin sticks, piled them methodically within the circle of stones, and had a great blaze going in no time.

"Well done," Terra said, turning toward the flickering dance. "The mosquitoes are fleeing, and the fireflies are arriving."

Chris snuggled up next to her. "A campfire is like having the sun stay with you into the night."

"That's very romantic."

"That's me."

She punched his shoulder.

He said, "Are you going to call me a dork?"

"No, sir," Terra said. "I'm going to kiss you."

chapter **ninety-six**

"SMOKE FOLLOWS beauty," Chris said.

As if dancing, Terra moved around the campfire. "That's a great old saying. My father said that to my mother when we camped at Thunder Bay. Mom hated camping, but she did it for us. I remember how beautiful she was in the firelight. I thought I could see her soul shimmering in the smoke. I was five years old, and it seemed like my mother was the most alive creature in the universe. That camping trip is one of my favorite memories. My parents were so in love, and it all felt wild and dangerous and safe at the same time."

Chris took a deep breath. Many perfect moments for the proposal had already vanished, and it was time to finally make it happen. The moment was now to kneel, to kneel at the door of eternity, and ask Terra to walk down the death-defying aisle for him.

All aglow, she paused on the other side of the campsite as if inviting him to dance, and then whisked away into the dew-sparkled grass while he slowly pursued through swirls of smoke. At the crown of the hill, Terra stood and arched her neck as if the stars were drops of golden rain and she wanted to drink them all in. Following that beauty to its logical conclusion, Chris knelt in the grass at her feet while the fireflies, gentle luminists of the North, blinked like holiday lights. The nervous knight brought out the shimmer-flashing ring and held the heirloom of love in his palm as if offering up to Terra a lifetime of holy fire.

"Oh, Christopher," Terra said, leaning forward but not taking the ring. "I suppose I shouldn't be surprised. But I am surprised. It's shocking to be confronted by so much reality. Please don't misunderstand my actions. Just let me sleep on this, okay? I'm not saying no."

All Chris heard was no.

He failed to hear the yes within the context of Terra's hesitation.

Tears in her eyes, she offered Chris a hopeful smile. "We should talk more about this."

No. He did not want to talk about it. He did not want to hear Terra's explanation, not in the woods and not all the way back to Duluth. After all, why would she need twenty-four hours to think about it? Nothing would be different in twenty-four hours, he thought. So this is probably the end of the relationship.

"I'm not saying no," Terra repeated when Chris dropped her off at the hospice.

He nodded, numb with rejection. "Whatever you say."

chapter ninety-seven

THE NEXT morning at Saint Francis, Trevor already seemed to know. He was smugly dusting around the consignment crosses and stained glass. "You were setting yourself up for a fall, Sacramento. Guys like you don't marry girls like Terra. It's just a simple fact. You are not worthy of her."

Having stayed up all night, Chris was slouched in an overstuffed chair, sipping his seventh shot of espresso. "Did you say something, Trev?"

Moving on to dust the icons, the failed seminarian said, "Girls like Terra marry professors at the Sorbonne. Or Oxford dons. They don't marry guys that barely got through high school."

Chris took an angry gulp of coffee. "Thanks for your support, buddy. Glad to know that you think the guy who writes your checks is worthless."

Trevor laughed at the feet of a large, carved crucifix. "I didn't say you were worthless, Sacramento. I'm trying to help you out here. I'm trying to point out the reality of the situation. Listen. What would you do when Terra went away to graduate school?"

Chris squirmed in his chair. "Graduate school?"

"Yeah. Terra mentioned it several times. Don't you pay attention to her?"

Staring out into the mist, Chris did recall a few off-hand remarks about Oxford and Cambridge University. "I listen better than you think, Trev. And you know what? If my wife wanted to go to graduate school, anywhere in the world, I'd go with her."

"Is that so?" Trevor stepped over to Chastity's Belts, and fondled one in his hands. "If Terra wanted to go to someplace like the University of Dallas, you'd pack up and move to Texas?"

Chris gulped the last of his espresso. "Yeah, I would move for her."

"Is that right? And what about Saint Francis Market?"

Standing to face the failed seminarian, Chris said, "I'd leave the store in your capable hands. And I'd start another one in Dallas. After all, Texas probably needs Saint Francis as much as any place. Same goes for Cambridge. Or Oxford. Or Hong Kong. Or New Zealand. I'd go anywhere in the world for Terra."

The look on Trevor's face was a mix of disbelief and pity. "Well, thank God you don't have to pack up and start your life over again." He fondled another one of Chastity's Belts. "I mean, it's over between you and Terra, right? You're probably thinking about getting back together with Mary Joan, right?"

You wish, Chris thought. Man, talk about living in unreality. Pixieless Trevor wants Terra for himself. The obsession is obvious.

"Sacramento, don't worry about Terra Corwin. She'll end up with someone at her level. I have no doubt that she'll marry a man who is worthy of her."

Chris stood up woozily from his chair. "I'm worthy of her."

With a sarcastic shrug, Trevor said, "If you say so, boss."

To make his employee earn that shrug, Chris decided to take the morning off. "I'm out of here."

"Whatever. I've got everything under control. And Skunk comes in pretty soon. He's better with the customers than you are, anyway. So you just go in peace to love and serve the Lord."

Fists clenched, Chris marched in full fury toward Trevor. If ever a guy deserved a punch in the mouth, it was him, standing there smiling in a benedictory pose.

"You know what?" Chris growled, raising his right arm.

"Um, ah, no," Trevor stammered, suddenly realizing the danger.

The words that Chris wanted to say to vent his rage and justify his attack were at the tip of his tongue. In a moment he would unleash them, followed by the punch and the crunch of Trevor's broken teeth. If ever a guy was worthy of a good smack . . .

"Oh, man," the young knight said in a defeated voice. He lowered his arm. "Oh, man. Oh, man."

"Wh-wh-what?"

Chris stared out at the great ghost of a lake. "You were right, Trev."

"I was?"

"Yes. I'm not worthy of her."

The failed seminarian gasped with relief. "I was only kidding about that. You know me, always playing around. You shouldn't take anything I say too seriously."

Chris turned and headed for the door, muttering, "I have heard the voice of God . . . spoken by an ass."

chapter ninety-eight

"YOU ARE not worthy of her."

The phrase was like an addendum to a death certificate. Chris had passed the night as if he were a corpse, trying to figure out what had gone wrong, his mind festering with a thousand ways he could have controlled things better. Maybe it was the diamond ring. He could have bought something new instead of offering his beloved a hand-me-down. And who proposes marriage in the middle of a swarm of mosquitoes? Maybe vampires. Probably not even them. Man, oh, man, is it really all vanity?

Driving through the early-morning fog, Chris continued to misremember and misinterpret the proposal. He was convinced that there was something within his power that he could have done, there on the ancient campsite, to have made the event more romantic, so perfect that Terra would have said yes.

"You are not worthy," echoed in his sorrowful head.

Chris drove the El Camino out of Duluth, ascending and descending the southern hillside. Slowly passing through the invisible valley, his mind shifted from the nothingness to images of color — mosaics of magenta and azure in the sky, and swirls of ocean green covering the whole earth. Shaking his head to see the fog again, Chris turned the wheel and exited the interstate. He felt like taking an untraveled road, going where nobody knew his name, and just being lost. Crawling up the half-wilderness highway, he journeyed through the misty, tree-lined streets of Elmwood . . . Mahtowa . . . Barnum . . . Moose Lake . . . Sturgeon Lake . . . Willow River . . . He admired the small towns in the woods, one appearing hazily after another. Chris scratched his morning shadow of whiskers, and wondered: who lives here? What do they do? Are they lumberjacks, hunters, tanners, smiths, fowlers, pagans, Christians? Are they lovers? Are they worthy?

The El Camino passed through the shrouded communities. Water towers, churches, schools, houses, cafés, and banks were swallowed up in the smoky mist. The Miracle Kid of Superior Street rolled into the next town, historic Hinckley. "I know where I am now," Chris whispered. He'd read about this place — how a spark in 1918 had flamed into catastrophe, scorching the community to nearly nothing, leaving the survivors almost no shelter in which to battle the ensuing plague of flu. Chris recalled a story about the burning of a family Bible, how it had gone down to ashes with the house, and yet a fragment had arisen above the fire and ridden the smoke all the way to Duluth — to a tree above the harbor.

The surviving Scripture proclaimed the liturgy of Heaven and earth, and was found by a little girl who had climbed high — her father beneath with open arms — to retrieve the treasure. The girl had shouted the found words: "Holy, holy, holy!"

I know, I know, Chris thought. And he kept rolling through the small towns for more than an hour, his mind sometimes wild with colorful stories, and sometimes drab as the fog all around him. At the edge of the Twin Cities, he pulled over to a shoulder of wildflowers, and made a call from that patch of blue.

"Hey, Trev. Are you busy?"

"Not really. Where are you?"

"Sodom and Gomorrah."

"What?"

"The Twin Cities."

"Yeah, that's probably a good place for you."

He is such a freaking jerk, Chris thought, and then said, "The reason I called, Trev, is that I need you to do me a favor."

"I already did."

"You did?"

"Yeah. I found the ring on a side table, among your trash of espresso cups. Don't worry, the ring is safe and secret in my pocket."

"Umm, good. But don't you think it should go into the safe?"

"Yeah, I was meaning to do that. But it got so darn busy around here. The early berries are flying off the shelves."

"I thought you said it wasn't busy, Trev."

"Nothing I can't handle, boss. So. Are you coming in for the afternoon shift?"

A tease of sunlight brightened the Twin Cities' towers. Chris gazed southward, feeling a hint of warmth. "I don't know, Trev."

"You don't know, Sacramento? Then who should I ask? Will your mom know? Should I call her to find out if you're coming in to work today?"

Killing the call, the young knight sped toward the great cities on the plain, the El Camino swerving through the rush-hour traffic like the wind among statues. Chris would not be going in to work that day, and he thought he might be finished altogether with buying and selling. His mind raced with imagined heroics, epic journeys, and literary illuminations, and he had the lunatic idea that he might want to go to graduate school.

"Oh, crap. I should probably get an undergrad degree first."

The fog lifted on the other side of the Cities, showing a silvering glimpse of the mighty waterway. Old Man River made Chris feel a bit smug. "Sometimes you just have to get away from the source of trouble," he told himself. "Just look at the

Mississippi. All it does is go with its own flow. And everyone loves it."

The Miracle Kid allowed himself to be a lost soul on the highway; and he reveled in that lostness, the exhilaration of faux freedom. The grin on his face was clown-like, made worse by his sudden breaking into song. "The Long and Winding Road" was the first thing that came to his mind. He wailed the lyrics as if he were stranded by the side of the road, all alone in the universe. And loving it.

And the phone rang.

"Hey, Trev. I was just singing."

"Let me guess. 'Achy Breaky Heart'? 'Free Bird'? 'The Long and Winding Road'?"

"How did you guess? You must be a prophet."

Trevor did not disagree. "Okay. Where are you?"

"You tell me. You're the prophet."

Pause.

A long pause.

"As your vision should plainly show you, Trev, I'm entering Red Wing."

"What? Where?"

"Red Wing."

"You're still going south? You haven't turned around yet?"

"I will. I'm just having some fun."

"You're going to break down."

Chris laughed. "No, Trev. Listen to this."

He held the phone out the window so the failed seminarian could hear the sound of the open road.

It was the rush of nothingness.

Trevor responded, "You better turn around before you go too far. There's nothing for you down there."

chapter ninety-nine

THE HILLS of Winona, like prehistoric whales surfacing above the river, are one of the ancient wonders of Minnesota. While glaciers leveled the neighboring land with recurrent crushes of ice, the hills of Winona remained arisen.

Chris continued his descent, into a deep preserve of hardwood forest. The dark pines were thick with red squirrels, flying from branch to branch. Above the road, an eagle stared down from its lift of wind, talons clenched peacefully.

The young knight journeyed through the forest, down into the Root River Valley. He paused at the riverside and climbed out of the El Camino to reflect upon his own roots. Chris wondered about the lives and early deaths of his grandparents. He'd never gotten to know them, beyond a few memories of toddling around some rooms for the dying. He recalled a woman at the Sacramento hospice who seemed like an angel, ministering to his grandmother as if she knew the language of Heaven. Tears flowed in that room day and night, and Chris had tried to comfort his mom while her mother drifted further away into grace.

"Well, that's enough," Chris whispered, wiping his eyes and leaving the Root River.

The El Camino climbed slowly out of the valley and wheeled around the curves of the higher elevations. Wispy clouds veiled the view, so when Chris looked at the mirror to see how far back the visibility went, his focus was stuck on his own face. How mournful he was, the countenance of his eyes like paintings he'd seen of Adam banished from the Garden.

Chris descended from the hills and bluffs and crossed the border into Iowa. The place appeared more exotic than he'd expected. There were undulating fields not only of corn but also of beans, alfalfa, and fallow acres of pretty weeds and wildflowers. The young knight stopped for gas, water, and sunflower seeds in a small town called Decorah. He exchanged pleasantries about the weather with the cute cashier, noticed the engagement ring on her hand, and got quickly back on the road. Teeth-gnashing the sunflower shells and chewing the seeds, he thought about turning the El Camino around and returning to Saint Francis. He was sure that Terra would be there, waiting patiently for him, willing to talk more about the possibility of them. Talk, talk, talk, he was so tired of it. His mind flashed to a memory of adolescent Pixie, and how she believed they were soul-mates. Did such a state of relationship really exist? Could souls be mated? Or was every soul a solitary shimmer, just as lonely and desirous as a body?

Chris picked up the phone and called Terra.

She did not answer.

"Hey," he said, leaving a message. "We need to talk."

In a world after Babel, there was always more to say. And Chris wanted Terra to know a secret. There was something he should have told her at the ancient campsite. There was something that might have swayed her to accept his proposal.

Now he saw a sign in the ditch, a hand-painted piece of plywood in the shape of a catcher's mitt: "Field of Dreams. 70 Miles."

The movie was one of his favorites. Not so much because he was sentimental about baseball, but rather because he and his dad had watched the DVD together. They had sat on the sofa in the house above Two Harbors, munching popcorn, keeping their thoughts to themselves, until the end of the film, when Joe wiped his eyes and said, "Look at how the father and son worked things out, playing a game of catch, tossing a ball around like a whole world of forgiveness. How cool is that?"

"Very cool."

The Iowa sky brightened as if the sun had burned everything — including the blue — clean away. Near the Field of Dreams, a stand of unharvested pine trees gave shade to a herd of heifers. Chris turned away from the movie site, knowing it was not a place to go alone, and he accelerated east toward the riverboat town of Dubuque. He thought he could feel the presence of the river before he could see it, the Mississippi being his favorite mystical body of water other than Superior. "Proud Mary" came rolling from his lips, a song he didn't especially like. And yet he was rolling, rolling, rolling . . . And the moment Chris saw the soiled water, he dammed the song in his mouth, thinking that the Mississippi was not so much the Holy Spirit River but rather a metaphor for going down a spiritual drain.

Chris drove warily into Dubuque. "I can't keep going south. Trevor will run the store into the ground. And I need to meet with Terra and tell her the secret. I need to turn and go back."

Just a little further . . . a little more of the river . . .

The El Camino chugged down the Iowa coastline, the engine spluttering as if submerged and drowning.

Just a little further . . .

The Quad Cites appeared, and there was a sign for an airport. Chris thought that maybe he would abandon the car-truck, and fly home. "I need to be there now."

Turn, turn, turn . . .

He missed the road to the airport and kept on going down, following the river to Muscatine, and connecting again with Highway 61. The old road made him remember his personal marathon up the North Shore, how he'd attempted to run all the way to the cathedral-house to win Terra's heart. If only he had been faster, or at least kept going through the rain. Then maybe he would have made it to her house, or at least met the Corwin car on the road. Everything would have been different, easier. He and Terra would have grown up closer, even in their distance, and not dated other people, and simply sweet-hearted their way into engagement and marriage. They would probably be on their honeymoon now, starflowers in Terra's hair, and no more dragons.

Chris kept going down . . . passing through the small towns and thinking about his secret. Why hadn't Terra called him back yet?

"She needs to know. I should have told her when I offered the ring."

Chris had taken private instructions all winter from the priest at Star of the Sea, and was presented to the Bishop for Easter Confirmation. The gift of the Holy Spirit was given to the young knight, and he was commissioned to receive the Body and Blood. However, he had opted to abstain, wanting to make his First Communion the same day as his wedding. The plan was to live a day and night of love that would be as wild as Scripture — a communion with Heaven and Terra — like another *Song of Songs*.

What more could a man want?

If only he were worthy.

The day was losing ground to shadows, giving fair warning of the approaching night, but Chris stayed on the road, descending all the way into the hint of hills that suggested the wilds of Missouri. The landscape should have intrigued him, but he yawned, having been too much awake for too many hours; and he thought about listening to some music. The stereo system could pound the doldrums out of any sleepy driver, but Chris pushed the wrong button and was pummeled by talk radio. Eerie voices from several stations came in and out of the static.

"... it was the first triple-play of the season ..."
"... high-pressure system out of the North ..."
"... those sneaky Democrats are at it again ..."
"... Jesus Christ our Lord and Savior ..."
"... killer is loose in Saint Louis, and ..."

A large bird strutted across the road, a ring-necked pheasant with glowing eyes. Chris swerved to avoid it and nearly collided with an oncoming semi-truck. Give or take a moment of chance, decision, or grace, the Miracle Kid would have been crushed.

That's enough, he thought. That's more than enough. It's time to go home.

So near to death, his heart was drumming like crazy, missing a beat, missing his beloved, missing everything. Hands tightly gripping the wheel, Chris tried to catch his breath, his mind racing yet lucid. Why go any farther? What's out here that isn't at home? Is this trip really part of my calling?

Chris knew that being randomly on the road was merely an exercise in escapism, and there was no worthiness in that. Saint Francis, however, had real work for him — physical and spiritual. And all of his relationships in the Zenith City needed his body and soul.

Chris glanced at his phone. "Why didn't she call me back?"

The El Camino sputtered southward, and the young knight didn't turn around.

The sun continued its late-afternoon descent, and the land grew more lush, smoldering like green fire. There was a sign on the road for a "Mystical Cave" that gave Chris pause, and he slowed to a crawl. All sorts of underground images arose in his well-read memory, from the paintings in the caves before history, to Plato's Cave and its prisoners of unformed perception, to Elijah's mountainous retreat and the Still Small Voice, to the drop-down depths of the Cyclops, to the lairs of a thousand dragons of medieval lore, to Becky Thatcher and Tom Sawyer and their three days in a Missouri tomb.

Tempted, Chris wondered if he should take a tour of the Mystical Cave. He imagined the underground journey might be the purpose of this road trip, with enough adventure to get the wanderlust out of his hurting heart; and then he looked up the road and saw another sign.

AVENUE OF THE SAINTS

The El Camino accelerated in a flash of rusty light above the catacombs, and Chris considered the lives of the saints. In this swoon of existence, with mortality like a fainting spell, how had the saints achieved such everlasting fame? From Saint Paul to Saint Louis, here was the road to commemorate a man of Damascus and a king of Paris.

"I need more gas," Chris muttered.

He drove down the holy avenue and stopped at the first station he could find. After filling up with premium, hoping that would cure some of the car-truck's sputtering, he went inside to use the restroom. And then Chris bought a bottle of spring water, joking with the cashier, an elderly gentleman with mischievous eyes. "You ought to sell Deep North down here."

"Ought we?" the gentleman said. "Ought we, indeed?"

"Umm . . . or maybe not," Chris said. "Anyway . . . where am I?"

The cashier shrugged. "Do I look like Google Maps?"

"You look like a man who knows things. And I'd like to know how close I am to Saint Louis."

"There was a killing today in Saint Louis," the cashier said in a foreboding voice. "My sources say a monster did it."

"A monster?"

"Yes. It has the traffic all snarled. If you go down to Saint Louis, you might get stuck, and . . ."

"And what?"

The elderly gentlemen seemed amused by the idea. "You might entertain the monster."

Okay, okay, Chris thought, hurrying back to the El Camino. Are all gas-station attendants cryptic? Is it listed on the job application? *Must say crazy things and freak out the customers.*

Leaving the Avenue of the Saints, Chris sped up the ramp to the interstate and joined the flow of drivers on their way to Saint Louis. Despite the weird warning, he wanted to see the crossroads of the country, where East meets West beneath the glittering Gateway Arch.

Just before sunset, the car-truck sputtered through the suburbs and into the city. "Man!" Chris was struck by the proximity of glory to ruin. Some of the brick buildings were stately mansions, and some had windows that seemed blown out as if by war. On the river side of the road, there was a chain-link fence topped with barbed wire, as if the abandoned warehouses needed extra protection. The traffic was slow and sometimes stalling, allowing a good view of the Arch and the wasteland.

When he was a kid, Chris had been enthralled by stories of Lewis and Clark, and now he was at their point of departure. Named for the quintessential medieval king, Saint Louis was one of the most adventuresome places on earth, where the Mississippi was a royal road, where Lewis and Clark had battled killer beasts and currents to find the source of a darker water: the Missouri. And from there, the brave explorers had pushed on to the Pacific, the seemingly infinite water of peace.

Chris recalled that one of the explorers — Lewis — in misery, had committed suicide after having found what he was looking for. Sadly, the waters weren't enough.

"What am I doing here?" Chris whispered, and turned west onto a less-traveled road. Among the projects and nondescript structures, a decrepit church seemed to be grasping at the falling light, the bone-white spire leaning as if ready to break. The El Camino also threatened to break down in a neighborhood where Chris may not have been most welcome. However, without fear, and with a friendly wave to the street-corner congregants, he turned south and drove the sputter-bucket into an area of refurbished big houses and actual mansions, the majesty of the old city sparkling in brick-red sunset.

"Looks like this place is on the rise."

And around the next corner arose a green dome of Roman and Byzantine proportions, guarded by twin towers also glowing with green as if alive and in full bloom.

"Holy . . . man . . . this is what Professor Corwin was talking about."

The young knight laughed and teared up, remembering what Terra had said about the death of her grandfather, how the great medievalist had proclaimed that he and Silvenshine were going to Saint Louis to slay a dragon.

"Well, old friend," Chris whispered prayerfully, "here I am at what looks like an ancient cathedral. But I don't see the dragon . . . yet."

The parking lot was full, so Chris had to leave the El Camino on the street near the front door. Making the Sign of the Cross over his linen shirt as if to turn it to armor, the young knight braved the door of the heavenly vision.

chapter one hundred

"SOLD OUT," the pretty lady said, perched at the ticket counter.

"I can't go inside?"

"Sorry."

Dazed by a lack of sleep and the long drive, the Miracle Kid could not understand how a cathedral could be sold out. He scratched his shadow of whiskers, and asked, "Is the Pope here?"

The ticket lady laughed. "No, not tonight. It's a concert of sacred music."

Chris listened for a few moments while the Gregorian chant whispered under the door like a rumor of glory.

He sighed, and muttered, "No ticket . . . no wedding garment."

"It's not a wedding," the sweet-voiced lady replied. "Just a concert. But people are here from all over the place. It's a packed house."

Chris gazed into the ticket lady's batting eyes, and lamented, "I drove all the way down from Duluth. I wasn't sure why I was doing it, other than to get away from some decisions. And when I saw the green dome in the sky, it was like an epiphany, as if an old prophecy were playing out."

"Prophecy? In this day and age?"

"Yes. And if I went along with it, and perhaps confronted some great danger here, then I could go home and propose again. And this time . . ."

"I'm sorry," the lady said. "If you do not have a ticket for the concert, you cannot go inside."

The music beckoned. "*Benedictus es super thronum sanctum . . .*"

Chris glanced up at a mosaic of King Louis in the entryway. The warrior who became a Franciscan was all serenity, the bits of broken glass transformed into a perfection of art and theology. Royal eyes were still commanding from centuries past, as if the orders always remained the same: "Fight for love."

"You'll have to find something else to do tonight," the ticket lady said. "You seem tired. Maybe you should check into a motel and get some rest. But be careful if you leave this neighborhood. Things have been scary down by the riverside."

A scratch of fear made Chris flinch. "The monster. I heard something about that."

The lady whispered, "They almost caught him this afternoon, but he got away again. Traffic has been horrible where the last attack occurred, near the Arch. Take my advice and stay away from there."

"Duly noted," Chris said.

Heart pounding, he abandoned the cathedral, jumped in the El Camino, and drove straight toward the Arch.

chapter **one hundred one**

THE CROSSROADS monument, a steel megalith splashed red with sunset, was one of the world's most famous gateways, the secular conclusion to the Avenue of the Saints. Chris wanted to pass through as a sort of ritual, a rite of passage to mark the end of his secular days. And then he would go to the airport, and fly home to be with that Catholic girl. Forever, he hoped.

"Why won't she call? C'mon, Terra. It's your turn."

The traffic was slow but flowing better than expected, considering the number of law-enforcement vehicles. Some were speeding by, and some were parked on the shoulder with lights flashing — as if something invisible were under arrest.

The road descended, and the Gateway Arch disappeared behind a wall that was splattered with graffiti, and then it suddenly reappeared like a bridge to the sky. A flock of fiery birds flapped over the top, and Chris, now within a few blocks of the monument, realized that all of the roads went around. The Gateway was accessible only to those with wings, or on foot.

"Maybe I should park. But there's yellow tape everywhere."

A waving cop made everyone get on the interstate where the flow of traffic quickened and pulled Chris out of the city. Caught in the current of a thousand cars and trucks, the next thing he knew he'd crossed over the river from Missouri to Illinois, where he was immediately lost in a flood of concrete and metal, winding through a torrent of ramps and roads branching in every direction.

"Damn. Damn. Damn."

It was twilight now, and the young knight accelerated forward, hoping to find a way back. He imagined that Professor Corwin was in the passenger seat with a big frown on his face. Or not a frown, but a great curve-down of mustache. And what was that word he kept saying under his whiskers and breath? What was that word he kept laughing?

"Silvenshine. Silvenshine. Silvenshine."

Chris took the first exit, despite its lack of a sign, and found himself in a scraggle of dusky trees at a crossway. Without thinking, he turned the wrong way and drove toward the country instead of the city, the El Camino sounding like its engine was ready to combust into ashes. Down the road, the darkness did not seem to fall as much as arise from the earth, and Chris flicked on his headlights at the first hint of civilization. A billboard flashed bright as a movie screen: CAHOKIA.

The word meant nothing to him. He searched through a billion files in his brain, and came up empty. Chris kept driving, and passed a dark and strangely shaped hill, and turned left at the entrance to what seemed to be a picnic area. The El Camino crawled down to the lonely parking lot, and stalled.

"Good . . . the end of the road . . . finally."

Chris slowly opened the door and climbed out. The sun had set without diminishing any heat, and moistness festered on his face. The young knight stepped forward, looking warily at the silhouette of the hill. It was shaped like a monster — the biggest dragon's head in the world.

"I'm here," Chris muttered, lightheaded and swaying. "I'm here to slay you."

chapter **one hundred two**

THE DRAGON'S HEAD was made during the Middle Ages by a tribe of sun-worshipers and cannibals who piled up tons of mud and yet remained infinitely closer to the earth than to the heavens. When the primitive society died out, the monstrous mound stood fallow of ritual for generations, becoming a mere undulation on the horizon as seen from the site that would become Saint Louis.

Eighteenth-century French monks, revolted by the revolution that was destroying their country, did what Benedictines have always done: they brought the Scriptures, Sacraments, and culture into the depths of a new wilderness. They journeyed to New France, to the shores of the Holy Spirit River, and established a mission. The wildly noble and intrepid monks discovered the bloodstained dragon, climbed its muddy scales, and planted a garden on its head.

The site became fondly known as "Monks' Mound."

Ethereal chant and charitable ritual lifted the Benedictines ever higher, but their ministry was short-lived. Like monarch butterflies, the monks flitted about in the spiritual sunlight, and were suddenly gone. While caring for the sick, they took on the virus themselves, died, and were buried beneath the dragon, among the bones of the cannibals.

chapter one hundred three

THE YOUNG KNIGHT continued his quest. Even if the dragon were only a symbol and already dead, he would still confront it as a form of therapeutic theater. Chris already had a good story to tell, and he hoped the climax — his stomping on the head of the dragon — would lead to many tellings in Saint Francis Market. And he imagined that Terra would deem the story worthy of a Holy Grail Adventure.

Chris staggered forward through the gloaming, his heroic aspirations weighted down with many worries, including getting the El Camino towed and sold for scrap, and finding a taxi to bring him to the airport, and eating some real food before he got on the plane . . . and as he stood before the Dragon's Head that loomed nearly as large as the sky, he paused.

What was the point, he thought, of climbing? Wouldn't people think he was a fool for acting like a little kid? Who does things like this, other than overly imaginative children and lunatics and poets?

"And lovers . . ." he whispered.

Chris opened his cell phone to see if there was a connection. And he heard a noise. At first, the sound seemed to be something in his phone. Perhaps he'd accidentally set it on vibrate and was about to miss a call from Terra.

"Hello? Hello? Terra, are you there?"

Chris heard the noise again, outside of the phone, as if the sound were emanating from the Dragon's Head. The young knight leaned forward, listening intently.

It was a still, small growl.

Chris flinched and lurched backward, almost falling. Regaining his balance, he squinted through the mist and searched for signs of life — human, animal, or other. Knowing it was not possible for the earthen monster to make such a growl, Chris considered all of the options, from a farm cat to thunder, and then began to laugh at himself, thinking it was his stomach growling. After all, he was starving to death.

"I need to finish this," he said, stumbling toward the incline. "I need to get back to Duluth and get on with life. Hopefully, with married life."

Chris's legs remembered their strength, and he slowly but powerfully ascended the side of the mound, grasping the long grass for support. Birds flew up as if to greet him, their blur of wings disappearing above the crest and into the first stars. Higher and higher, the Miracle Kid climbed to the top of the dragon, to where the monks had made their stand against the world to lift all things in the rapture of the Grail.

"This . . . is . . . amazing," Chris said, trying to catch his breath. "Why is this mound . . . a secret? Why didn't we read about this . . . in school?"

Although the sun had set, there was light everywhere at the summit. It seemed as if the many heavens were housed in one cathedral, with more candles appearing by the moment. Chris lay down on his back in an area where the grass was burnt away, and he took in the fires above. Among the myriad constellations, the knight's eyes were drawn to what appeared to be a lion, and he saw an infinity of crosses within the king of beasts . . . and even deeper into the formation were galaxies rising like spiraling ghosts of resurrection.

There was another growl.

Chris stood, legs shaking, and walked over to the western edge of the mound. He peered down, searching for the source of the warning. It was not his stomach. And there did not seem to be any other forms of life around. Could it possibly be the Dragon's Head growling? Should he prepare for some sort of battle?

For the next several minutes, Chris bravely investigated, looking over the edge in all four directions.

There was nothing. At least nothing that seemed dangerous or out of place. Just a scattering of dark trees reaching out in silence across the plains.

Chris looked farther . . . and above the great river, the moon was reddening over Saint Louis, hovering above the Gateway Arch. The young knight took an enthralled step back, and bumped into a wooden sign that had been planted into the Dragon's Head. His first thought was that it was a large crucifix or icon left behind by the monks. However, the placard showed a glowing image of the ritual of human sacrifice. Chris squinted to read the red letters. The placard proclaimed the historical importance of the natives, calling them, "The Great Society of the Middle Ages."

Chris smiled and shook his head, thinking: The Great Society? Do people really believe that? While Oxford and the University of Paris were elevating medieval Europe to the heights, creating scholars, artists, scientists, and saints, this part of the world was still lost in darkness, illiteracy, and cannibalism.

"A mound of blood-soaked mud," Chris said, "compared with the Cathedral of Notre Dame. Illiteracy compared with the *Summa Theologica*. Human sacrifice compared with holy vows of hospitality."

The glories of Christendom were easy for Chris to love, but the checkered history of Catholics had always made him hesitant to swallow the whole Faith. He'd been living off the crumbs of the Church, one way or another, his entire life. And Saint

Francis Market had been more of the same — scrounging among the goods while not giving in to the great: Communion. Well, now he was prepared to give in. With Terra, or even without her, he was ready to receive the quintessence of grace.

The moon rose scarlet above Holy Spirit River, and Chris reveled in what was self-evident and revealed. Standing on the Dragon's Head, he could see everything — from the Tree of Life to Manna in the Desert to Loaves and Fishes to the Last Supper to the Cross. The Sacrifice was being offered at that moment, all around the world. And the monks on the mound, timeless in God's time, were bearing the Holy Grail to the heavens and to Heaven . . . now . . . Christopher knew it was all now . . . and he could not wait to join the Feast.

"Uh oh. What was that?"

The growl was not still or small. And it was not internal. Down near the snout of the dragon, the sound arose.

Chris thought it might be the monster that everyone was talking about. "God . . . God help me."

Up the side of the hill of sacrifice, the killer prowled, while the young knight held his breath beneath the scarlet moonlight and torching stars. Chris's awareness of the world intensified, from the scent of flowers around the placard to the flash of heat lightning at the horizon. Had he not been in danger, the subtle splendors may have sent his soul flying heavenward and earthward in a paradox of ecstasy.

A large, tawny head appeared over the crest of the mound, fiery eyes glaring. The mountain lion growled with a low rumble and sucking of saliva, the blood-lust rising. A scream may have erupted from the throat of a typical victim, and Chris did feel a surge of panic, yet he stood his ground in trembling silence.

The lion showed its whole body, rising above the ridge, the ferocity increasing with each step, as if it were famished. Chris was filled not only with panic but also with wonder. Had the hungry firecat prowled, mostly invisible, from the wilds of the

North and down the Avenue of the Saints? Or had he spirited out of the Big Sky country to hunt for blood on the Plains?

Weaponless, but with a plan to survive the attack, Chris offered up his left hand. He hoped the impending dismemberment would appease the lion; and he clenched his right fist to make a good punch. The knight would go for an eye, and hope for a howl and retreat. After all, it was just an animal, and the fear of man should be manifest.

I will fight you, Chris thought, the words echoing and growing in his mind. I will fight you to the death.

The mountain lion stood on its hind legs and slashed the air above the offered hand, the sharp claws nearly reaching the knight's chest. Chris knew the next slash would open his ribcage, and the one after that would rip out his heart.

"Good-good kitty," he rasped, "play nice."

Chris let his hand drop limply to his side, knowing there was no way he could defeat the lion in battle. The thought crossed his mind that perhaps he could tame it, like Saint Francis had tamed the wolf. However, the holiness needed for that was not at his command, and so the best course of quick action was to play dead. He would fall to the ground and give himself up to the intercession of the otherworldly, but the beast lunged forward for the kill — as if there had not been enough death on that hilltop altar, as if another spill of blood was due — and suddenly placed his heavy paws on the young knight's shoulders. The claws were out, like tiny swords, but did not break the skin.

"Good-good kitty . . ."

The natural smile on the firecat's face disappeared with a loud growl, the hot breath wild and deadly sweet. Chris felt as if he were dreaming and perfectly awake, and the lion reared its head toward the heavens, mouth open insatiably wide, and roared. The sound was like the song of doom. And the deepest melody of resurrection.

The knight was resigned to the providence of his death. Of all the ways to leave this world, this was a great one. Worthy of a song, or an epic poem, or at least a line within the heroic liturgy.

And then the image of Terra filled his head, the image of her saying yes.

Trembling to the point of shaking, with the weight of the lion on his shoulders, and the weight of his beloved in his soul, Christopher raised his hands to the king of beasts, to what no longer looked like a killer.

"God . . . Almighty . . ."

The firecat licked the knight's face, blinked, and leapt over the side of the mound.

Within moments, the flashing lights of law enforcement colored the landscape below, the impossible chase continuing toward the east.

"God Almighty . . ." Chris whispered, falling to the earth. "Man alive."

chapter **one hundred four**

The phone rang like church bells while Chris sat cross-legged on the mound.

"Hey, Terra."

"Christopher, I've been meaning to call you all day, but the hospice had two residents pass on, and we were understaffed. Mrs. Narneski had no next of kin, so I made all of the arrangements for her, and everything is fine — she died wonderfully — and the funeral is Saturday at Star of the Sea, and, well . . . I'm sorry, Christopher. You left a message saying you wanted to talk."

The young knight cleared his throat, and paused. He thought he could hear the firecat roaring far away, or it might have been the wind. "Is Mrs. Narneski the old teacher who had a one-room school out in the woods?"

"Yes, that's her. How sweet of you to remember. She was amazing, giving her whole life to her students, beginning in International Falls and ending up at Cathedral High."

"She volunteered at the literacy center during her retirement," Chris said, as if recalling the life of a Saint. "We delivered coffee at the center a few times, and Mrs. Narneski told me her story."

"I love how the story made an impression on you. I love how you care. And I . . . um . . . love . . ."

Chris entered the pause, smiling. "You love what? You love who?"

Terra laughed nervously. "You know."

He joined the laughter, reassuring, "Yeah, I know."

"Anyway, Christopher, tell me. How was your day? Did anything exciting happen?"

Gazing at the shimmer of Saint Louis and the light above the silver Arch, he said, "It was a day for the ages."

"I had an intuition," Terra said. "I know something has changed, but I can't explain it."

Chris knelt on one knee. "I can explain everything. Listen, love. I'm ready for Communion. Are you ready for the ring?"

chapter one hundred five

CHRIS AND TERRA were married the following June in the upper room of the cathedral-house. The Historical Society was kind enough to rent it out to them, and the Catholic Church was kind enough to offer two thousand years of blessings and navigations for the marital journey.

The bride was beatific in white, and Chris was a knight in shining linen. Victor Corwin, long-bearded as a monk, had returned a few days early to help his daughter decorate the chapel with forty bouquets of flowers, all in medieval patterns of spiritual significance. There were apple blossoms for hope. Daisies to focus on God. Purple lilacs as reminders of romance. Morning glories for affection. And roses the color of Communion wine.

During the Scripture readings, sunlight poured a northern heaven through the clear and stained-glass windows. And while a small choir chanted angelic responses, Chris glanced outside to see that Lake Superior was a golden reflection of a sky that seemed all sun. He gestured for Terra to see, and she nodded, her eyes brimming with light.

In a great cloud of prayer and incense, the Bishop of Duluth gave his blessing to the continuation of Eden. "And for the love of God," he said in his homily, "do not forget to forgive, every day, and to laugh. And may you love each other more than anything in the world. And love God more than that."

Terra and Chris exchanged looks of shimmering recognition when they exchanged the rings, and again when they lit the unity candle. Yes, they knew the secret of life: relationship with the ultimate *Mysterium Tremendum*, the Holy Trinity.

Trevor, in the back row with Moosehead and Skunk, whispered loudly, "I knew this wedding would happen. I knew it from the beginning. It was obvious that Sacramento and Terra belonged together."

"Shhh," mouthed Grant Mudgett, "it's starting to get good now."

When Chris drank from the Holy Grail, with all eyes upon him like seraphim, he was not subsumed in fire. There were no dragons at the altar, and the cool sip of transformation was almost anticlimactic. The lionhearted knight had expected the Blood to be a taste of lightning and to linger on the tongue with otherworldliness. In fact, the Blood tasted as it was described by the festive saints and poets of the Church.

What did Communion taste like?

Like faith . . . pure and simple.

Christopher drank it in, the joy completing itself in his submission to the Gift. It was like a marriage already made, and he had a knowing beyond human passion — to passionately share with Terra — the bliss of being perfectly known.

"They're not going to the Bahamas," Trevor whispered loudly. "They took my advice, and they're taking a Mediterranean cruise. And then a tour of Italy. Rome, Assisi, Florence, the whole Italian thing. Man alive, and woman alive! They're going to have great adventures!"

About the Author

DAVID ATHEY is the author of a previous novel, *Danny Gospel,* and has published nearly two hundred poems, stories, essays, and reviews in literary journals such as *The Iowa Review, California Quarterly, Southern Humanities Review* and *Harvard Review.* He is an Associate Professor of English at Palm Beach Atlantic University.

Acknowledgments

THANK YOU, Kathleen Anderson, Christopher Jensen, John Barger, Regina Doman, Nora Malone, and Sheila Perry.

An Invitation

Reader, the book that you hold in your hands was published by Sophia Institute Press.

Sophia Institute seeks to restore man's knowledge of eternal truth, including man's knowledge of his own nature, his relation to other persons, and his relation to God.

Our press fulfills this mission by offering translations, reprints, and new publications. We offer scholarly as well as popular publications; there are works of fiction along with books that draw from all the arts and sciences of our civilization. These books afford readers a rich source of the enduring wisdom of mankind.

Sophia Institute Press is the publishing arm of the Thomas More College of Liberal Arts and Holy Spirit College. Both colleges are dedicated to providing university-level education in the Western tradition under the guiding light of Catholic teaching.

If you know a young person who might be interested in the ideas found in this book, share it. If you know a young person seeking a college that takes seriously the adventure of learning and the quest for truth, bring our institutions to his attention.

www.SophiaInstitute.com
www.ThomasMoreCollege.edu
www.HolySpiritCollege.org

SOPHIA INSTITUTE PRESS

THE PUBLISHING DIVISION OF

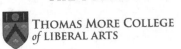